Love,
Lies
& Lipstick

Rod Cornelius

Copyright © Rod Cornelius, 2017
An Akirim Press Publishing
Copyediting By Mirika Mayo Cornelius/Akirim Press

www.akirimpress.com
www.rodcornelius.com

Love, Lies & Lipstick

Whatever It Takes

Cash rules everything around us and that's not excluding the rent. Quay stepped into the strip game not by choice, but because she didn't have any other options. After her good-for-nothing man puts them in a bind that could get her and her daughter thrown out in the harsh, rough streets of Jacksonville, Florida, Quay makes a decision to cross the ultimate line. When her brash plot to get deeper in the game puts her life on the line, Quay has to do whatever it takes to survive.

Diggin' Gold

There's not a woman alive that wants a man that doesn't have anything.

The same holds true for Kizzy Washington. Now, Kizzy doesn't want any old, average dude that's trying to make ends meet. She needs a man that can provide her with plenty of cash and all the glamorous things her heart desires. Kizzy Washington is a gold digger and there is no shame in her game! So when Kizzy zeroes in on that guy that can provide her with everything she lusts for, she's willing to do anything, and I do mean ANYTHING to snag him.

Kizzy has been spending the last couple of years working as a waitress at a small town diner waiting for a Rich Casanova to come in and sweep her off her feet so she can take him for all he has. When she finds out one of the elderly patrons that's been sitting up under her nose for years could possess all the riches she's been in search of, she goes in for the KILL. But will her gold digging ambitions get the best of her and give her much more than she bargains for?

The Trusted

Rick Reed is a convict on the run from the law. He's been convicted for committing over two dozen homicides, and he just escaped facing the death penalty. With the help of his sexy girlfriend, Keisha, Rick is well on his way to Mexico, trekking from back road to back road. Things quickly go awry when Rick and Keisha lose their wheels and find themselves in the middle of nowhere in the strange, country town, Stony Creek. Stony Creek is a virtual ghost town with only one family remaining, the Havertys, and the secret this family holds could spell disaster for Rick and Keisha.

He Beats Me

When Ashley first met Keon, she thought she had met the love of her life. It wasn't long after she cut herself off from all of her family and friends that Keon revealed his true abusive nature. Ashley quickly went from being the target of his affection to the target of his strikes and stomps. It's not until Keon's big move into the drug game goes tragically awry that he realizes the usefulness for Ashley again. The problem is, if he can't get his plan to work, they all could end up dead.

Acknowledgements

This book is dedicated solely to my lovely wife Mirika Mayo Cornelius. Love you.

More Akirim Press Books

Books by Rod Cornelius

Single Again

Ghetto Eyes

UGLY

Books by Mirika Mayo Cornelius

Secret

Colored Lily: Poppa Took My Innocence

Ain't Quite What I Thought

Ain't Quite What I Thought 2

Sunny Sides of My Shade

Murders At Gabriel's Trail: The Complete Series

First Degree Sins

Paton

Books by Cyan Deane

Dead Man's Mayhem

Execution's Karma

Table of Contents

Whatever It Takes

When she pranced onto the stage, she was surprised to see the building was practically a ghost town. The tiny gentlemen's club was nearly empty with the exception of one lone patron. The man sat in a chair directly in front of the stage with his hands resting calmly on his knee caps. With his dark, black suit and the cheap red tie hanging from his neck, he wore a large brim fedora hat that made it difficult to see his eyes from the way he was tilting his head downward, towards the floor.

Her favorite song to perform to, R. Kelly's 'Twelve Play', started to play, but when she looked towards the corner where the deejay booth was located, she noticed no one was there manning the station. She thought it to be weird, but not weird enough to make her lose out on taking her only customer for everything he brought in there to spend.

She took to the pole, eased out her smooth caramel hips and began to slowly rotate them from side to side as a bit of a tease to let the mysterious man know what he was about to get himself into. As she got deeper into her dance while allowing the music to dictate her risqué body movements, she turned her attention towards the area where the man was sitting to see if he had moved closer to the stage to begin compensating her with some cold, hard cash for her work thus far, but she quickly realized he had abandoned her.

She promptly refrained from her dance routine and cautiously walked towards the edge of the stage, baffled by the man's disappearance and even more so by the venue's emptiness. She surveyed the landscape from wall to wall. It was now a complete ghost town. It was all so freakishly strange. No matter how hard she tried, she couldn't put her thoughts together fast enough to figure out what in the world was going on.

"Quay!" yelled a deep voice from behind her.

She whipped around and was surprised to see the lone customer standing on the stage before her with a pistol pointed at her face. This time it wasn't just the tilt of his hat that made it difficult to see his eyes, but the big, black barrel of the gun he was grasping in front of her.

"Wait!" she yelled while swaying her hands in front of the pistol.

Before she could even get out another word the man growled, "Die, you filthy whore!" The gun went off.

Quay bolted up from her sleep in a cold sweat. While breathing ferociously, she was relieved that it was all just another terrible nightmare. She clasped her hands over her face and let out a deep sigh of relief. She raked her fingers through her long dark hair a couple of times and plopped backwards onto her pillow.

Another damn nightmare, she thought. As she rested on her back in a daze at the popcorn texture on the ceiling, wearing nothing but her bra and panties, she couldn't shake the eerie dream from her mind. It just seemed so real. Ever since she started dancing, three months prior, the nightmares began, and they were only getting worse. She never imagined living the life of a stripper, but when the opportunity presented itself from her sorry man's, cousin, Cy, she reluctantly took it. Not because she wanted to, but because she literally didn't have much of a choice.

When Spud propositioned it to her after his hours were sliced in half on his job, it sickened her to her stomach, and it really made her begin to see him for the poor excuse of a man everyone else had claimed he was long ago. *What kind of a man asks his woman to give other strange men lap dances and proceed to get groped and fondled throughout the wee hours of the morning?* she asked herself while he

16

explained it to her as the only way they could possibly generate enough cash fast enough to keep the bills paid and a roof over their heads.

Times were tough, but she figured the worse the times got, it would have been the perfect opportunity for him to stand up and be a real man for a change, but to her dissatisfaction, he chose to fumble the opportunity once again and put the burden of being the man of the house all on her. The only reason she even went along with it was to make sure her baby wasn't submitted to being thrown out in the cold, an experience she was all too familiar with during her own youth when her father decided to leave her and her mom for his chick on the side. She'd do anything to make certain her child would never have to worry about being in a safe place to rest her head at night, and if it meant hopping on a stage and dancing in front of a few perverts for a couple of hours on a nightly basis, she was up for the task. She just never imagined she'd be doing it for as long as she had and that it would be freaking her out the way that it was.

Her moment of relaxation quickly came to a halt when she heard knocking on the front door from the living room. She rolled off the bed and slipped on one of Spud's oversized t-shirts and a pair of jogging pants. She scurried to the bathroom, took a quick peek at herself in the mirror, and ran her brush through her hair a few times. She then made her way through the house to the front door. "I'm coming. I'm coming," she said as the knocking on the door became more frequent. She took a look through the peephole and her mouth almost hit the floor as she immediately unlocked and swung the door open.

"Baby!" she exclaimed as she bent down on one knee and gave her daughter, Breelyn, a hug. She could tell by how she wasn't hugging her back that she wasn't happy at all. She looked up at Joyce while embracing her daughter and then at the new model Cadillac that was parked out on the edge of the road with the woman's grouchy old husband staring dead in her face.

"So what's going on, Joyce?" she asked.

"He didn't call you, did he?" the old lady asked.

Quay let out a hard sigh and told Breelyn, "Go inside, baby. I'll be in there in a minute. Your Auntie Joyce and I need to talk."

Breelyn didn't say a word. She just sadly walked into the house with her head down.

"He didn't call you," Joyce repeated as she handed Quay a small duffle bag with Breelyn's things in it. "I knew he wasn't going to."

Quay shook her head and said, "If he's locked up somewhere, he knows not to call me. Spud already warned him once about calling me and begging for bail money. We're well beyond that point in our lives."

Joyce nodded, "Well, you can see he didn't show, Quay. He done messed around and got caught up in some type of robbery mess down there in Orlando with them hoodlums he be dealing with. He's in jail as we speak, and to be honest with you, he's just gonna have to sit and wait there until his trial comes up, unless one of his other kid's mommas get him out. Lord knows me and Lester don't have the money to get him out. We barely making ends meet as it is."

Quay's eyes glanced over to the new model Cadillac that Lester was still mean mugging her from. *Yeah, ends meet*, she thought to herself. "Yeah, I can see that," Quay said.

"Well, I would keep Breelyn, but we're too old to be running around with lil' ones for more than a few days. You know how it is, Quay. We're old now. When Lester's sugar starts to getting up, he just gets as grouchy as he wanna' be, and…"

"Look, Joyce, it's all good," Quay interrupted. "Breelyn wanted to spend this week with her daddy, not her daddy's aunt and uncle."

Lester harshly honked the horn of his brand spanking new ride, which prompted them both to look in the vehicle's direction. Joyce nervously whipped back around to Quay and handed her a sheet of paper. Before Quay even grabbed it, she could see the big, bold red letters that spelled out 'Eviction Notice' on top of the paper.

"It was on the door before I knocked. I snatched it before Breelyn saw it on there for her and the whole world to see." She moved towards Quay's ear and whispered, "Everybody in the neighborhood don't need to be knowing all your business."

"Well, thank you," said Quay. She did her best to hide her anger from the old woman as she did a quick glance over the letter. She was so upset about it she could just scream from the top of her lungs, but she refused to let her baby daddy's people see her shaken, ever.

Lester bashed on the horn once again, this time more violently and longer. Quay just cut her eyes at him as Joyce looked towards the car and began to frantically rub her hands together, "Oh, there he goes."

"Look, you better go, Joyce," said Quay. "Obviously, Lester has some place he needs for y'all to be."

"Yeah, I better get going, Quay," she uttered nervously. "I don't want to keep this man waiting any longer."

"Please don't," Quay added. She didn't wait for the woman to get to the car before she retreated into the house and slammed the door shut. The first thing Quay noticed when entering her home was the miserable look on Bree's face as she sat on the edge of the couch with her chin resting between the palm of her hands. The somber look on her child's face immediately had her heartbroken and furious at the same time. Her good for nothing baby daddy managed to screw up everything once again.

"Hey there, sweetie," she said while approaching the seven year old. She sat beside the child and wrapped her arm around her. "There's no need for the long face because when momma gets home tomorrow, we're gonna hit the mall like

21

some big time boss chicks and shop till we both drop. And when we're done, we're gonna get some ice…"

"My daddy don't love me," Breelyn offered in a deep, unsettling voice.

"What? Wait? No, sweetheart," Quay said as she dropped to one knee before her daughter and grabbed her hands. "Your daddy does love you."

"Then why didn't he show up?" she asked as she lifted her head with tears slowly streaming down her cheeks. "He never shows up."

"Baby, your father…," she stopped herself. Although she knew Lorenzo wasn't about anything and hadn't been about anything since she dropped out of high school when she got pregnant, she never wanted to pass that image of Breelyn's father onto her.

Despite his constant screw ups and frequent run ins with the law, if there was one thing Quay knew about Lorenzo, it was that he truly loved his daughter. He just didn't possess the maturity to consistently display it, which was part of the reason they weren't together anymore. Her days of waiting on Lorenzo to stand up and become a man were long gone, and she'd hoped her daughter wouldn't have to wait as she did. From the way things were beginning to look, it appeared to be inevitable. "He loves you, baby. He really does."

"It don't feel like it, Mommy."

Instead of making up any more excuses for her father, she simply embraced the child and held her into her bosom. "Bree, if there's one thing I know about your daddy, it's that he loves you. He just got a lot of growing up to do. We all do." As she held Bree close, her eyes were transfixed on the eviction notice that laid on the sofa beside her. If it wasn't one darn thing, it was always another. She pulled away from her daughter and looked her right in her eyes, "Your daddy is going to make this all up to you, I promise. He just has to take care of some very important business right now, but when he's all done, he will set things straight, you understand?"

"Yes, I understand, mommy."

"Good, baby," she said as she engulfed her in her arms once more while mumbling to herself, "If he doesn't, there's gonna be hell to pay."

****

Breeze ripped the dime across the hidden area of the scratch off lottery ticket he had positioned on top of a rolled up newspaper that was never meant for reading. Once he cleared away the hidden surface, he carefully scanned each number on the ticket in hopes of having a winning number, but once again, he managed to uncover another loser. He flipped the ticket over and began scratching off the surface to the next ticket.

As he tried his luck with another ticket in his huge stack, Loc slept in the driver seat with a 9mm pistol on his lap and his hand resting on top of it. The brawn, dark-skinned man was about a foot taller than Breeze and sported a bald head and a neatly kept goatee. They were backed in at the rear of the hotel parking lot and were supposed to be observing everyone that walked in and out of the building.

Loc awakened from his nap and glanced over at Breeze as he peeled away on the ticket. "You gonna clean up all that scratch off shit you're getting over every goddamn thing."

Breeze paused from his scratch-offs and looked over the junky mess surrounding him in the old, beat up Impala. He dug down towards the floor of the car and picked up a couple of used party cups and empty soda cans and said,

"Nigga, is you for real? Who the hell normally ride shotgun with your filthy ass, Oscar from Sesame Street?"

"That's alright tho, nigga. My shit's paid for."

"How much did they give you back when you gave 'em the twenty?"

"Fuck you! Smart ass mouth," said Loc. "You just clean up all that lotto shit when you're done. My car, my mess."

"Fine with me, Oscar," Breeze replied with a brief chuckle.

Suddenly, a dingy clothed homeless man pounced on Loc's window with an empty vegetable can in his hand. It caught Loc by surprise as he grabbed his pistol while rolling down his window, and brandished the gun towards the man.

"Fuck outta here with that!" Loc shouted at the poor soul.

"Hey, man," said the homeless guy as he fell backwards onto the ground and hurried away from the vehicle on his elbows. "I'm sorry, brotha. I just wanted some change."

"Change them nasty ass duds you got on and find yourself a fucking job. This ain't the damn Goodwill, nigga."

The poor vagrant climbed to his feet and darted off down the parking lot, leaving his rusted can and Loc behind.

Breeze giggled, "Man, why are you so damn mean?"

"I ain't eat breakfast," Loc answered as he sat the gun on his lap and rolled his window back up.

"Don't blame it on that. You just a mean motherfucker, that's all. That shit ain't good, you know. What's your blood pressure looking like?"

"The fuck you suppose to be—the surgeon general?"

"The surgeon general," Breeze laughed. "Nigga, that's for cigarettes."

"Shit, I don't know," he scratched his head for a moment as he briefly entertained the question, but in the blink of an eye, he quickly got fired up again and yelled, "Fuck all that! Don't be worrying about me. You just worry about getting that lotto shit cleaned up out of my car before you make me put my foot in your black ass."

"See how you is, dude?" Breeze chuckled. "All that ain't even necessary."

As Breeze continued with his laughter, Loc's eyes beamed in on the man they were staking out as he walked down the hotel sidewalk wearing a bright red, oversized robe, slippers and a box of donuts in his hands. "There go his punk ass right there," he said pointing in the man's direction.

"That nigga went to Dunkin Donuts like that?" Breeze asked.

"How in the hell did he leave his room and we didn't catch it?"

"Don't look at me. You were the one knocked out over there with all that snoring."

"And you were fucking around with them dumb ass lottery tickets," Loc said as he swiped the tickets off Breeze's lap.

"Shit, nigga, you were the one asleep," Breeze explained while retrieving his tickets from the floorboard.

"We're suppose to take turns watching this nigga's ins and outs when the other is sleep. What if this clown had

27

to left for good right up under our noses? Then how are we suppose to get paid?"

"Hell if I know. You can't be expecting me to be on the lookout all day and night while you take them long ass sleep breaks. That ain't how it's suppose to work."

"If you wanna get paid, you better do what the hell you need to do and make it work, nigga."

"Man, whatever," said Breeze as he waved his hand out of frustration. "And when are we gonna get to put the hit on this nigga? I'm getting tired of all of this stalking shit, anyway."

"When we get that call, my nigga." said Loc. "As soon as we get the call." Once the man disappeared into the building, Loc repositioned himself in his seat to get comfortable again. "Just make sure that nigga don't leave the spot again while I take another nap."

Breeze stared at him in displeasure as Loc nearly fell into a deep sleep immediately. He couldn't believe he was going back to sleep after the discussion they just had, but he simply decided to let it go, and tackle the rest of his scratch off tickets. The last place he wanted to be was on a crazy nigga like Loc's bad side, especially when he didn't have any way to get back down to Miami. Loc was one of those dudes that just didn't have a conscious about anything he did, and leaving a so called homeboy stranded miles away from home to fend for himself, would be something he wouldn't even flinch to.

****

Quay paced back and forth in the den with the her phone glued to her ear as her eyes periodically glanced over to her sleeping daughter. She was trying to get in touch with Mr. Riley, her landlord, in order to get to the bottom of the eviction notice he posted on her front door. She knew he was getting his money because she was sending it to him through Spud once she scraped it altogether. She was running a few days late gathering this month's payment, but he never had any problems with them being a couple of days late in the past, at least that's what she thought.

"Yes, Quayla," answered a deep, uninterested voice.

"Mr. Riley," Quay uttered into the phone, surprised he finally picked up. She called him at least thirty times over the past hour and couldn't get anything but his voicemail. "Mr. Riley, I got your–"

"Look, Quayla, I know what you want, and I'm afraid I can't give it to you. Now you and your guy, Spud, have left me no other choice. I haven't received so much as one red cent from you people in three months and–"

"Three months?" Quay interrupted. "Spud hasn't given you the rent in three months? Mr. Riley, you have to be mistaken. Three months?"

"Well, if I were mistaken I guess I wouldn't have to be going around placing eviction notices on people's doors at the crack of dawn. And I gotta say, I've been more than patient about all of this, hearing excuses after excuses. I even feel a little bad about having to throw you people out because your little Breelyn reminds me so much of my granddaughter, but unfortunately enough is enough. I don't have any other choice. I need my money."

"Wait, Mr. Riley, I had no idea Spud wasn't paying you the rent money."

"Well, he wasn't, and the joy train has finally stopped. I'm going to need you people to pack up your things and get out by five tomorrow because that's when I'm coming over there with the sheriff."

"Mr. Riley, no.. no.. no," Quay begged.

"I'm sorry, Quayla, I can't fall for the pity party again. I need my money. Now if you don't mind…"

"And you'll have your money, Mr. Riley. I just need a little more time. I'll have it all, plus a little extra. Just don't throw me and my baby out. Please!"

"Quayla…," her name cracked out from the back of his throat. "I can't.."

"Please, Mr. Riley. I'll get it. I will get it all to you," she promised. "You just said Breelyn reminded you of your own grandchild. Please, just give me a chance to get you your money and keep a roof over my daughter's head. I know if your granddaughter was in the same situation, you would want somebody to give her mother a chance to make things right." She felt wrong for playing with the old man's heart with his granddaughter, but she had to say something to buy some time from him, and besides, he was the one that brought her up in the first place.

He let out a hard sigh after a few seconds of silence, "Friday, Quayla!" he barked. "I want the three months I'm owed and the next two months, all in one, and not a penny less. Next Friday by five o'clock or there won't be any amount of begging or crying in the world that's gonna stop me from throwing you people out. I'm sorry, but that's just the way it's gonna have to be."

"Thank you. Thank you, Mr. Riley," she said.

"Yeah, whatever, Quayla." He hung up.

"Mr. Riley… Mr. Riley.." she said into the phone but when she glanced at the phone screen she realized he had already ended the call. She tossed the phone on the bed, bowed and just shook her head. She was ecstatic about getting some time to get him the cash, but she didn't have a clue as to how she was going to get him the amount of money he was demanding in so little time. Then her mind quickly switched to Spud. She was furious she had been giving him all of her earnings to pay the bills and he wasn't paying them. She couldn't fathom what he was doing with all the money she had given him over the past several months.

She heard keys jingling at the front door and quickly marched off into the living room with the eviction notice in her hand. She looked over to Breelyn as she remained fast asleep on the couch and awaited for Spud to swing the door open.

Spud unexpectedly stumbled in through the door sipping on a straw sticking up out of his jumbo fast food cup. He paused in his tracks as he shut the door behind himself. "What's wrong with you?"

Quayla stood her post with her arms folded. She hadn't seen him since yesterday morning, and she couldn't wait to hear his excuse as to what he was doing with himself for the past twenty-four hours. She disregarded his question completely and went straight to asking her own. "So we're coming back home in the middle of the next day now, are we?"

"Man whatever," said Spud as he trampled in. He froze in his tracks when he caught a glimpse of the television across the room. "Who turned off the X-Box?"

"What?" Quay asked aggravated as she looked over towards the TV stand and the X-Box.

"I left the X-Box on, and now it's off," he said as he walked over the television and bent his chubby self over to get a closer examination of the game system. "I was on a hard ass part of Call of Duty, and now the shit's off. I done told y'all not to be touching my shit."

"Keep your voice down," she said. "Nobody touched that stupid video game."

"Then why is it off then? Damn!"

"Do you mind?" She looked towards the innocently sleeping Breelyn.

"Man, whatever," he brushed by her and down the hall towards the kitchen.

"Anyway, where were you?"

"Out," he said.

"Oh, so you were just out?"

"You were out," he said as he placed his cup in the fridge.

"Yeah," she nodded perturbed. "I was out working."

"That's still out!"

"You're just unbelievable," she said.

"What?" he asked dumbfounded.

"You know what? Since you have such an outstanding sense of humor, let's just see how good it is when you take a look at this. Here!" she handed him the eviction notice.

"What the hell is this?" he asked.

She let out a huge glob of air in frustration and yelled, "Look at it!"

He unfolded it, took a glance at the big red words at the top of it and slung it onto the table, "I don't want that. I don't know what you giving that to me for. I paid my half of the bills."

"What? Your half of the bills? What do you mean your half of the bills? I've been giving you almost everything I pull in at that old dump of a club you got me working at to pay this rent, and Mr. Riley says he hadn't gotten one damn penny from you in three months. Now where is the money?"

"He told you three months?"

"What difference does it make? He hadn't been getting any of it? We're about to get thrown out on our asses if we don't get the last three months plus the next two months of rent into him by next Friday."

"How in the hell are we gonna do all that?"

"Hell, I don't know, *Mr. Man!* Why don't you step up for a change and figure something the hell out," she replied as she smashed the side of his head with the tips of her fingers.

He snatched the letter from the table and skimmed through it once more as she walked over to the window and glanced out of it with her arms folded and her lips poking out.

"Damn," he said as he balled up the paper and threw it in the trash. He slowly walked up behind her and said, "Look, I was gonna tell you this last week, but I didn't know how to. I thought I was gonna be able to recoup the cash, but…"

She whipped around, "What the hell happened to all that money, Spud? Do you think I like prancing around in that grimy behind club all damn night?"

"Well hell, I'm trying to tell you what happened if you would just let me talk for one second, shoot."

"Oh, just man up and say it already." If looks could kill he would be spread out on the floor beneath her feet. As much as she wanted to hear his reasoning for him not paying the bills with the money she gave him, she also wanted to slap his lips off his face just as badly. "Well! What are you waiting for? Say it!"

He shrugged his shoulders and looked towards the ceiling, "I lost all the money betting on the fight."

"What?" she yelled. "You lost all of my money betting on a fight? Gambling, nigga? You lost all our money gambling?"

"Now, now, now, wait a minute," he stuttered as he scrambled to give her all the details before she went totally ballistic. "Now, I won and I won big, but the nigga ain't pay up. He ain't pay nobody. His punk ass skipped town."

"Well you better go find him," she said. "As a matter of fact, you need to be looking for his ass right now."

"I already did," he said. "Well… five-o did. They found him laid up in Memphis with a slug in his dumb ass head. Apparently, I wasn't the only one he did the shit to."

"So where does that leave us, Spud?"

"We can't stay at your momma house?"

"Are you a fuckin' retarded?" she asked with a short, sarcastic laugh.

"Well, you ain't gotta be talking like that."

"No!" she said. "Hell no, we can't stay at my momma house."

"Well that's all you had to say. You ain't gotta be calling people out their name and stuff."

"Somebody needs to call you out your name," she said. "I need to do more than that." She paused, took a few deep breaths and clasped her hands together while saying calmly, "What are you gonna do about this, Spud?"

"Me?"

"Don't play dumb. Yes, you. You lost all of our money, now you need to come up with a solution." She took a seat at the table and waited for his answer. Spud, stood before her dumfounded and speechless. "You can't do it, can you? You can't step up and get us through the crap you put us in, just one time."

"Look, I've been asking for…"

She jumped out of his chair and into his face. "We need money, Spud! We need the money you lost on some dumb fight! You put us here. You did this to us."

He backed up a step and let her yell as her finger would not stop wagging in his face. When she finally stopped, he said, "You don't think you can work a few extra nights at Oasis?"

His words almost made her fully unload on him as she raised her hand to smack him, but she just walked off to other side of the kitchen, shaking her head in disgust at the man she decided to spend the best years of her life with. She then became disgusted with herself. "Look, I'm about to get Breelyn's things together. I'm gonna need you to run us over to my mom's house and me over to Oasis later."

"I can take you one place but not both."

"What do you mean, you can take me one place but not both?"

"Gas, man! Gas is high as hell and just like you said, I gotta go figure some things out."

"You know what Negro..."

"Why can't you ever just let Bree stay with me?" he asked.

She gave him a cold stare. Quayla barely trusted Bree with her own daddy and his creative ways of getting in trouble. There was no way on God's green earth she was going to trust her to be alone with any other man but her father. "You know what, just take us over to my momma house. I'll find a way to Oasis."

"Fine with me," he shrugged his chunky shoulders as she darted off into the den.

★★★★★★★★★★★★

Spud drove his lime green Crown Victoria in front of Quay's mother's apartment building. He turned the car off and leaned back in his seat, gazing at Quayla, who was looking straight forward as if he didn't exist.

"Mom has the door opened," Quayla said to her daughter. "I'll be right behind you, sweetie."

"Okay, Mom," she said. "Bye, Spud."

"Bye, lil' shorty," said Spud. "You be good at your grandma's."

"I will," she said as she anxiously unbuckled her seat belt, grabbed her Dora the Explorer backpack and dashed out of the car.

Quay smiled as she watched her daughter sprint into the building and up the stairs to her grandmother's apartment.

"You need some help getting her other stuff out of the trunk?"

"Nope, I got it," she said. "I just need you to find a way to get what we talked about done. We don't have a lot of time, Spud."

"Baby girl you know I'm on it. Now give me some of that, suga." He leaned over and poked his lips out for a kiss.

"You're kidding me, right?" she said as she rolled her eyes and turned away.

"So it's like that, Quay? You gonna give your boy the cold shoulder like that?"

"It's gonna be like that until you find us a way out of this mess you got us in."

"You ain't even right, Quay. I told you got this, girl."

"For your sake, I hope you do, Spud." She grabbed the door hand and exited the car.

When Quay got up the stairs with the rest of Breelyn's bags, her mother was waiting just outside of the door sipping on a cup of hot tea. "So he's locked up again," said Deloris.

"Ma," said Quay, "Don't start."

"What, I'm not starting," said the middle aged woman, that looked like an older version of Quay. "I'm just stating the obvious, that's all."

Quay just shook her head as she eased into the apartment with her mother following behind her, closing the door.

****

"So, you gonna tell me what happened with Lorenzo?" asked Deloris as she chopped carrots on the cutting board across from Quay, who was sitting at the table.

"You already know, Ma."

"What was it this time?"

"I don't even know. Joyce said he got mixed up in some type of robbery or something. I didn't ask her for the details. The only person I'm concerned about is Breelyn."

"I told you I never liked that boy. I don't even know what you ever saw in 'em. He's a bum."

"Well, he is your grandbaby's daddy."

"And who fault is that?" She gave Quayla a stern look. "Anyway, my grandbaby is probably the only good thing he's ever been associated with in his entire life. Every time you look he's behind bars over some foolishness. This time I hope they give him more than just a slap on his wrist. Maybe a kick in his ass will work out better."

Quay said, "Ma, don't start this today, please. I'm just not in the mood for it today, now."

"And what about the one you're with now? I see he got them big dumb rims he been talking about getting on that stupid looking, old police car he got y'all riding around in. He can't come up and speak no more? What, he too good come up and say hi to your momma?"

"You know what, Ma? Spud is good right where he is."

"Humph! I can tell by the way you said that, he's screwing up again, too. What he do this time?" Deloris asked. "I know he done something. I can tell by how you

43

looking. I saw it all over your face when you walked up them stairs"

"It's nothing, Ma. He just.." She bowed her head as thoughts of him blowing all of their money rushed through her mind.

"Say it child. If you can't talk to your momma, who can you talk to?"

She let out a hard sigh and looked towards the ceiling. "He just blew all of our rent money gambling on some fight. He said he won but the guy that was suppose to pay him ran off with all the money and got himself killed."

"Humph," she chuckled while shaking her head. "Pardon my French, Quayla, but Spud ain't shit!"

"Momma!" Quay quickly responded. She looked behind her to see if Breelyn was anywhere around listening to them.

"No, no, don't you no momma me. Spud ain't shit. Lorenzo ain't shit, and none of them other ones ain't shit neither, Quay," Deloris declared while swaying her knife in the air. "Take time and look at things honestly, chile. It's a pattern. A pattern that begins with you and finishes with one of them sorry niggas you end up with between your legs and wasting your time. It's time to grow up and cut your losses."

"So this is all my fault," she asked.

"If you stick around and continue to let it happen it is. Quay this is no longer just about you. You got a little girl to look after. She keeps seeing you with these sorry behind Negroes, how do you think she's gonna pick 'em when she gets old enough to?" Deloris asked. "It's beyond time for you to stop thinking about your own needs and to start thinking about the needs of your daughter. That's what I had to do for you when your daddy skipped out on me with that heffa. If you want to set the right example for my grandchild, one that she can be proud of, you will. She's the only one that should matter now."

"Well, Ma, I assure you, Breelyn is my first priority. She always is."

"You need some money, girl? I don't have much, but I'll give you what I have. You've always been too proud to ask for anything. Now ain't the time for pride. Just tell me what you need. I can start a fund with the girls and we could go and…"

"No, Ma, no. I don't need for you to do any of that. And you can keep my business to yourself. I got it. I'm old enough to handle my own battles, and that's what I plan on doing," she declared. "I don't even know why I even said anything to you about it."

"Well, you better do what you gotta do. Them streets are cold, and I'm not trying to see my granddaughter nor you in 'em."

"I got this, Ma."

"And I'm not trying to take anything to do with your business, but, Quay, you have to make some changes. And speaking of business, since you so grown these days, what kind of work you be doing at night where you don't get back until the morning? I've been aiming to ask you about this for a couple of weeks now."

Quay pushed away from the table and hopped up. "You know what, Ma, I'm gonna go check on my daughter."

"Don't runaway when I start asking you questions you don't wanna' answer, chile."

"I'm not, Ma. I'm just gonna go check on, Bree."

"Well she fine out there, as long as them cartoons running. This here, me and you time. We're not finished."

"We'll talk later, Ma. I'm 'bout to check on Bree," she inisisted as she skirted out of the kitchen.

She tiptoed down the hall and stood at the doorway entering into the living room. Bree sat with her legs crossed in front of the television, watching cartoons with her teddy bear gripped closely by her side. Quay decided not to even bother her as she simply watched her young child, relaxing and enjoying herself, utterly unaware of all the horrors that existed beyond the walls of the apartment building. There was no way on God's green earth she would ever allow her daughter to be exposed to the harsh rigors of the world subdued to living on the streets as long as she could help it– not in this lifetime.

She reluctantly pushed herself away from admiring her young adolescent and slowly made her way down the hall into the bathroom. She stood in front of the mirror and solemnly gazed at her own reflection. She was disappointed by what she saw in the mirror, possibly even despising who she saw. She never imagined her life would turn out the way that it had thus far, and it was becoming increasingly difficult for her to see any improvements any time soon.

Quayla sat at the bus stop a few blocks away from her mother's apartment building in a trance watching the passing cars. She waited at her mother's apartment as long as she could before going to the bus stop. She hated waiting at the stop for too long because she would always get bombarded with ride offers from perverted and strange men. She got her fill of those types when she got to the club.

A dark colored sedan passed her by and quickly slammed on brakes a few feet from her. She slipped her hand inside her purse and grabbed her pepper spray when she noticed the driver placing the car in reverse. "And here he comes," she said under her breath.

The driver blew his horn twice to get her attention as he backed up a little more. She simply looked in the opposite direction, pretending not to see or hear him at all. She didn't have a clue as to who was behind the wheel, but she knew he was persistent as hell. The car stopped in front of her, and the dark tinted window on the passenger side began to roll down.

"Quayla? Quay!" said the driver. "What are you doing out here waiting on a bus?"

She rose from the bench, squinting her eyes to get a better look at the driver. She was surprised to discover that it was one of her old girlfriend's older brother, Zeke. "Oh, hey Zeke!"

"Girl, what'cha you doing out here?"

"Minding my own." She always thought he was nice, and he had always been kind to her, but she wasn't trying to rekindle any old relationships today. She had too much thrown on her plate for one day, and she always felt that the less people in the past knew about her present, the better.

"Still got that quick tongue on ya' I see."

She nodded with a pithy, fake smile.

He looked at her then around her. "Hmm, looks like you're waiting for the bus."

"You're a genius."

"Well girl, you know good and well someone as pretty as you shouldn't be out here waiting for the city bus. Where you headed? I can give you a lift."

She took a moment to think. She didn't want to ride the bus, and if he took her there, they'd be going straight

49

there without her having to make the constant stops the bus needed to make that always made a short ride much longer. Arriving to the club a few minutes early would allow her to get a much needed jump on some of the other girls. She just felt too embarrassed to tell him where she was headed. "I got it, Zeke. Thanks for the offer, though. The bus will be here any minute."

"Girl, you better get in this car. You know we go way back."

She could tell by the look on his handsome, clean cut face, he wasn't taking no for an answer. She took a deep sigh, gathered her things and hopped into the car.

"So where we headed?" he asked as he eased his car in drive.

"Oasis."

"Say what?" he replied with his mouth wide opened. "Oasis? The strip club? Ho-asis?"

"Look, you know what," she said grabbing at the door handle. "Just let me out before…"

"No…no..no, I got you. I was just playing around. I'll take you there."

She gazed out of the window while second guessing herself about getting into the car in the first place. Zeke was three years older than her, and she always had somewhat of a puppy-dog crush on him when she used to hang out with his sister, Nisha. When they were growing up, whenever he came around she always paused and fell short of breath when he spoke to her. She felt that was part of the reason for her getting into the car in the first place.

As she broke away from her window gaze, giving him a brief look over, she couldn't help but think he was even finer than she remembered. She hadn't seen him since he went off for college, years ago. He lost some of that baby fat he always carried and had a nice muscular build with a smooth temple fade to go with his neatly trimmed full beard. She went back to gazing out of the window, thinking, what if? She always thought he was a little sweet on her too, but with their age difference at the time and her being his little sister's best friend, she figured that sat a decent sized barrier between them.

As silence continued its occupancy in the car ride, Zeke glanced at her a few times, yearning to strike up some type of conversation with her, but he was a little nervous about saying the wrong thing again. Not able to bare the silence any longer he said, "So… what do you do at Oasis? Hostess? Bartend?"

She smiled and bowed her head. She was surprised the question took as long as it did to part his lips. She said, "If you must know, Zeke, I'm a dancer. Surprise."

"No way! A dancer?"

"Yes, I'm a dancer," she said. "I get on that pole for those who make it rain. So you can release all of your astonishment and disappointment now."

"Nah, nah, I'm not trying to judge you, Quay. I wouldn't do that," he said. "I just thought… never mind."

"What? What is it?"

"It's nothing."

"No, what is it? Just go 'head and say it, Zeke. Trust me, I can take whatever you throw at me."

"Well, when I used to see you with my sister back in the day, you always seemed to have things so well put together. I just thought you'd be doing something major, like managing some fortune five hundred company or something." He was quick to add, "Not to say there's anything wrong with what you're doing now. I just didn't see that coming."

There was an awkward silence that followed his comments, one that sent her mind reminiscing of her naive teenage years. Yeah, she even thought she had everything put together well her darn self. She was going to marry Lorenzo, have plenty of kids while staying home and raising them as he went out and made an honest living on a real job. There's rarely been a day in her adult life she didn't want to smack the hell out of herself for dreaming up those outlandish fantasies. Through all the roadblocks and misfortunes she had to brace through, she even wondered to herself how she ended up doing what she was doing.

She said to him, "Well, we live to disappoint, I guess." She went back to quietly staring out of the window. Despite all the scenery they passed by, she couldn't see any of it. Her mind was now concerned with getting Mr. Riley his money, maybe rectifying her life, and possibly even living up to the expectations she once carried for herself, if she could just work through her current mess.

He figured his questioning her about the club was the reason for the abrupt silence, so he took another shot at breaking the ice. "Well, guess what?" he asked.

"What?"

"I'm a cop."

"What?" Her neck snapped around as she leaned away from him like he was harboring some type of infectious disease.

"Yup," he said as he dug into his pocket and flashed his shiny gold badge. "I knew that would surprise the shit out of you."

"Zeke, now you know me…"she said nervously.

"Whoa…whoa, whoa! Girl, chill out," he laughed. "I'm off duty right now. I know you aren't about no shady stuff. What? You think I picked you up because I thought you were at the bus stop trickin' or something?" He laughed harder.

"No!" she added with a hint of an attitude and a roll of the eyes. "So how long have you been a cop?"

"Not long, about seven months. They say I'm still wet behind the ears."

"Humph! You're right. That shocks the shit out of me. I never knew you wanted to be a cop, but you were always a do-gooder," she said with a chuckle.

"Yeah, whatever you say," he said. "But I don't know, it's not something I planned. I could've saved myself a whole bunch of money in student loans if I did. I just watched the news and constantly saw all these young brothers out here getting shot and killed by the city's finest, I thought it would be a good idea to stand up and be a part of the solution."

"I hear you, Zeke, but a police officer? Really?"

"Hey," he shrugged. "You can be a part of the problem or a part of the solution. We need more people looking like us to represent us. Trust me, I was never a fan of po-po back in the day, but change starts from within."

"Yeah," she said. "I guess you're right. That's a drastic change, though."

"You ain't never lied about that. Cats from the hood that know I'm on the force now won't even fart in a brotha's direction. And the ones that do speak, think I'm some kind of a sellout. I get it from all sides, I guess."

"Well, you knew what you signed up for, do-gooder," she laughed.

"Very funny," he smiled. "I bet you wouldn't have gotten in the car if you knew before hand, huh?"

"Hell no!"

They both laughed.

He took another look at her as she went back to drifting her focus through her window. He couldn't believe how beautiful a women she had grown to become. Back in the day, she was just his kid sister's annoying best friend and the both of them got on his nerves. Now, however she was a full fledge woman. A very attractive full fledge woman. "Hey, whatever happened to that guy you used to date? Lawrence... Lonnie..?"

"Lorenzo."

"Lorenzo, yeah, that's his name."

"He's around. Let's just say he's in your profession also, but just in reverse."

"Oh, I see. I always knew he was a knucklehead."

"He's also my child's father."

"Damn, my bad," he said with caution. "I didn't even know you had kids together. My bad."

"Just one child, and we're not together anymore, Zeke. I closed that chapter in my life long ago. We just share a beautiful daughter and that's it."

"Oh, okay. Well... how does your current man feel about you working at Oasis?"

"Wow, Zeke, you know you got a lot of questions. What are you a crime scene investigator, too? Back in the day, you barely said anything to me besides get out of your face when me and Nisha used to hang."

He laughed, "That's because you two used to be annoying as hell, and I didn't ask you all that! I'm just keeping the conversation going."

"Well, Mr. Nosey, here's another shocker for you. He was the one to recommend I work there. He got me the job."

"What? Are you serious?"

"Long, stupid story," said Quay. "Anyway, how's Nisha?"

He wasn't quite ready to jump into a new subject after she revealed to him that her man actually had the gall to ask her to strip, but he respected her mute request to change the subject and said, "Oh, Nish, she's doing real good. She went and got married, became a nurse and moved out to Colorado with her family. She's doing real good."

"Wow," Quay replied. "She really has done good for herself."

Hearing about Nisha's successes and family life placed Quayla in instant reflection mode about her own missteps and shortcomings again. It seemed like yesterday, her and Nisha were sitting on the porch in the hood, talking about which boy was the finest and which one of them they were going to get to spend their money on them. Although she was thrilled to hear that her best friend had made a good life for herself, she couldn't help but feel bad about how her life was turning out. Basically, she was a single parent, a stripper at a rundown gentlemen's club, and just a few days away from being homeless–yup, she felt like a complete failure.

Zeke continued to ramble on about his sister's successes as Quay's mind became occupied by thoughts of the money she needed to get to her landlord by Friday. She knew Spud was just too unreliable to come through, and he was really on some other stuff, so she couldn't help but believe it was all on her again. As she peered through the window, the thoughts just kept beating within in her head. *How in the world am I gonna get this money in the time this man is looking to have it?*

****

Loc and Breeze eased into the parking lot of the strip club called, Bottoms Up. They slowly passed by the man they've been tailing for most of the week. They parked a few spaces down from the heavy set man's late model Lexus. Dressed in a dated Hawaiian shirt, black slacks and a red flax cap, he strolled towards the entrance completely unaware that he was being followed.

"Look at this corny ass nigga, looking like a black Magnum P.I.," said Breeze leaning back in his chair observing the man's movement from the passenger side mirror. "I just don't understand this dude. This nigga got us driving all up through Florida to these bum ass strip clubs like they going out of style. What in the hell is wrong with the clubs in Miami? Shit!"

"The nigga can't eat where he shits," said Loc as he reclined back in his chair, preparing to take another nap. "Simple as that."

"You think he taggin' any of them broads up in these spots? A little side action in the V.I.P.?"

"Who knows?" said Loc. "All I know, is when the time is right, we gonna tag his fat ass–permanently!"

"Why you think they want his ass smoked?"

"I don't know. I don't ask no questions. All I ask about is how much I'm getting paid and what I gotta do to collect, that's it. Things are less complicated that way."

"This gotta be one rich mutha fucka, though," he said looking towards Loc as he made himself comfortable in his own seat. "All these fancy ass hotels, these bougie restaurants and strip club money for days, this nigga living the high life and don't even know it's 'bout to be time for that ass to expire. They ain't never lied when they said ignorance is bliss."

"Yeah, well, he can't say he didn't get his rocks off on the way to the checkout line, that's for damn sure."

****

Zeke rolled up in front of the club and stopped his car at the entrance. He took a brief look at the brawn, bald bouncer standing at the front door and then back at Quay as she gathered her things.

"How much do I owe you, Zeke?" Quay asked, digging in her bag for some cash.

He frowned. "Girl, go 'head with that. You don't owe me a thing. I just wish I was dropping you off somewhere other than this place. I've never had any calls to go up in there for anything, but some of the other gentlemen clubs in Jacksonville... it's just not a good thing, Quay."

She blushed, delighted he felt she needed some protecting–an expression of concern she never received from Spud. "I'm a big girl, Zeke. I think I can handle myself."

"Oh, I'm sure you can," he nodded, still hung up on how beautiful she had become. "I just want you to be careful out here that's all. In these streets, one minute you can just be chillin' and everything can be poppin' off good and the next thing you know, all hell is breaking loose over some petty crap."

"Well, thanks for your concern, Zeke, and the ride," she said as she grabbed the door handle. "It was really good seeing you again."

"Quay," he said. She paused with one foot hanging out of the door, looking back at him. "Take this." He dug into his pocket and retrieved one of his cards. "If one of them jokers in there get to be too much for you, or if you need something, anything, or if you just want to talk, you call me. It don't matter the time."

She took his card and smiled at it. "Okay, Zeke. I'll do that."

"Quay, I'm serious."

"I am, too."

"Quayla, there's more options for you than in there. I don't know what your situation is right now or why you're even doing what you're doing, but you're better than that. I'm not judging, I'm just being a friend, like I've always been."

She nodded with a bit of a smile and hopped out the car. She knew every word he spoke was truth, and the feelings were even mutual, but she understood she had to do what she had to do to get by and at this moment in her life, it was Oasis.

He wanted to say something else, anything, to prevent her from going up in the tiny club and doing whatever she felt she had to do, but he knew he didn't have the right to tell her not to. Hell, before the short drive to Oasis, it had been nearly a decade since they last spoke. He resigned to the fact that she knew what she was doing and he simply let his eyes trail her movements as she greeted the brawn bouncer standing at the door. Moments later she disappeared into the club entrance.

****

Quay strolled into the club, her backpack hanging off her shoulder, as she waved and smiled at the scattered assembly of people she passed by to get to the dressing rooms in the back. Most of the greetings from the other girls she passed by were cold and unenthusiastic. To them, she was still the new chick on the block, and they knew as well as she did that she was by far the most attractive woman in the joint. They couldn't stand it.

Unfortunately, being the most attractive dancer didn't automatically translate into garnering the most earnings by the end of the night. She may have been the meaning of the word fire, but the less attractive, veteran dancers were consistently collecting the most bank, and they flaunted it in front of her every chance they got. When she made it to the dressing room, she immediately spotted the only girl she considered to be a friend since she started dancing, Déjà, sitting in front of her mirror getting her make up just right for the night.

"Hey girl," she said as she dropped down on a bench positioned behind the woman.

"What's up, suga," Déjà spoke, not turning around to face her, but greeting her from her reflection in the mirror. "You up in here early tonight. Trying to catch yourself one of them old geezers before they rush home to beat their wives' curfew?"

"Girl, I wish. You know nobody pays me much attention in here except the tourists that accidentally find themselves down this way."

"You just ain't working it how it need to be worked, that's all," she said as she popped her lipstick. "I done told ya', you stick with me, I'll get you right. I'll show you how to get them perverted bastards spitting them dollars out at you like a cash machine."

Quay moved up and sat in the chair next to Déjà. "Girl, I know you know the business like the back of your hand and all, but these dudes just come in here and they only deal with the same chicks, over and over. They act like I got the cooties or something. And by no means am I trying to be cocky, but I know I look better than most of the broads up in here."

She whispered, "Awe, you know what is, girl."

"No," she said. "I don't. Tell me so I can fix it. I'm not coming up in here for my health. I got bills I gotta pay."

"It's Cy's ass. That's all it is. You know he's had his eyes on you since you first walked through that door and probably even before that."

"What? Girl, you crazy. Cy is shady as hell, but not that shady."

"Humph! He probably done claimed you for himself to all the lame niggas he knows that come through here. Them niggas scared of his ass anyway," she continued to whisper. "This club ain't nothing but a front for the other stuff he into. His fat, disgusting ass, know good and well you his cousin's girl. His first cousin at that; his lame ass."

"I don't think he would try and stab Spud in the back like that. They've always been pretty tight."

"The hell he wouldn't. And you can act like you don't know, but Spud would do the same to him," said Déjà. "And to tell you the truth, you should give Cy some. If you don't mind a big, fat, disgusting, sweaty bastard huffing and puffing, gasping for air on top of you. I give that fat bastard ten seconds tops. Six of them seconds to find his little business. I know he can't see that little ass Vienna sausage he packing." They giggled.

"Girl, you stupid," said Quay. "I gotta do something, but I'm not that desperate. This idiot back at the house done lost all of our money gambling, and now we're behind on the rent. Lord knows I can't let my baby get kicked out in these streets. I had to go through it for a spell when I was growing up, and I just can't let her go through that mess, not like I did."

"Spud, say he lost all y'all's money gambling, huh?" Déjà questioned. "How do you know he ain't been spending that money on some other, bitch? I don't try to be all up in your business girl, but I could've sworn I saw Spud's trifling ass in the Avenues Mall with that heffa, Nadia, a few weeks back. I just know that was him and her together. We should beat her ass if she works tonight just for the possibility of her running around town with his stankin' ass."

"Girl, I'm at the point in my life, that if he is running around with that chick or any other trick, they can have his sorry ass. I just don't give a damn anymore."

"Well, she still deserve an ass kickin'," said Déjà. "Let's just make something up so we can just beat the bitch ass."

"Chile, go 'head with that. You know we are both entirely too old to be fighting people. You more than me," Quay laughed. "Besides, I'm just worried about getting this rent to this man in time. Not only is our landlord asking for all the back rent we owe him, but he's talking about he wants two months in advance, too. How in the hell am I gonna come up with all that money by next week?"

"Well, you better get with the program then, girl." Déjà said pointing towards her.

"What program are you talking about, Déjà? And I hope you're not talking about what I think you're talking about."

"Girl, just like the old saying goes, closed legs don't get fed."

"And you are talking about exactly what I thought you were talking about," she said rolling her eyes. "Girl, I am not a hoe."

"Well, if you're fucking a man that you're not married to, and he's not doing nothing for you or your little girl, not only does that make you a hoe, but it makes you a dumb hoe."

"Thanks a lot, Déjà. Why don't you tell me how you really feel."

"Hey, baby, I'm just giving it to you the only way Déjà know how," she said. "And trust me, I know you're not some random hoe, but you better open your eyes and realize where you're at. I mean, you're giving up the cookies for some old, sloppy man that don't wanna work, for free, and he can't even bring home the bacon unless that shit's on a sandwich. On top of that, he's spending up all the money that you're bringing to the table for bills he should be paying.

I'm sorry, but that just don't make any fucking sense to me at all when you can get one of these niggas up in here that will give you top dollar just to sniff it. Girl, you better wake up and use your assets. That pretty face don't last forever. As the beauty goes, so does a man's attention. If all these little ass thots running 'round here, chasing behind these worthless Negroes without any potential whatsoever understood how the game is really setup, they wouldn't be broke as hell with a bunch of damn bey bey kids wandering around wondering where their daddy is."

"I know but...

"Look, Quay, you can't be a stripper with morals. Go and find you a job at somebody's customer service center for that shit. No matter what the circumstances were that brought you in here—you are now a stripper. You have to do whatever it takes to make that bread. If it requires laying on your back for a few minutes when nobody's fuckin' looking, then you do what the hell you gotta do and keep it moving. 'Cause suga', life ain't handing out shit for free."

As Quay absorbed the impromptu lecture from Déjà, one of the girls peaked in from the door at the entrance and said, "Quay, Cy wants to talk to you in his office."

"Okay," she replied.

"Gone and give Biggie a chance, girl," Déjà laughed as she returned her focus to the mirror and her makeup.

"Girl, I'm not messing with you," she said as she headed for the door.

****

Cyprus reclined in his huge leather executive chair behind his fancy oak desk as a sparingly dressed dancer massaged his neck and shoulders. He was leaning back in his chair with his eyes shut and a smile plastered over his face.

"Girl, your hands feel like they been dipped and bronzed in some purified holy water fixed up by the Lord himself, you heard me," he said.

Quay knocked on the door and crept in. Cy jolted forward onto his desk as his lady took a few steps back, yielding her massage.

"Awe, there she is—Quay, just the fine feline I wanted to see," he said. He turned to the lady behind him. "Go on and get with me later baby cakes. Cyprus gotta talk business."

The girl made her way towards the door but not without rolling her eyes at Quay as she passed by. Quay approached Cy's desk and said, "What's up, Cyprus?"

"Nothin' much, sweetie, nothing much at all. Why don't you have a seat," he said as he signaled her to sit. "How we doing tonight? We doin' good? I know you doing good. You sure as hell looking good. Look at you."

"I'm alright, Cy." She plopped down in the chair in front of him. "I know you didn't call me in here to find out how I was, so what's up?"

"We'll get to that. We'll get to that," he said. "So how's everything with the girls? Y'all getting along, fine? I don't really see you mingling around with the other ladies like you should."

"Look, Cy, if you're calling me in here to snitch on what the girls are doing, you got the wrong one. Besides, they don't really talk to me no ways."

"No, no, no, baby doll," he said. "I just wanna make sure the girls treating you right, that's all. 'Cause you know, you're the special one. I like to know how my dimes are doing up in my spot. Make sure you're well taken care of."

"Really," she said unenthused as he looked at her with a demented smile. He was staring at her like she was a piece of meat, and it made her feel uncomfortable. It made her think about what Déjà said about him taking a liking to her, and it disgusted her. What irritated her even more about the six foot, three hundred and fifty pound man that sat before her was his annoying breathing. It resembled someone shoveling snow, and it made her skin crawl. "So you called me in here because I'm special."

"Hell yeah! Now, not just because you're dealing with my lil' cousin right now, but it's 'cause you really are special."

"Well, since you seem to be so high on me right now, I guess you won't mind me asking you if you're blackballing me? Telling people not to get dances from me?"

He placed his hand over his chest, "Now, why in the hell would I do some stupid shit like that? Girl, I'm a business man."

"Umm hmm," she replied.

"I got financial goals I'm trying to accomplish. You don't make no money, I don't make no money. Now we are here in hot ass Jacksonville, Florida. It's so damn hot down here, my sweat don't roll down my face it just evaporates as soon as it formulates. It is so damn hot down here, these niggas' brains is fried like some southern fried chicken. Brains so messed up, they won't know a good woman if one jumped up out one of them stupid looking Crown Vic's they be tricking out and smacked 'em right upside their goddamn skull. These niggas brains are fried, you heard me?"

"I hear you."

"And that's the reason I called you in here, Quay. These niggas' brains is fried."

"That's all fine, Cy, but please can we get to what you called me in here for?" she asked. "I gotta be on stage soon, and I need to get ready."

"Well, I know you gotta get on stage, girl. I own the place," he said in calmer tone. "Now, it disheartens me to show you what I have to show you, but I gotta do it, Quay. I just got to."

"What do you have to show me, Cy," she said. By now, she was just ready for him to say what he had to say so she could be off on her way. The quicker she could get out on stage, the sooner she could begin gathering up some money to present to her landlord when the time came.

"Now I want you to brace yourself because it's about Spud," he said. "The nigga's family and all, but sometimes things go above and beyond family, you heard me?"

"I hear you, Cy."

"Now, if you really, really want to know the truth about it, I don't even know why this nigga let you work up in here in the first place. And that's saying a lot because I own this mother fucker, you heard?"

"I hear you, Cy," she said rolling her eyes.

"Got you all around these musty ass men, and…"

"Cy!" she yelled. "Will you just show me what you got to show me?"

"Alright. Alright," he said. He slid open the draw behind his desk, pulled out a manila envelope and threw it on the desk in front of her. "There you go. Open it up."

"What is this, Cy," she asked staring at the folder, apprehensive about even touching it.

"Just open it and see," he said. "Now, normally Big Cy mind his own damn business about most things because I ain't from down here in this country ass, big city, but when something ain't right and bear down on a nigga soul for too long, he just gotta release it."

She slid out multiple photos of Spud with different women. He was hugged up with them, kissing on them, holding hands–just doing the most. The crazy thing about it all was that most of the pictures were taken of him with the chick Déjà had just warned her about, Nadia.

"And I know lil' cuz might be feeding you some jazz about that nigga that got his wig split up in Memphis scamming him for his loot. Some of that's true. That little terd got me for a few hundred, but he ain't get cuz for half of what them broads on them pictures been gettin' him for."

She took a break from staring at the photos and looked Cyprus dead in his eyes. She didn't know what he expected from her for snitching on his own blood that way. She was almost more inclined about the reason behind him throwing his own cousin under the bus so easily.

"What's in this for you, Cyprus… for showing this mess to me?"

"Why it gottta be about my ass, baby doll? This is all about you and your man. Don't shoot the messenger, sweetie?"

"It's always about you, Cyprus."

She began flipping through the pictures some more. With each photo of him and his flock of ladies she knew all too well as to why he wasn't able to come home at a reasonable time every night, and him always coming up missing when she called him from the club to get a measly ride home. While she was out hustling hard, he was out in the streets playing–out playing hard. She continued to thumb through the photos.

"Now, don't get me wrong, this dude is family and I love him like family, but when shit ain't right, sometimes you gotta walk away from family, you heard me? And it's just you and Big Cy here. Let's just be honest for a minute between one another. You know you're too good for this nigga. I say it all the time. You need to gone and get your shit from back there in them lockers with them mediocre chicks and let Big Cy take care of you. Big Cy know how to treat a real woman. I ain't gonna wrong you."

Even though she expected Spud was up to something for a while, seeing him in the act, in all those pictures with them other women infuriated her. She looked at each picture several times, each angering and hurting her at the same time.

She looked at the ratchet pictures until she couldn't look at them anymore, then said, "I need to leave, Cy."

"Did you just hear what I just said about you packing up your stuff and letting Big Cy take care of you?"

"I need to leave. I gotta get ready to work tonight."

"I'm sorry, Quay."

A brief frown spread across his face. He then signaled her to return the photos back to him. She slid them across the table and rose from her seat.

"Baby doll, that offer will forever be open to you," he said. "In the meantime you can go back out there and make Big Cy some money after you're done boo-hooing over that sorry nigga."

She didn't even entertain him with a response as she walked towards the exit. He carried a smirk on his face as she excused herself from his office.

"Just a matter of time, baby doll. Just a matter of time."

After leaving his office, she stood a few feet from his door and did her earnest to hold back her tears. The last thing she ever wanted was for any of the other girls to see her down. She slipped out her phone and dialed Spud. She had a few choice words to say to him, and the first thing she was going to demand of him was that he get the hell out of their house. When she put her phone up to her ear, she could hear his voicemail pickup immediately. She suspected he was out living it up with one of the chicken heads his cousin had just revealed to her. She ended the call.

****

When Monty walked into Oasis, he stopped at the entrance and surveyed the place from wall to wall. He was used to the thin crowd, and although he was quite a ways from home, the seclusion at this particular gentlemen's club made him feel even more relaxed. Not only did he favor the isolation of this club, but there was this one beautiful lady that danced here he just enjoyed seeing perform more than every club he hopped around to on a nightly basis. Unfortunately, after his quick survey of the place, he realized she was nowhere in sight. He strolled towards the bar, feeling a lot cooler and more attractive than he actually was.

Monty leaned up against the bar and glanced towards the stage at the bare naked dancer groping the pole. With her slight belly pooch and worn down physique, she definitely wasn't the dancer he had come to see. He waved the bartender over.

"What will it be for you, my man," the bartender asked.

"Bud Light–make sure the bottle's ice cold, too" he said as he took a seat on a barstool, glancing back at the dancer on the pole.

The bartender plucked the cap off the bottle of beer and dropped it on the counter in front of Monty. Monty pulled out a crisp ten dollar bill, slid it across the bar and said, "Keep the change."

"That's what's up," the bartender replied.

"Hey, is that real pretty, brown skinned chick with that long, natural looking hair here tonight? Did she dance yet?"

"Who?"

"Destiny, I think is her name."

"Oh, Quay?"

Monty shrugged, signaling to the man he had no idea as to the woman's real name.

"Yeah, that's who you're talking about. She's here, but she didn't get on yet."

Monty nodded and removed himself from the bar. He strolled towards the stage and took a seat in one of the chairs a few feet away. He took a quick look over his surroundings, pausing every few seconds at the sparingly draped women scattered throughout the floor with his fellow patrons. He slouched in the seat while chugging down his beer as he waited for his favorite dancer to come out and send his mind on a journey.

Quayla sat in front of the mirror wearing nothing but a bra and thong, her face motionless, heart throbbing, and her mind rummaging through a million thoughts per second. After seeing the photos Cy revealed to her, she wasn't even certain if the no-good man she had been shacking up with over the past few years even lost their money in gambling at all. The only thing she was certain of was that she gave every cent she had left to him, and he didn't have it anymore. Money most likely spent on all the whores he found more time to be with than working on his job trying to make an honest living for her. She was finally tired of all the bullshit him and the world had shoveled her way.

Déjà crept into the dressing room, minutes removed from her performance, with her sights set on the young woman she had taken in as somewhat of a protégé. "Hey girl," she said as she claimed the chair next to Quayla. "You okay?"

She nodded and said, "Yeah, I'll live."

"How about that one guy that's been sweatin' you all week just walked in. I know he's waiting on you," said Déjà. "He only drop them bills on you, so you better get out there while he's still hot for you."

"Who?"

"Girl, don't act like you don't know; that chubby dark skinned nigga that always be coming in here with them damn tired ass Hawaiian shirts. The only one that comes in here looking like he should be a bad guy on Miami Vice."

"Oh, okay, I know who you're talking about. I think he said his name was Monty or something like that."

"Even his name sounds corny," she said. "But he makes damn sure he gets in here before you get on."

"Yeah, I noticed that."

"Shoot, girl, you say you need that money and he seems to be extra charitable with you. You better get him before one of them other heffas get slick and snag him up. They're not all innocent like you," she said with a chuckle.

"Okay, thanks," she said.

Déjà squinted her eyes, concerned by her friend's disorientated behavior. She could tell something was wrong, but she was never one to pry too much in the other girl's business. One minute they're your best flippin' friend, the next minute you better stay the hell away from their client. "Girl, you sure you okay?"

"Yes, I'm good," she nodded. "I'm good."

"Alright," she said as she jumped out of her chair. "Go'on and make that bread like I told you. I'm 'bout to go back out and work this floor some. Do what you gotta do baby girl. Don't be shy about it."

****

When she marched onto the stage, she was no longer Quayla Wilson. She was now the exotic dancer known as Destiny. No longer was she a caring mother, a loyal girlfriend, or a obedient daughter–she was now an exotic dancer. The life she lived during the day was left behind the walls of the neon stage.

As she hopped on the pole and gave it a few twirls, she glanced over the club at the usual suspects–few and far between–occupied by the girls that frequented their time. As she went about her normal routine, she noticed Monty sitting a few feet away from the stage with his eyes trailing her every movement. She turned all her attention to him and slowly curled her index finger for him to come closer to the stage. He jumped up and mindlessly approached the stage, pulling out a gold money clip that straddled a nice chunk of cash. Before he even met her at the stage, he began throwing bills at her with each step he moved towards her.

Since he's been stopping in, he's been the most consistent with dropping the dough, so she made him her priority. She could tell what he liked by the ways his eyes followed her body. She stood before him and dangled her unmentionables in front of him as if she was toying with a hungry dog yearning for a bone. She wasn't attracted to him, only his money and the more attention she gave him, the more dough he removed from his clip and onto the floor beneath her stilettos. It didn't take long for her to know what he really liked, so she turned away from him and began twerking her round hump of pleasure in his face. His money came falling down her backside like a waterfall.

When the music stopped, she went walking towards the back, but paused before she made it to the door that led to the dressing room. She turned, looked around the club and observed all the other girls working the floor, seducing their regulars, doing whatever it took to bring in the dough. Their clients knew what they were coming for each night, and the girls, their girls, were going to make damn sure they were going to give it to them. It became obvious to her that the possibility of Cy blackballing her wasn't the only reason she was lacking in nightly revenue. It was time to get with the program or wind up sleeping on the streets.

She turned her attention over to Monty, who had resigned into his plush chair while sipping on his beer. She knew it was time to make a change, to finally see what Monty was working with.

She walked up to him, stood in front of him and said, "Monty, right?"

When he looked up and saw her heavenly crafted physique in front of him his face lit up like a fireworks exhibit. "Uh, yeah, Monty. You remembered."

She giggled, while channeling her days of playing the young guys back in her high school to get whatever she wanted. A few batting of the eyes and a soft, gentle voice and they were hooked like a fish. She said, "How could I forget?"

"Right, right," he said nervously.

"You mind if I sit?"

"Sure," he said waving her to the chair next to him.

Unexpectedly, she resigned on his lap. She purposely grinded her hips along his manhood to get him aroused. She said, "I'm glad you made it out to see me again."

"Oh yeah," he nodded, his loins beyond stimulated. "I can't miss my, Destiny. You're the sexiest thing up in this piece."

"Call me, Quay," she said.

"Quay," he buffoonishly repeated. "So umm, what made you come back out here? I thought you were done for the night."

"I don't know," she said as she leaned on him and began running her fingers up and down his chest. "You looked kinda lonely, like you needed some company."

"Darling, you must be read my mind," he said with a sleazy chuckle.

"So do you wanna go back in V.I.P.? There's a lot more privacy back there if you want to be in a more private setting." The words that exuded from her lips were foreign to her ears. She knew she had to get him in a position to where she could get more cash quickly, before she stopped and really thought about what she was doing. Stopping and thinking about what she was trying to do would've most likely made her gag all over him, or find the nearest exit–neither an option at this point.

He looked around, licked his lips and said, "Nah, I was thinking about something else. You know, a little more private."

She was reluctant to ask but had it in her mind to do what was necessary. "And where's that, Monty?"

"Well," he said as he took a quick look around to make sure no one was eavesdropping on their conversation. He leaned into her ear and whispered. "I know you guys got rules and all, but I was thinking maybe we could head over to my place a little later. I got this fancy suite back at the Drayton Suites and you know, I'm all alone."

"I see," she replied. An undesirable vision on him naked and profusely breathing on top of her seeped into her mind.

"I mean, I got money. So you'll get paid whatever you're asking for. Money's not even an issue. I just need a little company for tonight, that's all."

Before she could give herself a chance the talk herself out of it she said, "Okay."

"Really?" he asked, nearly as surprised as she was on the inside.

"Yeah, you said Drayton Suites, right?"

"Yeah, right down the street from here, just off the beach."

"I know where it is."

"So are you really down for this?"

"Are you really gonna pay me whatever I ask?"

"Hell yeah, sweetheart. Like I told you, money is not an issue. I'm just an old guy looking to have some fun tonight."

"Okay, Monty," she moved towards his ear and whispered, "Meet me on the side of the building in about twenty minutes."

"Cool. That sounds like music to my ears, baby. I'll be right there."

When she got up and retreated back to the dressing room, his eyes didn't leave her smooth, chocolate behind. He had a million different desires he planned to fulfill with her once he got her back to his room. He slouched back in his seat, closed his eyes and took in a deep, relaxing breath. Heaven, to him, was indeed on its way.

When she walked through the dressing room doors, reality struck. Along with reality came the thoughts of *what in the hell did I just do?* She grabbed a chair beside Déjà who was busy counting her take so far for the night.

"I don't know what I just did."

"What? You jacked him off in V.I.P.?" Déjà asked.

"No, I told him I'd go back to his hotel room with him. I think he's expecting some sex."

"Damn, girl, I didn't expect you to do all that," she whispered. "But them fat niggas be giving up the most dough for some good trim."

"Déjà, I don't know what I just agreed to do with this man," she said nervously. "I don't think I can do this."

"Well, the shit you just negotiated is dangerous as hell, that's for sure, but that nigga out there is a square. I don't think you got nothin' to worry about."

"Oh no, Déjà, I didn't even ask him if he was a cop."

"Girl, hush up," said Déjà. "That dude out there ain't no fuckin' cop. Cops try to blend in, not stand out. That fool around there ain't blending in with nothing but a bowl of fruit cocktail."

"You ever did anything like this?"

"Every fucking chance I get," she said. "I can't pay my damn rent off these tips alone. The real ballers don't waste no big cash up here in Jacksonville, not when they can go further down South and blow their money on some premium thots. You just gotta be smart about the shit you do

in here and not let Cyprus, nor none of them other hatin'
bitches know about it. They do the same shit too, but they'll
be quick to rat your ass out if they find out your ass is doing
it."

"I told him to meet me on the side of the building in
twenty minutes."

"Good girl, you're learning already," she said as she
walked over to her locker, made sure no one was coming,
and pulled out a small box cutter. When she returned to the
chair beside her friend, she grabbed her hand and placed the
blade in the palm of it. "Take this shit with you. Slit his
fucking throat if he try something shady."

Quay reluctantly grabbed the weapon. She glanced at
it for a second before stuffing it back into her hands. She
said, "No, I'm good. I don't need it."

"Girl, you better take this damn thing," she said
shoving it back into her hand. "You're about to step into a
whole new world with what you're 'bout to do. If you want
to survive, you best be prepared. This ain't a game, girl."

Quay paused for a moment while gazing into the
seriousness set in her friend's eyes. Déjà was right. She was
about to journey into a whole new realm that everyone

warned her she would eventually drift into one way or the other. Since she was going there, there was no harm in being more safe than sorry. She nodded as she clasped the blade with full intentions on using it if she was forced to. "Alright then."

Déjà continued, "Go on and get your stuff together. I'll tell Cy's fat ass that you weren't feeling well and you needed to leave early."

Quay nodded, "Okay."

"And you call me when you get home," said Déjà. "'Cause you may not cut the nigga, but if he gives you some trouble, I promise you I'll find his Professor Klump looking ass and slice his shit up like some fresh tomatoes in a heartbeat."

"Girl, you crazy," she said as Déjà left her side. She was still uncertain if she could go through with it. She knew she had to make her decision quickly and soon. Between Spud cheating on her all around Jacksonville while spending all their money doing it, and having her and her daughter kicked out of their home into the cold, cruel streets of Jacksonville, her choice was never more clearer.

****

91

Breeze's concentration was engulfed with skimming through the timelines of all his social media accounts until his instinct told him to lift his head. When he looked up, he noticed Monty had slipped out of the club and was pacing back and forth on the side of the building, directly in front of their car. He tapped Loc on his arm with the back of his hand to wake him out of his slumber.

"Look at old boy."

"What?"

"Looks like he's waiting for something or somebody."

Loc zeroed in on Monty while swiping the mucus out of the corner of his eye. "I guess hopping from club to club is finally about to work out for his fat ass."

"You think he waiting on some snatch?"

"That's what the hell it's looking like."

Suddenly, Quay emerged from the shadows of the back of the building and joined Monty at the side of the club. They exchanged a few words, then briskly began walking towards his car.

"Goddamn, that chick he rollin' with is fine as hell. That hole in the wall got 'em up in there like that?" asked Breeze.

"Nah," Loc chuckled, "Not all of 'em. She's just an exception. I've been in there a few times. Ain't never seen a dime looking like that up in there before. Most of them broads in there either old as hell or looking like they on the pipe."

"I hear what you're saying, but if they got some more of 'em in there looking like that, we gotta hit these cats back later," Breeze said, rubbing his inner thigh. "For real."

"Fuck them tired bitches in that shit shack. We finish this gig, with the type of money they paying us, you'll be swimming in some top notch panties back home in South Beach. Never mind them trap hoes coming outta there." He grabbed Breeze firmly by his arm and told him, "Now look here nigga, I need you to stay focus, 'cuz when we do this shit, we can't be 'bout no clown shit."

"Alright dude, calm down with your bipolar ass. All that touching ain't even necessary," he said, snatching his arm away. "I wanna get paid just like you. I'm just waiting for the word."

He nodded, "Now that's what the hell I'm talkin' 'bout." After giving Breeze a stern look, Loc started up the Impala in preparation to trail Monty to wherever he was headed with his new found friend.

As Monty began maneuvering out of the club parking lot, Quay looked around the vehicle in efforts to figure out a little more about the man that told her he had a suite down the street in the fancy Drayton Suites. The car he was chaperoning her in was darn near spotless–too spotless–like rental car spotless. She'd never been in a Lexus before, and she figured the ride would be slightly more desirable from what the commercials she saw on television portrayed it to be.

"You know, I'm kind of surprised you agreed to leave with me. Most girls only want to handle their business in the VIP–like they're scared of something."

"You dangerous?"

"No, of course not. I'm as harmless as a baby, baby."

She said, "All right then." It didn't matter. In her backpack, she had the blade Déjà gave her, and if things went south, she knew she'd have to do whatever she needed to protect herself.

Monty glanced at her and smiled as she gazed out of the passenger window. She was wearing a white t-shirt and some snug blue jeans with cuts running down the leg, but his eyes saw past all of that. He knew what was in the candy shop, and he couldn't wait to get his hands all over it. He was so aroused by her simply being in the car with him, he was surprised he hadn't messed over himself yet. He figured he was going to explode on contact, but he was already planning to pay her whatever she asked for to stay the entire night and allow him to hit it until he got what he felt his money's worth was.

"You're not the talkative type, are you?"

"Talking does nothing but waste time, and we have things to do," she said. She was thinking the quicker she got the night over with the better. She still couldn't believe she was actually going through with it, but the reality of sitting on the side of the road with Breelyn with no place to go was something she would never allow to come to pass.

"A woman about handling her business. That's exactly what I like," he said while reaching his hand over and extending it across her thigh.

Before he could initiate his intentions of finagling his grasp any further up her thigh than his initial landing spot, he was met with a quick smack of his hand by Quay. Her delivery was in a playful manner, almost like a mother giving a warning to her child, however internally, she loathed his touch with a passion. She said, "Uh, uh, uh, no sneak previews before we get to the room."

"Yeah, that's fine," he said licking his lips, in his mind–thinking of himself as a handsome Denzel Washington look-alike. "You're right. We got all night."

She turned her head towards her window and rolled her eyes while praying Déjà was right in assuming he was only a two minute man. The thought of being intimate with him any longer than a couple of seconds sent chills down her spine.

After a short drive, they were at the hotel, and he escorted her out of his vehicle and through the hotel's entrance. Unbeknownst to them, Breeze and Loc were right behind them, easing into a parking space in back of the lot.

"Boy, I know he got to be paying her a pretty penny," Breeze said, staring at them walking into the building from the back window.

"You ain't bullshittin'," said Loc.

Monty opened the door and guided her into his room. It was definitely a fine suite with a mess of a man residing in it. The suite was cozy, yet roomy, accommodated with a petite kitchen and living room space. Very nice, but extremely messy with pizza boxes and drink cans scattered all about. It wasn't the worst she'd seen from a man, but she figured he'd be a little neater judging from his tidy car.

"You got to excuse the mess, sweetheart," he said locking the door behind her. "It's just me and I really wasn't expecting any company tonight."

"Sure you didn't," she replied.

He brushed past her and said, "Follow me."

He couldn't wait to get her walking through his bedroom doors, his manhood was rock solid and was just about ready to explode through his pants. They walked into the room, and the moment Quay laid eyes on the king size bed, it all became reality. She immediately felt like throwing up.

Loc and Breeze bopped their head simultaneously to the latest Wiz Khalifa song that spewed faintly through the car's radio speaker. Suddenly, Loc's smartphone, that he'd laid idle on the dashboard, vibrated from an incoming text message.

He grabbed the phone and unlocked the screen. The text on his device screen read: PROCEED. The first smile on the trip spurred onto his face as he looked towards Breeze and said, "Let's do this shit. We got the word."

"Bout damn time," Breeze replied.

****

Monty had Quay pinned up against his dresser as she leaned away from him while he kissed and licked her up and down her neck, his hands crawling and groping her back and rump in no systematic fashion. One would think Quay was more to him than just a dancer he hadn't known for more than a week in a town he wasn't even from. When she felt his hands slip away from her back and to the front of her jeans to work her pants unfastened, she knew it was time to stop him and set some ground rules.

She gently pushed him away from her and said, "Wait, wait, wait. Before we get good and into this Monty, we need to talk money." She walked around him and took a seat on the edge of the bed.

"Cool baby," he said breathing ferociously and holding out his arms as if money wouldn't be a problem. "How much you want?"

Quay had thought about everything from getting to the room to having to protect herself if Monty turned out to be a butcher knife wielding psychopath, but the one thing she hadn't considered was how much she was going to charge the fat slug for getting his rocks off. One thing she did take note of was how money didn't seem to be a big deal to him, so she quickly thought up the highest amount she assumed he'd pay and blurted out, "Two grand."

"Two grand," he said with a befuddled look.

She held her breath, awaiting for him to tell her hell no. If he declined to pay her, she felt it was no sweat off her back, she'd just have to scurry back to the club and make her rounds for the few newbies that regularly wandered in. At least she'd be able to keep her dignity for at least one more night.

"Two grand? Is that all? Hell baby, I'll give you double that just for you to knock it down every time it gets back up the entire night."

"Four grand," she said, shocked but careful to not show it too much.

"Hell yeah," he said as he slipped his money clip out of his front pocket that was holding together his huge wad of cash. "All you got to do is earn the rest of it, baby." He pulled out and counted up some cash and handed it to her. "Here's your two grand up front."

She couldn't believe he just nonchalantly handed her half of the resolution to her financial problems in the blink of an eye and she hadn't done a thing yet but show up. She watched him as he threw his money clip on the dresser located at the foot of the bed and also emptied his phone, wallet and loose change onto it. Her eyes continued to glance at his money clip as he stared at her with a greasy look while shaking off his gold Rolex. She thought if she could only pull through the night she could solve all of her money issues with this one demeaning task. However, she understood it was going to be a hell of a lot easier said than actually done. She really didn't know how she was going to get through sexing this whale of a man.

"Now, where were we?" he asked as he pulled her onto her feet and began nibbling and sucking on and around her neck as if she was a savory piece of meat. She closed her eyes and tried to pretend he was someone else, anyone else. No matter how hard she tried, his touch and sharp cologne didn't allow her to trick herself into thinking that this man wasn't anyone other than the fat slob that he actually was.

He forcefully grabbed her hips, squeezing them frequently as she began pecking on his neck, in an honest attempt at kissing it.

"Yeah, baby, yeah," he groaned, his breathing became more intense. "That's what daddy likes."

He began guiding her towards the bed, not letting up from his tongue lashing of her neck and the groping of her buttocks. She fell backwards on the bed, slipped off her shirt, revealing her black laced bra, and positioned herself on the bed in a more comfortable position with her elbows.

He took a moment to admire her smooth, brown skin then looked downwards between her thighs with his tongue hanging like a starving rabid wolf and said, "Daddy gonna eat that thang, too."

She cringed at his words as he began unbuttoning his tacky, flowered shirt he became so well known for wearing. When he pulled his shirt off, she was even more disgusted than she thought she would be. Everything on him was hanging, sagging and hidden sparingly by his long stringy graying hairs that was spread out across and down his chest and stomach area. It was obvious the only crunches he knew about was Crunch 'N Munch.

As she made an attempt to smile and put on for him as if she was enjoying his near naked display, she couldn't believe his breasts were darn near bigger than hers. By no means did she have any problems with big men because Spud wasn't slender to the faintest degree, but this dude was outright hideous.

He hopped between her legs and began kissing her along her belly button. His slippery wet tongue felt so nasty against her smooth skin. She had plans in mind to scrub each area his tongue met on her body for at least an hour when she got back home. Suddenly, she felt his hands crawling up her legs and against her waist as he began to unbutton her pants and that was when she said, "Wait!"

He popped up, backed up a little and said, "What? What is it?"

"Umm." Her mind felt like jelly as she tried to think of something, anything, to say to him to get a break from his overwhelming grasp. She quickly came up with, "I gotta freshen up for you down there." She slid from under him as he backed up further. "You know, after dancing and all, I just want it to be right for you."

"Oh, okay." He nodded, "Bathroom is back there."

She jumped up, grabbed her bag and ran to the bathroom. He fell backwards onto the bed. She burst through the bathroom door, locked it, immediately ran to the toilet and threw up.

His phone vibrated. "What the hell?" he asked. He jumped up off the bed and walked over to the dresser, looked down at the number on his caller ID and mumbled, "Oh, look at this shit right here–perfect timing." He looked towards the bathroom door, then back at his vibrating phone. "Hey, I gotta take a call–business. I'll be out in the hall."

"Okay," Quay screamed out from the other end of the door.

He threw his shirt on, grabbed the phone and briskly walked through the suite and out into the hallway. "Hello?"

****

"Goddamn it, man, we couldn't take the fuckin' elevator?" Breeze asked as stopped a few steps below Loc who was at the top of the stairs.

"Hell no, nigga. What we look like getting in the elevator right in front of the receptionist desk? Besides, it's only eight flights. You need to get in better shape if you're gonna be in this line of work."

"But damn man, those wasn't no ordinary eight flights of stairs."

"Man, shut the hell up," he said. Loc eased to the door and peaked through the door's window to get a glimpse of the hallway. "Now you sure this nigga is staying on this floor?"

"Yeah, nigga. I told you I followed his corny ass up to his room door that first night getting here. Eight Seventeen–suite."

"You better be right," he said as he grabbed the door handle that led into the hall. "Come on here and follow me closely."

Monty was pacing back and forth, several feet away from his room door. He spoke into the phone, "I didn't know you were going to have the paperwork ready this week. You should've advised me of this shit before I left town."

Just when they were about to turn the corner, Loc's peripheral vision caught a glance of Monty a few feet away, so he stuck out his arm to hold Breeze back around the corner, out of their target's sight.

"What?" Breeze asked as he slipped his head around the corner. "Damn, that's his ass right there."

"Why the hell you think I'm holding you back?"

"Oh," said Breeze. "Nigga bust a nut that fast?"

"No doubt," Loc answered. "Now we're 'bout to bust these slugs in his ass."

"Hell yeah," Breeze said while rubbing his hands, excited he was finally about to get into some action.

Loc pulled out his 9mm and screwed his silencer on the end of it. Breeze did the same with his gun. "Follow me quietly," he said. "When we get close enough, we hit him a few times and throw his ass back into his room."

"Cool," said Breeze.

Quay walked out of the bathroom and looked around the room. "Monty?" she said. She didn't hear him in the front room and noticed his money clip full of cash was sitting on the dresser. She stared at the cash, thinking that Monty's knot of money would make all her problems go away, at least for a little while. Her temptations to touch it got the best of her as she picked it up and began thumbing through and counting it.

With their guns by their sides, Breeze and Loc slowly crept down the hall towards Monty, whom appeared to be yelling quietly into the phone.

"Fuck you, too!" he said. As soon as he smashed the end button, he turned around to see Breeze and Loc running towards him with their guns at their waist. "What the fuck?"

Monty quickly began running towards his room door as the duo sped up and began spraying bullets Monty's way. The bullets hit everything but Monty as he grabbed his door handle and quickly slipped his card key into the door. He dashed through the door, and before he could slam it all the way shut, Breeze and Loc held it ajar, pushing it back towards him.

"Help, goddamn it! *Help!* They're trying the kill me," Monty yelled, trying to shut the door closed with all his might.

"Hold still," Loc said as he took a step back and shot at the door.

One of the bullets pierced through the bottom of the door and hit Monty in his leg. He screamed in pain as he fell backwards and tumbled towards a nightstand across the room, knocking over a lamp in the process. He began to drag himself across the floor, towards a dresser drawer he was determined to get to as the two men kicked the door open.

The commotion on the other side of the room door acquired Quay's attention as she stood frozen, trying to figure out what was going on in the front room without peeping through the door. She almost lost her breath when she heard two loud gunshots from the other side of the wall.

Monty was aimlessly shooting back at the two men as he managed to get his Saturday night special from the dresser drawer. They ducked and dodged until his weapon began making a clicking sound at each continuous pull of the trigger. Immediately, Loc aimed and shot Monty in his shooting arm causing him to drop the gun as if it was a hot potato. Monty bellowed in excruciating pain.

"Motherfucker!" Loc shouted. "You making all that goddamn noise."

Out of breath with a badly wounded leg and bloody arm, Monty just laid sprawled out, panting on the floor as the two hitmen hovered over his defeated body. "They... they.. they just couldn't let it." He wasn't allowed to finish his statement as they unloaded their guns into his chest, his body jerking with each bullet piercing into his flesh.

When they were done, Monty's eyes were still wide open as if he was staring at a ghost. Loc had a wild look on his face as he stuffed his gun into the small of his back. Gazing at Monty's blood drenched body seemed to bring him great pleasure.

Breeze walked closer to Monty's lifeless body and kicked his foot. "Whelp, he gone... with his lookin' ass," he laughed.

"Go back there and put one in that bitch he came here with," Loc ordered.

"Cool," said Breeze.

Loc walked closer to Monty's motionless body, stooped down and began to feel around his pants pockets. Breeze burst through the bedroom door and froze at the sight of the empty bed. "Shit," he mumbled. He quickly dropped to the floor, looked under the bed, and it was empty. He ran to the bathroom, kicked opened the door, and it was empty. He rummaged through the closet, yanking out handfuls of Monty's suits and Hawaiian shirts, but he didn't see a thing.

He raked his head and face while his eyes scanned the room from wall to wall, confused as to where the woman managed to skip off to. Just when he was about to exit the room, he stopped at the dresser. He picked up Monty's wallet and thumbed through the cash in it, then grabbed the gold Rolex that was beside it. He stuffed the valuables in his pocket, returned to the front room and said, "She's gone."

"What?" Loc asked in disbelief as he stood up and moved away from Monty's carcass. "Fuck you mean, she's gone?"

"She's gone. She's not in there."

"You sure? What the hell do you mean she's not back there? You checked up under the bed and shit?" he asked as he brushed past Breeze and kicked the bedroom door open. He stood in the doorway and scanned the room from wall to wall.

"See, I checked all up in there. She must've bailed on the nigga," said Breeze from behind him. "I don't know where the hell she skipped off to, but her ass ain't in there."

"Fuck!" he said.

"Man, we should've been gone like five minutes ago, anyway," said Breeze. "With all that fucking noise old boy made trying to hit back at us, I know twelve is on the way."

Loc punched at the wall a few times in frustration as he was never the one to leave loose ends, and this was definitely a loose end. "Damn it," he yelled.

"Loc, we gotta go man. You bullshittin' right now," Breeze said nervously.

"Where that bitch go?" Loc mumbled, his eyes still scanning over the room.

"What difference does it make, dawg? She ain't see us. Let's just fuckin' go."

He gave the bedroom one last glance over, stroked his goatee a couple of times and said, "Alright. Let's get the fuck out of here."

"Thank you, Lord," Breeze said as he made his way towards the exit. "Nigga, you acting like you wanna get caught."

Loc reluctantly trailed behind, giving Monty's limp body one last look as he followed Breeze out of the room. When they evacuated the suite, they left calm and collected, their eyes focused on each door they approached down the hall for any onlookers that could potentially become a problem for them. Their destination–the same fire escape they came up from.

Quay was rolled up tightly in the bottom corner of the closet with a couple of Monty's dark colored suits spread out over her head. She figured if the intruders came in rummaging through the dark closet, they may overlook her small frame underneath the clothing, and she was right. She knew she was dead if the prowlers placed a little more effort in their investigation by feeling around and exploring the closet more, but they didn't. She thanked God they didn't.

She held her breath as long as she could and was grateful the men didn't hear her whimpers when she realized they were in the room searching for her. She didn't need to see what had happened to Monty out in the front room to know they had put an end to him. It just freaked the hell out of her that they were actually looking to kill her also. Whoever got Monty knew she was with him and had to have followed them both to the room. It filled her mind with a whole new type of paranoia. Déjà always warned her about going home and being watchful of her surroundings because naughty girls often got followed by dangerous men.

She didn't know if the men came there for her or for some beef with the man that brought her there. What she did know was that she needed to get the hell out of there, and to do it quickly.

After a few moments of silence that felt like forever, Quay cautiously climbed out of the closet with her bag and sat it on the edge of the bed. She tiptoed to the bedroom door and cracked it opened. When she saw Monty's bloodied corpse sprawled out over in the corner across from her, she pushed her hand over her mouth to muffle her screams. She returned to the bed and began digging through her backpack for her phone. When she obtained it, she flipped opened the pocket in the front of the bag and pulled out Zeke's card. She speedily began dialing his number. With every ring of his phone, the intense thumping from her heart made her feel as if it was going to explode through her chest.

"Hello," Zeke answered. He was standing in the back of a convenience store, searching through the sports drinks, clothed in his workout gear–a plain white t-shirt and some baggy grey jogging pants.

"Zeke," she panted harshly into the phone.

"Quay... Quay is this you?" he asked as he backed away from the drink cooler and began to wander towards the front of the store. He could sense that she was bothered by something, and this sent him into full alert mode.

"Zeke... Zeke.. they killed him. My God, they killed him," she cried. "I think they want to get me, too. They were looking for me."

"Quay, hold up. What are you talking about? Where the hell are you?"

"I'm at the Drayton Suites just off Interstate 95."

"Drayton Suites? What the... who's trying to kill you? Do you know who they are?"

"No, I don't know them at all," she said. "They just busted in and shot this guy I was with. They killed him, Zeke. They shot him right in the head and all over his body. He's so bloody... so bloody... covered in blood and all."

"Are they gone?"

"Yeah, but they were looking for me, too. I think they could come back. Zeke, if they come back, I don't know what I'm gonna do."

"Quay, it's gonna be okay. Just calm down."

"I can't. I can't, Zeke. He's dead!" she cried. "They were looking to kill me too, man."

"Quay, listen to me. I'm not gonna let anyone hurt you," he assured her. "Look, just let me call the stat..."

"No, just you," she interrupted. "I just need you, Zeke."

He took a moment to think. Not knowing who or what he was up against were conditions he wasn't fond of at all, but he trusted her. If the situation involved anyone other than her, he knew his answer would be different. "Okay, okay, it'll just be me," he said as he hurried through the store and to his car. He looked down both directions of the street while his mind quickly processed through his next set of moves. He said, "There's a convenience store just on the corner from that hotel. I want you to see if you can make it there. Get around as many people as possible, Quay. I'm on my way."

"Okay...okay....Zeke."

"Yeah?"

"Hurry."

"I got you, Quay. I got you."

****

The two men jogged down the steps when Loc came to a complete stop. The woman that managed to disappear in thin air and slip through their fingers was still on his mind, and the nagging feeling of leaving a loose end was one he just couldn't shake.

When Breeze didn't hear his partner's foot moving behind his, he stopped also. He then whipped around and said, "What?"

"Something just ain't fucking right," he said shaking his head. "You sure you checked every place in that bedroom good? The closet? The bathroom? All that shit?"

"Yeah man, I told you I did. How many times I gotta tell you that?"

"Until I believe it."

"Come on man, let's just go. She's long gone."

"Then how the fuck we missed her?" he said. "Her ass is still in that fucking room, and I'm gonna go back up there and kill that bitch." He started back up the stairs.

"Loc, what the fuck man?" he said as he begrudgingly followed behind him. "We go back up there, and all we're gonna end up doing is getting caught, dude. I know somebody heard them gunshots from that jackass shooting back at us. Besides, she didn't even see us."

Loc froze in his tracks, turned around and asked, "And how in the hell do you know that?"

Feeling a bit intimated by Loc towering over him with his stark demeanor, he shrugged and said, "I don't."

"Exactly!" he said. "We're gonna go back up here, find her ass and put a slug in her–right fucking now."

"Ah man, come on. We're gonna fuck around and get caught!"

"Nigga, if she seen our faces, we're already caught."

****

Quay had a towel in her hands and was busy wiping every part of the bathroom she touched. When she was done, she roamed back into the bedroom, and looked around to make sure she didn't forget anything that could traced back to her. She grabbed her bag and pulled out the clip of money she had taken from Monty. She stared at it, knowing the money could give her an extension on life but now it was just blood money. She wanted to put it back, but she couldn't. It didn't feel right, but she needed it. She stuffed it down into her book bag, flipped the bag over her shoulder, gave the room one last stare and eased into the living room area.

She crept in, almost as if she was frightened to disturb Monty's deceased body. Seeing him bloodied with his mouth and eyes wide opened, gaping at her, made her feel even worse about taking the money, but she knew it wouldn't do him any good at this point. Where Monty was now, he no longer had use for any kind of money or stripper girls. Careful not to touch the door handle, she pushed it with her elbow and pulled the door open with her arms. When she was on the other side of the door, she closed her eyes and took a deep breath. She made it.

"There that bitch go right there," Breeze yelled from the other end of the hall.

Her eyes bolted open as she glanced down the hall only to see two men running towards her, brandishing their guns from behind their backs and pockets. Even though she never laid eyes on the men prior to that moment, she knew who they were, and she had no plans for letting them do to her what they did to Monty. She frantically charged down the opposite end of the hallway as bullets from their guns whizzed by her.

"Bitch, come back here," Loc yelled, frustrated that he couldn't get a clean shot on the woman.

Midway down the hall, Quay pulled down the fire alarm, immediately sounding it off. She hurried down the fire escape as the hotel residents began to flood the hallway.

"Put your shit away," Loc said to Breeze as he stuffed his own gun in his pocket. "Put it away."

The influx of people filling the hallway made them lose ground in their pursuit of Quay as she went barreling down the stairs, bumping into the residents that came squeezing into the stairwell from the lower floor levels.

Her heart was racing even faster than before. The haunting images of the two thugs chasing after her plastered in her mind as she couldn't help but repeatedly look upwards at the stairs above her. She knew without a doubt if they caught her, they would kill her. That was the only reason they were coming back to the room–to finish the job. When she finally made it into the lobby, she could see the hotel manger directing the rowdy guests through the front exit with other hotel employees. She finagled herself into the middle of the crowd in an effort to blend in with the other patrons. She looked back and didn't see the men.

The hotel employees directed them all to stand at least twenty feet from the building, away from the fire trucks that had their lights flashing at the entrance. Even though she was surrounded by people, like Zeke suggested, she was still nervous as hell. When she saw the two men scrambling out of the building with the other residents, she nearly passed out. The two men chasing her surveyed the crowd until the taller, angrier looking one, locked eyes on her. She could tell from the scowl on his face he wanted to do some serious harm to her.

"That's her ass right there," Loc said, leaning towards Breeze's ear, his eyes not leaving Quay.

"Word," Breeze replied, his eyes now locked on her, too.

"Go get the car. I'mma handle this shit real quick."

"Cool," said Breeze as he made a dash towards the rear of the building. Quay's eyes followed him only briefly. She couldn't help but keep her primary focus on the more dangerous looking man, who began walking straight towards her.

She knew she had a decision to make. She could stay there and wait for Zeke to come to her rescue but possibly earn the same fate of her fallen John upstairs because he might not make it on time, or she could make a dash for it and try her luck at losing the men. She understood whatever she chose, she needed to do it quickly because the tall, gangster with flaring nostrils and a face full of anger was heading her way.

The hotel manager brushed right by Loc with a police officer beside him. The stocky, middle-aged white man, with his massively receding hairline from the center of his head yelled to the crowd, "Alright people, I need for the guest that called in to the front desk about hearing possible gunshots being fired to step forward and tell Officer Howard here about what you heard," he paused for a moment and added, "And no one needs to panic. It was probably just some kids setting off crackers in one of the rooms, same ones that most likely set off the fire alarm." He leaned towards the officer and whispered under his breath, "Little rich brats always coming here doing crazy shit on the weekends."

She noticed her stalker had begun to back away from the officer in front of him. She wanted to come forward and tell the cop what happened, but she knew she'd incriminate herself for prostitution, and Lord knows what other charges they would bring against her. She could tell by the man's demeanor he wanted no parts of law enforcement and for good reason—he was a cold blooded murderer. His demeanor also said to her, this was her chance to get away.

She began to saunter down the row of cars, acting as if she was looking for her ride, leaving the man frozen behind the officer and hotel manager. When she felt she was far enough out of their vision, she began to speed walk through the parking lot. When she could not see them any longer, that's when all bets were off and she went into full run mode. With each step away from her would-be attackers and the hotel, her mind ran rampant with regret. *What the hell were you thinking, Quay? Look at the mess you've gotten yourself into. You could've gotten your stupid ass killed, lost everything, including Breelyn.*

As she crossed into an abandoned restaurant parking lot, she heard a loud screeching sound and noticed an older model Impala was headed straight for her. She paused for a moment, thinking it could be Zeke, but she remembered him having a different model car–a Camry. As the vehicle drew closer, she realized the driver was the other man that was hunting her down. She began running again, crossing through parking lot after parking lot, looking backwards at her assailant every few feet. He was hot on her trail. When she veered between two buildings that led to a walkway too narrow for his car to drive through, she saw him getting out of the vehicle from the corner of her eyes. Within seconds, she heard gunshots ringing out of his gun that were meant for her.

She didn't know where she was headed, but she was praying that none of the bullets hit her as she zigzagged in her sprint. She was too scared to look back at him, to see him with his aim on her, in fear that her last vision would be that of the man that was trying to kill her.

She saw another car, this time a familiar one, speeding down the street towards her. "Oh God," she stammered. "Zeke!" She yelled his name repeatedly, refusing to yield in her sprint, swaying her hands for him to come help her. He stopped his car a few yards away from her, crossing over the sidewalk. Breeze was still firing random shots at her as he drew closer.

Zeke jumped out of his car and ran towards her, "Quay," he said. "Get down." He whipped out his pistol as she dropped face first to the pavement.

Before Breeze could get a steady aim on Zeke, Zeke fired one shot at him, hitting him in his stomach. He tumbled to the ground like a set of dumbbells. When he realized the man had fallen with his lone shot, he immediately placed his focus on Quayla.

"Quay," he said. "Are you shot? Are you okay?" He helped her to her feet.

"No, I'm not shot. I'm okay," she nodded nervously with a stream of tears rolling down her face.

"What the hell is going on, Quay?"

"Another one. Another man," she said shaken and looking towards the man Zeke made short work out of. "There's another man trying to kill me. He's not too far away. We gotta leave."

"Quay, I can't leave here. I just shot a man. I have to call this in."

"No," she cried. "You can't. You can't. They'll take my child away from me, Zeke."

"What are you talking about, Quay?"

"I agreed to go back to a man's room with him. He was going to pay me for sex."

"What? Quay, are you serious?"

"It was the first time I tried it, Zeke. The first time."

"And it was about to be your last. You could've gotten killed doing some dumb crap like that, girl. It's not a game out here in these streets."

124

"I know… I know, but I didn't have a choice…"

"Awe man, nobody wants to hear that mess. There's always choice, Quay. Jesh!"

Suddenly, gunshots rang out. It was Loc, and he was shooting at them from behind the wheel of the Impala. Zeke pulled Quay onto the ground with him to protect her from the gunfire. Loc pulled up next to Breeze's fallen body. He could tell he was still breathing, but barely.

"Get your ass in! Quick," he said as he let off another shot towards the couple on the pavement. He popped the back door open as Breeze climbed to his feet while clutching the side of his stomach and stumbled into the car. Once Breeze was inside, the Impala skidded off.

Zeke looked up when he heard the car driving away. When he realized he hadn't killed the man he shot, he felt relieved. He didn't fully understand what he had managed to get himself involved with, but he was willing to get Quay to safety and give her an opportunity to explain herself before he determined his next move. "Come on, we gotta go before this place gets flooded with police cars."

"I can't go home, Zeke. Not yet."

"I know. I'm taking you to my place until we figure out what we're gonna do."

He escorted her to his car.

****

As Loc sped down the interstate, he glanced back at his partner that was spread out in the back seat of his ride, covering up his wound with his head tilted backwards and his eyes shut.

"Hey," Loc said to him while looking into his rearview mirror. "You okay back there?"

Breeze let out an uneasy moan and mumbled, "This shit hurts."

When he stopped at a red light, he looked towards the back at Breeze's abdomen area. He was tightly clutching the side of his stomach, his arm and shirt drenched in blood. "Damn, how many times did you get hit?"

"One," he mumbled faintly.

"I gotta make a few calls. Get to somewhere out of the way. We'll get you fixed up." He continued his drive down the stretch of road and glanced back at him in his rearview when he didn't get a response. "Breeze! Breeze, you hear me? We gonna get you fixed up, alright. Breeze!"

He slammed on brakes in the middle of the road, flipped on the dome light above him and looked back at his partner. He was still breathing, but very faintly.

As he forced the car back into drive and pulled onto the freeway, all he could do was shake his head. Things definitely didn't go as he planned, and he hoped the screw ups weren't going to make problems with him getting his money. However, the most annoying thing to him was the fact that he had a nagging loose end somewhere out there. He didn't like loose ends. They pissed him off. They pissed him off badly.

****

Quay was lying across the sofa, wearing an oversized Florida Marlins t-shirt Zeke had given her earlier. The television was broadcasting some random show as Zeke stood in the doorway leading to his bedroom behind her. On the way back to his house, she told him about the offer Monty made her and her reasons for going back to his room with him. He didn't like it, but he understood that's how life could be some times. People made decisions based on their circumstances–good or bad. Who was he to judge? Never in a million years did he see her as the type that would sell her body for money. Yeah, his sister and her played guys for fun back in the day, getting their nails and hair done from time to time, but nothing like this. He just couldn't see it.

Quay's head briskly popped up from the chair like a jack in the box. He walked towards her and said, "Hey, can't sleep?"

"No," she said as she raked her hands through her hair. "Still freaked out. I can't take my mind off of seeing Monty's dead body staring at me in that hotel room."

"I can imagine," he said. "I've seen quite a few deceased bodies during my stint on the force so far. It's not something you ever get used to, really."

"It's just…," she shook her head, tears sliding down her cheek as she envisioned the dead man in her mind.

"Don't get too worked up," he said as he walked around the chair. She readjusted herself on the couch to make room for him to sit. "We really gotta talk about this Monty thing. I'm going to need you calm to tell me all the details. And I need to know the complete details this time. I'm gonna do all I can to protect you."

She nodded, "I know."

"I mean, if this man is really dead and murdered, we gotta go to the station, but we must have all of our bases covered."

"I..." she stopped when she realized the news report on the television was broadcasting from the outside of the hotel Monty was murdered at. "Wait, turn that up."

"What?"

"Turn it up. Turn it up. That's the hotel."

He swiped the remote from the coffee table and turned the volume up. The anchor on the station reported, "The man was found dead, riddled with multiple gunshot wounds. We are getting unverified reports that the victim was staying in the suite under the name Belmont Patterson, husband of State Representative Lisa Patterson..."

A picture of Monty and his wife, Representative Patterson, flashed across the screen. The picture sent chills down Quay's spine as she rose and covered her mouth in fear. "Oh God... Oh God."

"Quay, please tell me that's not Monty—your Monty!" He rose behind her.

She looked at him and just nodded with tears streaming down her face. "That's him, that's him!"

"Ah, God, this can't be right," he yelled while raking the sides of his head. "Damn it, Quay!"

****

Loc stood several feet away from his car with the phone planted against his ear. They were parked on the stretch of highway just before getting on the Henry Buckman Bridge.

The man on the other end of his phone spoke in a calm, monotone voice. "I've had the luxury of watching your work on the late night news tonight–unimpressive to say the least."

"Slight complications," said Loc. "I got this shit all under control, though."

"If this is what you consider to be under control, I'd hate to see your definition of out of control."

"You're a funny man."

"This woman that was with him at the hotel, can she identify you?"

He chuckled, "Yup, but I'll find her. I'll put an end to her ratchet ass. She won't be identifying nobody for long, that's for sure."

"Hmmmm, indeed."

"The only thing I'm concerned with is that she took off with some dude. Looked like he could be a cop."

"Looked like a cop or was a cop?"

He grunted. He didn't want his client to think he was incapable of handling the job, but he knew it was far too late for him to not have that assumption. He begrudgingly said, "A cop. He was definitely a cop."

"Really." After a brief pause he said, "Seems like things have gotten fairly complicated."

"No..no.. they're not. I got this, man. I don't know why I gotta keep telling you that. It's just a little setback, baby, that's all. I will get the job done. You can trust that."

"Indeed." There was a few seconds of an uncomfortable silence on the line. "Mr. Leonard, I'll have you know that you were not my initial choice for this assignment. This entire ordeal was supposed to fly under the radar with little to no attention at all, and definitely without any witnesses. Had I known things were going to escalate in such a chaotic manner, I think I would've trusted my intuition a little more and made a much more professional selection.

"Fuck all that. You paid me to do a fucking job, and that's what the hell I set out to do."

"Then do it. You have one final opportunity to rectify this situation. If you can't perform to my original expectations of you, not only will my next selection be more apt at taking care of the girl, but he will be paid handsomely to take care of you also."

He let out a chuckle and returned with, "Yeah, I hear you, dude." He looked back at his car. He nearly forgot about his partner. "Look, there's one other thing. My man, Breeze, he got shot. It looks pretty bad. I don't think he's gonna make it."

"That's your man. You brought him in. My only concern is the task at hand, and I believe we've addressed all that needs to be discussed about it."

"Yeah, I know. In other words you give zero fucks." He was pissed by his lack of empathy, but he opted to just suck it up. Things were bad enough, and he didn't want to push his luck with his client.

"I do believe you have work to do, Mr. Leonard."

"Yeah, alright."

"No loose ends, Mr. Leonard. That's what you assured me. No loose ends," said the man.

"I know what the hell I said."

"Then I take it that you won't let your guy bleed to death?"

"Of course not."

"Good night, Mr. Leonard," said the man as he disconnected the call from his end.

"Yeah, fuck you!" said Loc. He knew the man was gone, but he wished he'd stayed on long enough for him to hear his words. "Shit," he said as he turned around to face his vehicle.

He slowly marched towards his car. He opened up the door and stared at his friend laying across the seat, struggling to breathe. The street light shined perfectly on his partner's bloody arm as he was still grasping his wound tightly. With the amount of blood that continued to ooze from underneath his arm, Loc was surprised he was still even conscious.

Breeze slowly rolled his head towards his friend. "Just drop me… drop me off… the hospital," he mumbled in short breaths. "You know… you know… I ain't no snitch."

"Yeah, I know," he nodded.

"Don't wanna die like this," Breeze said as he began to cry. "Can't… can't go out like this, brother."

"You won't," Loc said as he whipped out his pistol from the small of his back and shot Breeze once in the side of his head. He slammed the door shut and pounced both his fists on the roof of the car. "Fuck!"

He took a few moments to gather himself. Then, he placed the gun in the small of his back and walked to the rear of the car. He popped the trunk open and pulled out two plastic gas containers. From there, he looked around to see if anyone was coming down the road. The road was barren. Loc then walked to the back door, slung it open, and began drenching Breeze and the interior of the car with the gasoline.

Once he was done with the inside of the vehicle, he poured what was left of the gas over and around the car. He threw the gas cans on his old friend's limp lap and slammed the door shut. Once again, he looked up and down the desolate road to make sure no one was coming. He pulled out a pack of matches, lit a single strike and threw the match inside the car. The fire spread quickly as he walked calmly to the middle of the road. He gave his car one last stare and then proceeded to walk down the long, dark bridge.

TO BE CONTINUED...

Whatever It Takes 2

Diggin' GOLD

Business was slow as it had been for the past several months. There wasn't a soul occupying any of the empty booths that stretched from the double door entrance at the front to the sports photo filled wall that stretched all the way back to the far corners of the restaurant. Ever since the new truck stop across the street opened up, TJ's Mega Plaza, the diner had began dying a slow, miserable death. It wasn't unusual to go through an extended stretch of hours without a single customer to check in for a fresh cup of coffee or some friendly directions on how to get to the next town.

The competitors that harbored directly across the street offered state of the art dining, a comforting rest area with twenty-four hours of various entertainment options on their gigantic HD television screens that occupied every wall, sharply discounted gas and big breasted, flirty waitresses that had a knack for keeping all incoming truck driving customer hormones rising. With elements like those, Jimmy's Dinner had quickly become played out like a boom box equipped with only a tape deck.

A few customers, like Mr. Oaks, remained loyal to the suffering restaurant. Mr. Oaks had been dining at Jimmy's Diner every since Jimmy's father, Jimmy Sr., opened up the eatery over three decades ago, back when the tiny diner was the only meal offering on this particular stretch of highway. Mr. Oaks' loyalty to Jimmy's Diner began when the cookery saw brighter days with quality customer service, a cheerful wait staff and some of the best home cooking south of the Mason-Dixon.

Even though Jimmy Sr. passed away a few years back, and much of the original wait staff managed to move on to other places, namely the higher paying TJ's Mega Plaza, Mr. Oaks stuck around, defining the true meaning of thick and thin.

"Here you go Mr. Oaks," said Jimmy as he spun around from the open grill with a plate of three silver dollar pancakes, two eggs over easy with four strips of awfully burnt bacon on the side. He slid the sizzling, hot skillet directly in front of Mr. Oaks who had been waiting behind the counter, sitting at his regular bar stool for the first of his three daily meals as he did every morning.

"Oh my, Jimmy!" A huge smile sprang onto his wrinkled filled, copper toned face. "Just how I like it." He began unwrapping his silverware from the dinner cloth. He could hardly wait to dig into the sultry breakfast. "You cook my meals just like your father cooked them for me. Have I ever told you that, Jimmy?"

"Three times a day, Mr. Oaks. Three times a day," Jimmy chuckled. Jimmy was a nice looking dark skinned fellow; slim, clean cut, with a smooth baby face. "But you know what, Mr. Oaks? I never get tired of hearing it."

"Well it's the truth, son. You have every bit of talent that your father had," Mr. Oaks declared as he started chomping down his feast. No matter how many times he ate the same breakfast from Jimmy, it always tasted better each time.

"Thank you for the kind words, Mr. Oaks." Jimmy unwrapped his apron from his waist and laid it underneath the bar. He eased from behind the bar and gazed through the window on the other side of the diner. He became fixated from the view the window revealed. It seemed like there was a never ending line of patrons waiting to be served outside of the door at the restaurant that peered at him from across the street. "I wish everyone thought so."

Jimmy thought back to his younger years when his restaurant was a booming madhouse and his father was the one that manned the grill, slinging out hot servings of home cooked meals to all comers, and back then there were many. Jimmy shadowed his father every day, from sun up to sun down, mirroring his father's recipes to perfection, while enjoying every moment of it. There were only a few feelings Jimmy had experienced in his young life that gratified him the way that standing side by side with his father at that old rusty cooking grill did. A friendly father and son spat about who made the best ham and cheese omelet was not uncommon on daily basis.

Mr. Oaks took notice of Jimmy's sudden silence and slightly spun around on his stool to catch a view of the scene that had quietly captured Jimmy's attention. Mr. Oaks took a moment to swallow his food as he swiped his mouth with his dinner cloth. "That new diner over there is still taking all of your business, huh?"

Jimmy slowly nodded. The diner across the street was a vast contrast from his eating hub. Jimmy removed his attention from the window and sighed at the sight of the countless empty booths that resided in his facility. "Yup, it's pretty evident, Mr. Oaks. It's pretty much killing me and everything Pop built."

"You'll always have my business, son," Mr. Oaks assured him.

Jimmy smiled as he made his way back around the bar and grabbed a towel to wipe down the already spotless counter. "Thanks Mr. Oaks, but I wish that was enough to keep things afloat around here. I have bills coming out of the ying-yang, and it's not getting any better. I'm down to one waitress and I'm the only cook. No more third shift for Jimmy's Diner." Jimmy let out a sarcastic chuckle. "Not that it even matters. There's barely any first or second shift."

"Things will get better in due time, Jimmy. Good times are just around the corner." Mr. Oaks pointed at Jimmy, matter-of-factly. "You'll see. I can sense it."

"I sure hope so, Mr. Oaks." Jimmy shook his head, still overrun with frustration as he threw the towel down. "I try to stay positive, but it's getting tougher every day. I don't know how Pop managed to keep this place open as long as he did."

"This was his dream, Jimmy. He knew what he had to do to keep his dream alive, and he did it. He never gave up."

Jimmy let out a long sigh. "That, he didn't do. The man didn't know the meaning of folding." Jimmy glanced through the window at the congregation that patiently waited outside of his competitor's door step once again. "Then again, he didn't have to deal with TJ's Mega Plaza."

Suddenly, Kizzy rushed into the diner, running with her apron and notepad barely constrained underneath her elbow. Kizzy had a light caramel complexion and an athletic build. She wore her long sandy-brown hair wrapped in a medium ponytail that dangled up and down as she swiftly moved through the cafe.

"Kizzy," Jimmy yelled. She was late as usual, and besides the fact that she was sort of his girlfriend, her tardiness was beginning to get under his skin. She was late everyday this month, and each day, she was coming in later and later. In the diner's glory days, if she was anyone else, Jimmy would've let her go a long time ago. But she wasn't just anyone else and the glory days were long gone, so Jimmy did a lot of tongue biting and only rode her just enough to stay out of the doghouse when they were away from the job.

She swiftly walked past Mr. Oaks, "Hey, Earl!"

"Hi, Kizzy," Mr. Oaks blushed. He was so excited to see Kizzy walk in he didn't know if he should remain seated or stand. She breezed by him so quickly he thought it better to just remain seated.

"I know, I know, I'm late again," she rolled her eyes. "I'm sorry, Jimmy," she blurted out robotically as she didn't reduce her swift pace at all, strolling right pass Jimmy without making a smidgen of eye contact. She quickly dashed through the swinging doors that led to the back kitchen area. She knew his daily lecture about customer preparedness was abound and she wasn't trying to hear it this morning.

A befuddled look crossed Jimmy's face. He felt played, and her shortness with him made him even more annoyed. "I'll be right back, Mr. Oaks."

"Okay, Jimmy, but go easy on her, will you?"

Jimmy offered Mr. Oaks a quick, fake smile. "We'll see," he replied. He marched through the doors that led to the back kitchen area and further back into another set of swinging double doors that led to the break room and dressing area.

Kizzy was standing in front of a small mirror that rested on the back wall, checking herself out for any blemish that might be visible on her flawless, golden face. With the lack of paying customers coming in these days, she knew good looks increased the weight of the tips from the handful of customers that would find themselves into the struggling diner.

"So where were you?" Jimmy asked as he eased up into the reflection of the mirror from behind her.

Kizzy gave him a brief look and snapped back into her own reflection in the mirror. "Home! I overslept."

"Not this morning, last night. I called you several times throughout the night, but all I could get was your voicemail. I was actually kind of worried about you."

"I was okay. I went to see a movie," she stated as she began to apply lipstick to her full luscious lips.

"Alone?" Jimmy quickly rebutted. He couldn't suppress the slight hint of jealously that quickly developed in his voice.

"No," she shrugged her shoulders. "I went out on a date."

"A date?"

"Yeah, a date."

"Oh wow. Wow, Kizzy, I thought we had something going, you and I."

She capped up her lipstick and nonchalantly threw it in her purse. She turned around to Jimmy, who was clearly fuming from the inside out.

"Don't lose your head, Jimmy. It wasn't the kind of date that you're thinking about. I can look at your expression and see that you're already about to explode."

"Well, what the hell kind of date was it, Kizzy? That's all I'm trying to figure out right about now. Maybe if you tell me, you'll save me from *exploding*." He threw his hands up and made a quotation marks sign on exploding.

He was hot at the idea of the only woman he had been seeing exclusively going out on a date behind his back with another man. Although Jimmy was a handsome fellow, he had no real social life outside of the restaurant in years. The only reason him and Kizzy hooked up was because he needed more help shortly after his father passed away, and she emerged like an angel in disguise. A very attractive angel in disguise that appeared to show just as much interest in him as he had in her, right from the start.

"It was sort of a business date." She eased by him and walked towards the wall locker that stood behind him.

He thought if she was trying to make him jealous, she was doing a hell of a good job. "A business date? A business date with who?" He questioned as he whipped around to face her.

She threw her purse in the locker and closed the locker door. She didn't want to give him a name, but she knew if she didn't, she would never hear the end of it. She grunted and looked towards the ceiling. She was beyond regretting mentioning anything at all.

"With who, Kizzy?" Jimmy asked again, anxiously awaiting her answer. His day wasn't going to continue without knowing the identity of the man that was making moves on his lady behind his back. She was going to say it, or there wasn't going to be any peace this day.

"Trent Jackson," she reluctantly replied.

"Trent Jackson! Oh, hell no! Did you just say you went out on a date with Trent Jackson?" Jimmy's jaw almost fell to the floor. Trent Jackson was not only an arrogant, self serving jerk, but he was Jimmy's mortal enemy. Then there was T.J.'s Mega Plaza where the T.J. stood for the one and only, Trent Jackson. Trent was the sole owner of the diner that was putting a slow death to Jimmy's restaurant business. The simple mention of the man's name sent Jimmy ballistic. "TRENT JACKSON!"

She turned around and nodded her head. She wished instead of coming in late, that she didn't come in at all. "Yes, Jimmy, I went out on a *business* date with Trent Jackson last night. Emphasis on business."

"Trent Jackson! You went on a business date with the enemy. The restaurant devil himself! Are you sure it wasn't a put my black ass out of business-business date? Emphasis on put my black ass out of business." Jimmy threw his hands up and turned around and jabbed the wall. "How could you do that shit?"

She rolled her eyes and eased behind him. She knew he would be mad, but mass hysteria hadn't crossed her mind. She slowly placed her hand on his shoulder in an attempt to cool him down. "Jimmy, I did it out of the best interests of the company."

Jimmy snatched his shoulder away from her and spun around, facing her. "No, burning down his two-bit, business stealing truck stop is in the best interests of the company. And I'm certain you didn't do that because he still has about fifty million horny guys waiting outside to be served by his mutated breasted wait staff. No, going out with Trent Jackson was not in the best interests of the company." He dropped into a chair near him. As he stared at her, all he could see was betrayal.

"Jimmy, you're just over-reacting. Trent's really a nice guy. He's just misunderstood."

"Yeah, he took all of my damn employees and all of my customers, and now he's shooting for my girlfriend. Sure, Trent Jackson is one misunderstood dude. Give me a cigarette!"

She paused and gave him a stern look. "But Jimmy, you don't smoke."

"Well, right now is as good as time as any to start."

"Ahh, Jimmy, you know you can act like a big baby at times." She walked to him and sat on his lap. She wrapped her arms around his neck as he leaned his head back against the wall and gazed up at the ceiling. The sweet smell of her skin quickly eased his anger, but he wasn't ready for his fury to end yet. He wanted to be mad at her for just a little while longer. "Baby, you know you got exclusive rights to all of this. I ain't giving it away to nobody else," she said as she slowly rocked her bottom on his crouch. "Emphasis on nobody else."

Jimmy looked at her and smiled as his other brain began to take over all of his thinking duties. Kizzy nibbled on his ear and slowly trailed down the side of his neck with her lips. The woman had a way with his heart and he hated it at times, but outside of her and Mr. Oaks, he had no one else.

"And you sure you didn't give him any sneak previews?"

She let out a hard moan, "Ah, Jimmy." She took her hand and smushed his head. She quickly jumped up off of his lap. "What do you think I am? Some type of a hoe?"

"Nah, I'm not saying that," Jimmy rebutted, as he attempted to choose his words carefully. Jimmy knew that no one would be crazy enough to call a tramp a tramp even if they did an earnest job at earning the title. In his eyes, Kizzy wasn't a slut or a whore, but she was playing a suspect game. It raised an eyebrow. "I'm just saying, Trent Jackson is a human octopus, and believe it or not, I do know the guy. I know there's not too many women that's gone out on a date with him and haven't given up the cookies to him. I can tell you that."

"Well you know one woman now," she exclaimed as she checked herself out in the mirror one last time.

"Yeah," Jimmy said apprehensively as he leaned his head against the wall behind him again. He still had his reservations about her and Trent. He didn't like her going out with someone else and not telling him about it first, and he didn't like the fact that that somebody was Trent Jackson. He wanted to believe that it was just an innocent dinner date but something about the situation just didn't sit well with him.

She turned to him, "So what's going on, Jimmy? Why are you so stressed out lately? Something's gotta be bugging you, with you calling me a hoe and all."

Jimmy quickly shook his head. "I was not calling you a hoe. I was just telling you what I knew of the man. That's all."

"Trifling ass," She grunted. "What about what you know about me?"

He jumped up off of the chair as he wondered, how did her betraying him suddenly become all about him. He knew he stepped in a huge pile of dog crap, and he was going to have to move heaven and earth to fix it. His only problem was that he wasn't sure he wanted to even bother fixing it. Trent Jackson was trying to put them out of business, and it wasn't like she didn't know what the man was up to. Jimmy griped about it to her every day. But for the sake of peace, Jimmy folded. "Hey, look, I'm sorry, sweetie." He pleaded as he grabbed both of her arms from her side. "We cool?"

"No, we're not cool, Jimmy." Her eyes were as red as a fire engine as she struggled to suppress her tears of anger. She gave Jimmy a fierce look as if she wanted to sock him into tomorrow. "I mean, let's both be straight here. You were the one that told me that you didn't want to get too deep into a relationship right now. Am I lying about that? Or did I misunderstand you in the numerous times you said it to me?"

"No, I mean, that was just talk. I mean we can make this thing exclusive. I don't have any problems with that."

"Yeah, now that you think somebody else is gonna ease up behind your slow pace and snatch me from you," she said nodding her head.

"Well, I didn't know I was on the clock. Good grief!"

"There's no need to worry, Jimmy. All I did was go out on a friendly date with the guy to try and help you out."

"Okay, and I'm still trying to figure out how exactly you going out on a date with him is helping me out."

She snatched her arms away from him and gave him her back, "Oh, just forget it, Jimmy."

"Okay, so what did you two talk about?"

She rolled her eyes. She couldn't believe he was still pressing the issue. "Oh, Jimmy come on now. Is that really even important?"

"Fine then," Jimmy replied. "You want to know what's going on with me. I think I'm about to lose the restaurant."

Jimmy's news shocked her. The idea of not having a steady paycheck quickly kicked in. "You do? How is that possible?"

"Well, if you haven't noticed, business has been at an all time low around here, thanks to your boy across the street. But it's a little deeper than that at this point."

"What do you mean deeper, Jimmy?"

"Well, taxes deeper. I owe almost twenty grand. Pop laid a few bombshells on me when he passed."

"I don't understand, Jimmy," she shook her head. "What happened to all that money he left you?"

Jimmy bowed his head as he reminisced about the money from his father's insurance policy that left his hands faster than he received it. "His funeral arrangements, the food and supplies for the restaurant the last five years since he passed away, just a whole slew of things. I'm virtually tapped dry. Then finances really took a hit when that place across the street opened up. It's hard to compete with blueberry pancakes and big tits."

She moaned. "Damn, Jimmy."

He grabbed her hand and stared into her eyes. "I still got you though, right?"

A smile sprung onto her face. "You shouldn't have to ask that, Jimmy. I'm with you until the wheels fall off."

"Well… they're beginning to wobble quite a bit," he grinned. "You still love me, right?"

"Of course I love you, man." She gave him a quick peck on his lips.

"I love you too. Thank you," He was embarrassed but relieved at the same time. He believed her when she said she would stay, but he knew the odds of her loyalty wouldn't last long if he lost everything. "I'll figure this thing out. I'll get this place back on top - even better than when pop was around."

He heard the chimes at the door jingle, indicating that someone had entered from the front door of the café. He walked away from her and peaked out of one of the double doors and through a front line window that revealed the

154

dining area. "Oh snap, we got a customer! I'll take care of him. You just take your time freshening up."

"Thanks, Jimmy," she smiled.

"See you out front," he said as he migrated through the doors.

As soon as he walked through those double doors her smile quickly reshaped into a disgusted frown as she shook her head.

"Damn it, Jimmy. I don't know why in the hell you wanted to keep this stinking place up." she said to herself. She peeled her apron from her waist and threw against the wall, across the room.

****

It was eight o'clock, thirty minutes from closing time. It was another slow night and the handful of customers that did come in to enjoy their dinner were long gone. Kizzy was busy wiping down all of the salt and pepper shakers from the booths in the rear of the cafe. Mr. Oaks sat at the bar eating his last meal of the day while observing Jimmy scrub the grill clean.

"That overflow crowd from across the street really comes in handy some nights," Jimmy stated as he stepped back from the grill and wiped the beads of sweat from his forehead with the back of his hand. "Thank God for impatience."

Mr. Oaks laughed, "We gotta thank God for a lot of things, but I don't think impatience is on the top ten, Jimmy."

"You're right, Mr. Oaks," Jimmy laughed. "I just thank Him."

"Earl, do you need some more tea, honey?" Kizzy yelled from behind.

"No thanks, Kizzy. I'm good with what I have." Mr. Oaks replied.

"Okay, hun," she said.

"But you can definitely thank God for Kizzy," Mr. Oaks whispered to Jimmy.

Jimmy spun around and smiled at Mr. Oaks. He took a glimpse at Kizzy, who was still minding her own with the shakers. He admired her beauty as she worked. "Yeah, we sure owe Him one for making her."

Kizzy stood up and glanced over all the tables to make sure she covered each one. Her work was done. She stuffed her towel in her apron, grabbed her cleaning spray bottle, then made her way towards the guys at the bar.

"You sure you don't need any more tea, Earl? You know Jimmy's cooking can be a little on the dry side at times. I'd hate for you to go out on me choking over here," she joked while smiling at Jimmy.

Jimmy gave her a friendly smirk as he took no offense at all at her cooking jokes. Joking around was a big part of their nights since there was such an abundance of free time with business being slow.

"No, Kizzy, Jimmy's food is just fine," declared Mr. Oaks. "Did I ever tell you that Jimmy has every bit of talent his father had?"

Kizzy and Jimmy simultaneously, "Three times a day, Mr. Oaks. Three times a day." They all laughed.

Suddenly the bells at front entrance began to chime. Jimmy looked over to the entrance and his good mood dissipated in an instance. "Ah shit, look 'a here." He mumbled to himself as Trent Jackson strolled into the restaurant garnishing a suave black three piece suit as he carried a dozen roses in one hand.

"Jimmy Tyler Jr.!" Trent called out. His loud, deep voice sent waves through the building. "Ole, J.J.!"

Trent slowly cruised closer to the bar, as his huge muscular frame took each step with an impeccable vote of arrogance.

"Trent," Kizzy whispered to herself as she rushed towards him, meeting him before he could park himself at the bar counter. "Trent, I thought you were coming to pick me up at nine." She grabbed his hand.

"I was at first, but I just couldn't wait any longer. You have to pardon me for my lack of patience." He handed her the fresh bouquet of red roses. "I just couldn't bare another moment without your beauty in my presence. I guess you got that kind of effect on a fella'."

"Trent, they're beautiful." she sniffed the roses, as her eyes stayed glued on his huge grin. "You're so sweet."

"Yup, business date," Jimmy mumbled to himself as he removed his attention away from them and looked at Mr. Oaks. Mr. Oaks shook his head and shrugged his shoulders.

Kizzy rushed back to the bar counter. "Jimmy can I leave a little early?"

"Well, I thought we were doing inventory tonight, " he answered.

"Thanks, Jimmy. I knew you would understand."

"What?" Jimmy was stunned, but he was careful to not make a scene in front of his nemesis, Trent Jackson, as he glanced towards the pompous brown statue of a man. He stood with his fists in his pockets, in an attempt to contain himself from the latest stunt by Kizzy.

"I'll be right back, Trent." Kizzy fled to the back of the restaurant.

Jimmy, still stunned, simply stared at the flapping doors that led to the back kitchen area that Kizzy had just escaped through. He was pissed, but he wasn't about to show it. He'd rather die than to let Trent think that he's gotten the best of him.

"Jimmy, I'm not finished with my plate yet. I got to go to the wrinkled old men's room and take care of a little business," said Mr. Oaks as he began to stumble to the restrooms that were stationed in the front of the diner.

Mr. Oaks bypassed Trent, neither speaking to each other. Trent grinned, and slowly strolled closer to the bar near Jimmy. It was the moment he was waiting for. The chance to let Jimmy know, he got him again.

"Good Ole', Jimmy Tyler. Seems like you're losing at everything these days, my man."

"She ain't gone yet," Jimmy proclaimed. "And my name's not J.J. either. I know you thought that shit was cute."

"Ah man, lighten up," Trent said as he took a seat at one of the bar stools. "All is fair in love and war, my man. Besides, Jimmy, I think we both know she ain't nothing but a gold diggin' tramp." He swiped two fingers on the counter and rubbed the fingers together. He was impressed by the restaurant cleanliness, but with the lack of customers, he knew Jimmy didn't have much else to do but tidy up the place. "She belongs to whomever has the largest dollar amount and that would be me. We both know she ain't messin' with no broke nigga."

"And how would you know what I got, Trent?" Jimmy responded trying to withhold every urge in his bones to sock Trent in his freshly cut goatee. One sucker punch would be so easy and so refreshing. The temptation was killing him.

"Word has it on the street that you're having a little bit of a tax issue. Now that certainly sounds like a cash problem to me," Trent laughed.

Jimmy stared angrily into his eyes as he walked in front of him, with only the bar counter separating the two of them. Jimmy pressed both of his knuckles down into the counter and leaned towards Trent's face. "I'd be careful about what you gather from street gossip, Jackson, because word also has it on the street that you like to take it from the back."

Trent's conceited smirk transformed into an angry scowl, "I've bagged more bitches than your daddy flipped pancakes. Ain't no sugar in this here tank."

"Keep my pops name out your mouth and you'll do well with keeping your teeth behind them lips."

"Is that so?"

"Yeah, that's so," Jimmy nodded.

Trent leaned back and released a short chuckle. He was a lover, not a fighter. He had no benefits in getting into a physical altercation with Jimmy. He had already taken just about everything away from the man. The only thing left was his woman. "Jimmy, do you know why good guys always finish last?"

"Nah, enlighten me." Jimmy didn't take his eyes off of Trent as he stood in front of him, contemplating smashing him in his jaw one good time. He had already calculated what his projected bail money would be, and he estimated he'd have just enough to get out in a day if he were to beat Trent into a pulp.

"Because they're too damn worried about what everybody is gonna say about 'em if they do something wrong." He snickered. "As long you stand by and stay stuck playing that good guy role, I'll always be better, stronger and richer than you. That's just the way it is, my man."

"I think you need to get the hell up out of my restaurant while you can still walk out under your own recognizance."

"Oh, I will," he chuckled. "Once your bitch come on."

That was the final straw. Jimmy lifted his fist and was about to lunge on Trent, but Kizzy suddenly burst through the doors from the back. Jimmy lowered his hand, took a step back and leaned against the grill behind him. He folded his arms in an attempt to contain his anger.

"Trent, I need to make a stop by my place to take a quick shower and get dressed," she said walking towards the bar with her head down as she dug into her purse with her roses cradled in her arm.

"That's fine, babe," he said as he smiled at Jimmy, expressing a cocky disposition on his face. He knew he had accomplished his mission of pissing Jimmy off, and he knew Jimmy wasn't going to do anything about it.

"Jimmy, I'll see you in the morning, okay," she said as she looked up at Jimmy.

Jimmy looked over to her as he fervently struggled not to make a scene. "That's cool with me. Have a good time, if you can."

Kizzy eased up next to Trent. "You ready?" she asked him.

"Yeah, sweetie, let's go," he turned to her and pushed away from the bar. "We have a busy night ahead of us."

They began to march towards the front door. Mr. Oaks walked past the two as he made his way from the restroom.

"Goodnight, Earl," Kizzy said.

Mr. Oaks stopped in his tracks and turned around. He didn't realize he passed her by. "Ah, see you in the morning, Kizzy."

"The door's open, honey," Trent said as he guided Kizzy towards the door. "I got something for the old guy."

"Okay," she said as she continued to the exit.

Jimmy shook his head as he noticed Trent rushing up behind Mr. Oaks in an attempt to get his attention. "Hey, sir."

"Yeah," replied Mr. Oaks as he turned around and faced Trent.

Trent smiled and quickly decreased his pace as he realized he had obtained the old man's attention. It wasn't enough for him to be walking out the door with Jimmy's girl, he was determined to get one last dig at Jimmy. "Yes, sir," he said while digging in his pocket. "Why don't you spend some time in a real diner and not this here ghost town." Trent revealed a book of coupons from his restaurant. He grabbed Mr. Oaks hand and stuffed the booklet in his palm.

"Here you go old fella. A couple of real meals on me. I'm right across the street if you didn't know that." Trent looked over to Jimmy and gave him an arrogant grin.

Mr. Oaks looked down at the gift booklet and then at Trent. "I appreciate the offer son, but this old ghost town is where I get all of my real meals from." He forcefully stuffed the coupon book back into Trent's hand. "So I guess you can take these here coupons and shove them up your ass."

Mr. Oaks stumbled away from Trent, not giving him a second thought. The old man's rejection made him furious. Jimmy stood at the grill overjoyed with laughter.

"Have it your way old man," Trent yelled. "But don't blame me when your favorite place to eat gets shut down and is included as an extension of my parking lot. Crazy old man." He stormed out of the restaurant.

"You sure told him a thing or two," said Jimmy.

"Don't let the old age fool you, Jimmy," said Mr. Oaks as he reclaimed his spot at the bar. "This old rooster still knows how to cluck."

"That I do see, Mr. Oaks," laughed Jimmy. "That I do see."

Trent slowly cruised his late model, cherry red Jaguar into the driveway of his two story abode. It was a quiet night out in the ritzy neighborhood.

"So we're here," Trent announced. He turned his car off and slouched back in his leather seat. He turned to his sexy companion, Kizzy, who was draped in much sexier attire than her restaurant clothing–a short sun dress that revealed a generous view of her smooth caramel thighs. Trent licked his lips as he undressed her with his eyes. "My, my, my, you're looking good tonight."

She blushed, "I swear you've said that about a million times already."

"Baby, when does the truth ever get played out?"

"I guess it never does," she replied.

"Alright then. As long as you're holding it down the way that you do, then I'm going to continue with my bombardment of compliments. I want you to know that I like what I see, baby."

"You stupid," she said as she peered through the windshield at the humongous home. His two-story brick house was immaculate, and it impressed her. "All that house just for you, huh?"

"Baby, you know I do everything big. It wouldn't be me if I didn't." Her questions gave him the perfect opportunity to do his favorite thing–talk about himself.

"I see. You don't ever get lonely in there with all that space to yourself?"

"Yeah, it can get a little lonely at times, but for the most part, I don't have much time to think about being lonely because I'm always out there trying to make that cheddar," he chuckled. "But you know I got enough room for a roommate, or even a wife, if you play your cards right."

"Oh wow, if I play my cards right. Aren't you the confident one," she grinned.

"Sweetheart, confidence is a man's doorway to success. Without it, failure is inevitable."

"So does that make me some kind of conquest to you?"

"Of course not. I'm in a search for the right partner. One that I can overcome my conquests with. You just happen to be in the running, and your lead is overwhelming right about now."

"You're smooth, Trent, but I'll have you know that I'm not one of those little hookers out there that melt and ooze to any smooth words a handsome brotha' spits out at me."

"Oh, I know that. That's why when I first laid eyes on you, I knew I had to have you. I mean, seriously, I've had my share of fun and all, but I've gotten to the point where I just want to settle down."

She gave him a petite smile while shaking her head. "Now picture that - Trent Jackson calling himself settling down."

"You know I can do it, right?"

"Hey," she shrugged her shoulders. "I'm not disputing that."

"I can do it with you," he laughed. "Now I want you to picture yourself in that big ole' house of mine wearing nothing but a tee-shirt and some panties, fixing me up some pancakes and bacon right after I just got finished putting it down on you just before sunrise."

"Oh my God," she said as she burst out laughing. "You are so damn cocky." She gazed at him, while shaking her head. He simply stared at her with his big, boastful grin. "But you're so damn cute with it."

"That's me, baby. Cocky and cute with it," he said as he eased his hand onto her thigh and began caressing it. He had enough of talking, he was ready to get down to business.

"Did you lose something down there, Mr. Ego?" she asked.

"No, but I want to put something special down there."

"Yeah, I bet you do."

"You know last night was off the chain, right?" he said. "I mean seriously."

"So you think it was?"

"Hell yeah, it was," Trent declared. "So did you tell that clown about us yet?"

"No, not yet, but when did *we* become an us?"

He chuckled, "You gotta be kidding me right?"

"Well…," she held both hands out, in an attempt to have Trent explain himself.

"Shit, every since I was beating that thang on top of your bathroom sink last night," he recalled. "*More, Trent. Right there, Trent. Don't stop, Trent. It's yours, Trent.*"

"Oh, so it's like that?"

"Hell yeah. Just like that," he laughed. "Last night, I put my name on it, baby. You know that. Why don't you slide that dress up and let me get a peak at my imprint."

"You're a funny guy, Trent Jackson. I'm not mad at you though. A sister has to admit, you most certainly handled your business. I don't know about your name being on it…yet, but you did your thing."

"Damn right, I did. I got to handle mine. That's exactly why there won't be any lady of mine working up in somebody's restaurant as the help. You're gonna be right there in my spot, beside me, handling shit."

"Oh really?" She liked the way he talked about them working together, but she wasn't entirely sold on the idea of completely leaving Jimmy. Jimmy was her bird in the hand.

"Yes, really. How can that cat, Jimmy, call you his main lady, and he got you in his little drive thru shop waiting and bustin' on damn tables? That's weak as hell. Ain't nothing weak about Trent Jackson."

"Now, in Jimmy's defense, we weren't together when I first started working there. We just sort of evolved into something over time. Nothing serious."

"Well, now you've evolved into something else, and it's as serious as a mutha fucker." He continued to gently allow his hand to caress her inner thigh as he leaned over and began to nibble on her neck. The sweet smell of her soft skin had his manhood rising, and he was finding it increasingly difficult to compose himself.

"Hmmm, you're acting like you want a repeat of last night," she said as she leaned slightly away from him.

She wanted him just as bad as he wanted her, but just not bad enough to get it on in the car. She also realized that another round with Trent meant another day of lying to Jimmy, but what he doesn't know wouldn't hurt him, she thought. Besides, she was trying to come up and Jimmy's stock was falling fast. Trent had tangible assets, and she was almost ready to go all in.

"I told you earlier that I had a lack of patience for you. Now how about let's get up out of this ride and take a no-holds barred tour of my humble abode. There won't be a piece of furniture off limits. I promise," he said as he continued feasting on her neck.

She observed his house again, "I don't know if you got a back strong enough for the kind of tour that you're talking about. Your place looks like it has a lot of ground to cover. It could take the whole night to get it all."

He pulled up and backed away from her. "There's only one way to find out."

"Then why are we still in your Jag?"

He backed away further with a smile as she smiled right back at him. "Baby, it ain't nothing but a word."

"Then what are you waiting on?"

"Shiiiiiit!" he said. She finally told him what his ears had been waiting all night to hear. The green light was lit. He knew he could have pretty much any woman he set his sights on but Kizzy carried an extra spiff. Not only was she sexy and a freak in between the sheets, but she was Jimmy's lady. She was the last thing he could take from Jimmy and that was worth more than its weight in gold.

He quickly hopped out of the automobile and danced around the vehicle to open her door. He grabbed her hand to assist her on her exodus. He shut the door, not releasing her hand as they made their way to his front door.

As she stood behind him, she looked up and admired the huge brick home. She had never been in a house as big as his, and she couldn't wait to serenade it with him. "This really is a nice place, Trent. I could see you making me some pancakes in bed here," she joked.

"Oh we 'bout to make something, but it's not going to be pancakes, that's for sure." He led her into the dark house and slammed the door shut. Then he pulled her into him and gave her a passionate kiss.

"So I guess you mean business," she said as she backed away from his lips and rested her arms around his neck.

"Do I?" he smiled. He placed both hands on her rump and gripped it tightly, raising her up off of the floor as she wrapped her legs around his waist. As his tongue ran its slow, slippery course up and down her neck, he walked her through the dark living space and carried her to the leather couch. He laid her down and his tongue twirled around her bosom as his hands made their way down her thighs as he began to inch her dress upwards.

"I'm gonna make that pretty little kitty purr tonight," he promised.

Her hands raced up and down his back. "Stop talking and get to work."

"Oh, I'm 'bout to work your ass off," he said as he eased down to her stomach and began massaging it with his lips. She took her hands and forcefully pushed his head between her legs.

The door bell rang.

"What the hell?" his head popped up from her crouch.

"Just ignore it," she replied, wanting him to get back to business.

The door bell rang again.

"Nah, nobody comes to my crib this late. Anyone that knows me, knows better." He was pissed and was ready to share a few choice words with whomever stood on the other side of his front door. He came to his feet and stomped towards the entrance.

She let out a huge grunt and scooted up on the couch. She rolled up her panties and began straightening out her dress. "It's probably just somebody lost."

"Lost in this neighborhood? Hell nah," he said as he flicked on the lights. "Who the hell is it?" he barked towards the door.

"Davis County police department," recited a faint voice from the other side of the door.

Trent peeked through the peephole, "Who?" He recognized the two figures on the other side of the door as being two police officers, one white, one Hispanic.

"Davis County police department," the voice repeated.

He slung the door open, "What the fuck y'all want?"

"You Trent Jackson?" asked the white officer.

"Yeah, who the fuck wanna know?" Trent griped.

"The six head of kids you got waiting for your back child support payments and a judge," the Hispanic officer revealed with a hint of an attitude. On a normal night the cop would've been a lot more professional, but it was late and Trent was being a jerk at first contact.

"Man, what the hell are you characters talking about? Why the hell y'all ringing my doorbell this fucking late? Do you know what type of people live in this here neighborhood?"

"Mr. Jackson we don't have anything to do with that," said the white officer. "We just have several warrants for your arrest for unpaid child support, and we're gonna need to take you in."

"Child support? I don't owe no goddamn child support. What the hell are you toy cops talking about?"

"Trent, what's going on?" Kizzy questioned as she jumped off of the chair.

"Hold on, chick, let me handle this shit with these two toy cops." Trent snapped as he waived his hand back at her.

Her mouth dropped as she stood frozen. "Oh, okay," she mumbled to herself. She quickly realized his nice guy routine was just a façade, and she was now getting a glimpse at the real man.

"Now, I don't know what you dudes are coming up in my crib for, talking about I owe some fucking child support when I don't know what the hell you lames are talking about, but it's late and I'm trying to get some, so why don't you lames do us all a huge solid and go chase some cats out of the tree. You got the wrong man."

"This is 631 Sunrise Court?" the Hispanic cop asked.

"That's right! Paid for too. This house is worth more than twenty years of your salary too, son."

The Hispanic cop grinned and nodded his head as he attempted to keep his composure with Trent's hasty attitude. "We got the right name and the correct address, then I'm confident we have the right guy."

"Fuck you, toy cop," Trent replied.

"Now, Mr. Jackson there's no need for all this foul language with a lady present," the white officer intervened.

Trent looked back at Kizzy and sucked his teeth, "Man, whatever." He could see that she was mad by how she was folding her arms, and she turned away as he looked to her. He knew he messed up when he shunned her. He turned around, facing the cops again. "So these chicks are really

177

serious about this child support thing this time. Damn." He knew there was no need to prolong the inevitable.

"It's called responsibility," said the Hispanic cop.

"I don't need any damn lecture out of you, man."

"Look, Mr. Jackson, it's late, and we can do this the hard way or the easy way," The white policeman bargained. "And it's been a long night for all of us, so we prefer the easy route. So if you could just turn around so we can just read you your rights, you can get this whole thing sorted out in the morning."

Trent let out a heavy sigh. The gig was up. "Shit, you won't get any problems out of me," he said, as he turned his back to the officers and brought his wrist together behind his back.

"Thank you, Mr. Jackson," said the white officer as he whipped out his handcuffs. The Hispanic officer began reading Trent his Miranda Rights.

He pleaded out to Kizzy in an effort for some damage control. "Kizzy, this is some fucked up shit, I know. If you don't mind waiting by your phone in the morning, a brother may need some help out on the bail money depending on how much I got to pay out to these whiney broads."

"Really," she rolled her eyes. She couldn't believe the nerve of this dude. First he dissed her when she was trying to come to his side for support, and now he wanted some help with the bail money.

"Yeah, you don't even have to leave or nothing like that. If you need to run home and pick up some things, just take the Jag. It ain't no biggie."

"No, Trent, I think this *chick*, is going to call herself a cab and find her own way home. You just worry about straightening out your problems with those women you called whiney broads – and don't drop the soap."

"Baby wait! Why you trippin'?" he asked.

Kizzy stomped right by Trent and the officers, not giving her date a second look.

"Kizzy! Girl, why are you being some damn sensitive," he screamed as she continued her way right out of the door.

"Damn, it's just not your night, homie," the Hispanic officer joked as he grabbed Trent by his arm to direct him out of the home.

"Screw you, man. How about that?" Trent growled while shaking his head.

****

All of the lights in the barren restaurant were turned off except the set that lit the very back of the dining area. At the final booth in the back of the diner sat Jimmy and Mr. Oaks.

Jimmy sat with a cigar hanging out of his mouth and his back up against the window, with one leg laying across his seat and his other leg resting on the floor. "You know what, Mr. Oaks, I am so glad I didn't break my neck to get out of here tonight and rush home like I normally do. Ain't nothing home for me anyway."

Mr. Oaks sat opposite of Jimmy, "Home is where the heart is Jimmy," he advised his young friend as he sucked on a cigar of his own. "There's always something there."

"Yeah, well I wish it was where the money was," said Jimmy. Jimmy took in another hit from his cigar and slowly exhaled the smoke while staring at the end of the cigar. "You know, Mr. Oaks, I'm not much of a smoker, but with lung cancer and all the health hazards aside, I see why a lot of people smoke. This is relaxing as hell."

"Yeah, just don't make a habit out of it, son. All cigars aren't the same either. Very few are as enjoyable as the ones from Cuba," he laughed. "These were the last of my little stash."

"Yeah, well habits cost money, and that's one thing I don't have a lot of these days. So you won't have to worry about that from me."

"You know, money isn't everything, Jimmy. Trust me."

"Money may not be everything, but it sure solves a lot of problems."

"That may be true in a lot of cases, but money never solves the most important problems, son."

"Well, I'm about to lose my father's restaurant due to my lack of finances, and that's the most important problem to me right now. I mean, I'm about to lose everything my father worked so hard for. I feel like such a failure to him right about now."

"Jimmy, I've been thinking about this for some time now, and the longer I hold it in, the longer it burns inside me."

"What is it, Mr. Oaks?"

"I knew your father before you ever entered this world, and I was one of the first customers this here old place would consider a regular. I've seen you come in here and work summers as a teen, and I've seen you flourish at that grill as a blossoming young man, side by side with your father. Now I know, this here place is most of what you know because you were born into it, but Jimmy, is this place really all you want out of your life? I mean, I've been here from the beginning, and I've never once seen you take the chance to explore the world that's just outside those double doors leading outside of this place."

Jimmy sat idle as he took a moment to consider Mr. Oaks words. "I don't know how to answer that Mr. Oaks. I never thought about a life without this restaurant in it."

"Don't you think it would be a good idea to at least consider a life that may not include Jimmy's Diner? Son, just because this was your father's dream, doesn't mean it has to be yours, also. Your father was blessed with an opportunity to build his dream and to watch it flourish with his bright young son. That was his dream. I know. I was here to witness it unravel. It was a great vision, but it was his vision. He embraced it and he enjoyed it as long as he could."

"What are you trying to say, Mr. Oaks? You think I should let my father's dream perish?"

"No, I'm not saying that, but I want you to realize that this was your father's dream. He enjoyed it and he passed on. If this isn't your dream Jimmy, if this isn't what makes you happy, then you should find out what does. And when you find it, you should embrace it and enjoy it. That's exactly what your father did. I knew your father and I knew him well, and I know he didn't ask you to spend your life, continuing his."

"I hear what you're saying Mr. Oaks but this here, this diner, this is all I know," Jimmy said as he waived his arms around and looked around the restaurant. "This is what my father left me. I have to keep his dream alive."

Mr. Oaks gazed at Jimmy as he went from slouching to sitting upright in the booth."Jimmy, if I told you that I had millions in the bank, would you believe me?"

Jimmy chuckled while shaking his head, "I wouldn't be surprised at all, Mr. Oaks. Not one bit."

"What if I told you that at the ripe age of seventy-two years old, I've never made love to a woman?"

Jimmy laughed a little harder. Mr. Oaks was an old man of many tales, and Jimmy never had a reason to discount any tales his elderly friend told, but he immediately discounted his latest anecdote . "Then I would say, with all due respect, you're a damn lie, Mr. Oaks. Everybody's gotten a little bit throughout their lifetime. At least once."

"Not me. Never." Mr. Oaks claimed as he shook his head. "Now don't get me wrong, I love me some women, and only women, but I've never in my life have ever had an intimate relationship with one."

"Now, Mr. Oaks, I've listened to a lot of your stories, plenty times a day, but I refuse, I just absolutely refuse, to listen and believe that tomfoolery you're telling me right now," Jimmy said while pointing at Mr. Oaks. "Please don't continue telling me this nonsense."

"Jimmy, I don't want what happened to me, to happen to you."

"Well, Mr. Oaks, if it has anything to do with the foolishness you just told me, I think I'm well past that stage in life," he laughed. Jimmy thought there was no living man of Mr. Oaks' age that could live his whole entire life without scoring at least once. There was no way it could be true, and Jimmy refused to believe it.

"Oh, Jimmy, I have no doubt in my mind about that, but that's not the point I'm trying to get across to you, son."

"Well, my ears are wide open, Mr. Oaks. I can't wait to see how you're going to craft this one," he said. Jimmy was all ears.

Mr. Oaks paused for a moment as he considered reneging on telling his story as a flash of embarrassment rushed through his entire body as his story would be sure to change how Jimmy saw him. Unfortunately, he understood he opened a can of worms he couldn't back out of. He took a good look at Jimmy and decided his ego would just have to be a casualty if his story was going to help his young friend.

"Jimmy, I've been a millionaire ever since I came into this world. My old man was a pretty savvy business man up

185

north when it was hard for blacks to gain any ground in any profession back in the day."

"Yeah, we know that story too well," Jimmy added.

"Anyway, in my father's middle years, he took his businesses and ideas down south. Down here. After a few months of developing his base down here, he met this very attractive caramel complexioned young lady that unexpectedly turned his world upside down. My mother."

"Your daddy liked the red bones," Jimmy joked.

"Well, yeah, but anyway, my mother was a very intelligent woman, but she didn't carry the same work ethic as my father, nor did she have the same passion for success that he had. She just loved him. That's all she knew how to do for him," he said he bowed his head. "But some years after I was born, she realized she couldn't compete with his work. Daddy just worked all the time. So how can you stay in love with someone you only see for an hour out of the day, if at all? So eventually, after years and years of neglect, she wandered. Now, I don't know how it started, but I do know how it ended."

Jimmy's face was expressionless as Mr. Oaks took his time to continue his story. Jimmy couldn't help but notice the sadness that developed on his face as he continued to reveal his family's past. He wanted to stop him from continuing, but he knew the stubborn old man would just have to have his way and finish, so he listened on, without interruption.

"My father started hearing things around town about my mother and this man. This guy, there wasn't much to him, but I guess he gave momma what she needed. She never brought him around me, so I never knew anything about him. Not even his name." He paused as he took a moment to reflect on the idea of his mother being involved with another man other than his father.

His mother's affair happened many moons ago, but the pain it caused him was still there. Still in his heart after all these years. Still evident in his voice as he continued his story to Jimmy, who had his chin resting in the palm of his hand as he remained engaged with the story.

"Dad, he followed her one day, or I should say he followed them one day. They would meet up at some little run down, no-named motel, as the story goes. So dad, he waited outside of their little hotel room for hours as they shared themselves with each other, and he confronted them both as they made their way out of their room. Daddy pulled a pistol out on the man, and he told that man he would have him killed if he ever came around my mother again. My daddy had no problems out of that man because he knew my father had the resources to make good on his promise."

Mr. Oaks looked up and stared Jimmy right in his eyes. "My father didn't say one thing to my mother about it. He didn't fuss at her. He didn't even question her about why she did it. He just treated her really, really cold after the fact. That lasted for a very long time, Jimmy. Sure, they would appear at functions together and visit family and play the part of the happy couple for those looking, but behind closed doors, there was nothing. So much, eventually my mother couldn't take it anymore."

A lone tear slid down his face. The old man wanted to burst into many tears as he never whispered a word of his family's history to any other person, but he felt it important to continue for Jimmy's sake. "I remember that morning. My father had been gone away on a business trip for about a week. I was eleven years old at the time. It was the summer, and I wanted my mother to take me to see a movie. I forget which one, but I remember walking into her room, wondering why she was still in bed just after noon. She was an early bird since I could remember, Jimmy."

Jimmy gave Mr. Oaks a comforting smile, not knowing how else to respond.

"I cracked the door opened, and she was just lying in bed. She was still sleeping, so I thought. So I walked to her bed and tapped her on her shoulder, but I didn't get a response. I started to worry a bit, so I shook her a little harder. But as I shook her harder, I soon realized I was right to worry. I noticed she had an empty bottle of sleeping pills grasped in her hand," he cried. "She took her own life, Jimmy."

"I'm sorry, Mr. Oaks." Having lost his own mother to cancer at a young age, Jimmy could relate to his pain, and he truly felt bad for the old guy.

Mr. Oaks wiped his eyes and shook his head. He did his best to stifle as many tears as he could, but a few managed to expel themselves from the wells of his eyes. "My mother passed away on that day, but I think to my father she died years before she took her own life. When she stepped out on my daddy, his heart became black. Because of that darkness that infested in his heart he was determined to instill in me some type of hatred towards any woman that could have their eyes on my future fortune. And really, to him, that was any and every woman."

189

"Man, Mr. Oaks I had no idea you had to go through all of that. That's horrible," Jimmy said.

"No, what was horrible was being a young man with a father in his later years that had nothing else better to do but critique his choice of women. My father would constantly hassle me to make certain that the one woman I marry be the one for me and not the one for my money. Every woman I brought home to him, he found something wrong with them. He didn't give them an honest chance. I wanted nothing more but to impress my father because he was all that I had. So what he said went and also any chances of me having any meaningful relationship with any woman - good or bad."

"My goodness, man, how on God's green earth have you survived this long? No woman, I mean, jesh!"

"I don't think you want to know, son," Mr. Oaks frowned as he held up his two hands, signaling whatever he didn't do with the opposite sex, he did alone.

"Uh, you're right. I don't wanna know," Jimmy frowned.

"What I'm trying to say is, son, my father wanted me to settle down with one woman, marry one woman, any boring woman that he saw fit, and I was never able to bring one home to him. Hell, all I wanted was a fast and nasty hot momma. One that would make my hair stand up on top of my head. You know the type."

"Yeah," Jimmy laughed. "I sure do, Mr. Oaks."

"But I never got that," he said. He shook his head while thinking about how fast the years just flew by him. "Instead, I listened to my father and only looked for what I thought he wanted me to have. Every woman I met, I doubted, and because of that I ended up a lonely, old coot with a lot of money. Truth is, I don't think my father even wanted me to find happiness in a woman. I think he wanted me to live my life just as lonely as he lived in his. Lord as my witness, Jimmy, I'd trade every cent to my name just for the chance to change the path I've traveled."

"Damn, Mr. Oaks, I hope you don't mind me saying this, but that's one fucked up story."

"It is, isn't it," he laughed.

"Yup," Jimmy chuckled.

"Well, Jimmy, as hard as it was for me to reveal my story, I shared it with you because I don't want you to make the same mistakes I've made. If this restaurant business isn't for you, well hell, you should find out what is. Besides, how many meals does this old man have left?"

They laughed.

"Lots of them, Mr. Oaks. Lots of them."

"You're a good man, Jimmy Tyler Jr. Your whole life is before you. Don't sell yourself short."

"I hear you, Mr. Oaks. It's definitely something I need to consider," Jimmy nodded as he continued to let old man's story marinate in his mind. He never considered a life outside of the restaurant business, but with his recent financial issues, he was beginning to consider it. What bothered him the most was the guilt he knew he would feel if he let his father's dream go. Although his father was long removed from the earth, Jimmy still felt a strong loyalty to the man, and even in death, he didn't want to betray him.

****

After locking his front door, Jimmy flipped his shoes off in the middle of his living room floor and made a swift route to his bedroom. He had a long day and was ready to jump in the shower, then hit the sack.

As he began unbuttoning his shirt he pushed his bedroom door open. When he flicked on the lights he was hugely surprised by the woman dressed in red lingerie spread out across his bed. It was Kizzy.

"Yo, what the hell? Kizzy?" he said, befuddled.

"Hi, Jimmy," she said, greeting him with a petite wave. She wore a light red chiffon with lace cups that revealed her perky nipple outline.

Jimmy quickly turned away from her, not wanting to be tempted by her gorgeous physic. "I thought you were with your man, Trent Jackson. On another one of those business dates!"

"I was," she said as she slithered across the king-sized bed on all fours towards him. "But our date ended really quick when I found out what type of man he was."

She knew he was still mad at her, but with Trent getting sent to the big house, she had to repair the only sure thing she had going for her.

The idea of her finding out Trent wasn't the man he claimed to be intrigued him. He turned towards the bed and faced her. "Oh, really?"

"Yes," she replied as she grabbed his hand and positioned herself on her knees. She pulled him closer.

"So, what's all this?" he asked as she began to finish the job of unbuttoning his shirt.

"This is me, being where I'm supposed to be," she said softly as she began kissing him on his chest.

"Damn," he mumbled as he looked towards the ceiling. He knew darn well he couldn't let her get off with her betrayal that easy, but the sweet fragrance of her skin nearly made his knees buckle. "So.. so… what did you find out about him," he stuttered. He still wanted to know the goods about his nemesis, but the idea of making love to her one last time was superseding anything else.

"That he's a dog faced liar," she uttered out as she broke away from her oral massage of his chest. She began unbuckling his pants. She knew she had him. The only thing left for her to do was to seal the deal.

All Jimmy could do was look down at her and be the weak man that he was. He hated himself for letting her come in and manipulate him with her body, but her body was so good to him in the past. "What suddenly made you come to this con… conclusion?"

His pants dropped to the floor.

"I'll tell you all about it after I show you how much I missed you," she said as she spun him around on the bed on his back. She crawled on top of him and continued to kiss him across his chest.

****

Jimmy walked out of the bathroom with a towel strapped around his waist. He stopped at the door and stared at Kizzy. She sat on the bed with her back against the headboard wearing a pink robe. She was intensely engaged with the screen of the laptop that rested on her lap. After a few moments of feeling Jimmy's eyes peering at her she looked up at him and smiled.

"What?" she asked as she broke away from the computer.

"You were great," he replied.

"You weren't that bad yourself," she said as she took a pull from the cigarette she had sitting in the ash tray on the nightstand beside the bed.

"Well, I try," he said as he made his way over to his dresser and grabbed a pair of boxers. He threw the towel on the edge of the bed and slipped on his underwear. He then made his way under the sheets. "So what's all this talk about Trent Jackson being the scum of the world? As if I didn't tell you that already."

"He got arrested."

"What?"

"Yeap, right in the middle of our date," she nodded her head. "All that freakin' money he has and he's a deadbeat dad. The police were waiting at that bastard's house when we got there."

"Wow, really? I can't believe it. Him with all his big talk."

"Yup, I couldn't believe it either, but I just pulled him up online. This negro owes over three hundred thousand dollars in back child support for six kids by five different woman. Scum!" She angled her laptop so Jimmy could his mug shot online.

"Damn, he really needs to strap up."

"You telling me," she replied.

"Man, that's awful."

"Not really! Owing that kind of money, there's no way he's going to be able to keep that restaurant open."

Jimmy looked to her as he stuffed a pillow between his back and the headboard. "You think so?"

"How else is he going to reimburse all those women? He's going to have to sell everything. I know those women are going to be thrilled!"

"How can they be? " Jimmy frowned.

"Huh? Easy! All that money that's about to be rolling their way, that should be more than comforting."

"Nah, those kids, they don't have a father."

"With all that loot they're about to get from that bastard having to sell everything that he owns, they can all buy new fathers," she laughed.

"You don't get it, do you?"

"Get what, Jimmy? Everybody wasn't as lucky as you to have a father there when they were growing up. If my old man was about anything when I was coming up, my mother would've stuck it to his ass! But he was a drunk, with seven head of other kids scattered all over the place, and none of us got anything from his sorry ass. Everybody wasn't as fortunate to have somebody there like you did, Jimmy. Some of us didn't even care."

"So I should feel bad because my old man stuck around?"

"No, I'm not saying that. I'm just saying money is a good substitute for a daddy." She took another pull from her cigarette.

Jimmy chuckled, "You know, money isn't everything, Kizzy. I mean, look at Mr. Oaks…" He had no intentions to say anything about Mr. Oaks, but before he could stop himself, he'd already mentioned his name.

"What about Earl?" she snapped.

"Nothing." Jimmy knew he messed up. Kizzy sniffed information out like a bloodhound, and it would be a cold day in hell before he would get any sleep without disclosing his information about Mr. Oaks.

"Ooh, Jimmy, don't do that," she said as she nudged him on his shoulders. "How are you just going to mention something and try to take it back like that? I don't do that to you."

"Oh God, Kizzy," He let out a hard sigh. "I shouldn't even tell you this, and you better not let him know I told you, neither."

"Oh shut up, Jimmy. You know I can keep a secret."

He considered keeping his mouth shut one last time, but she had her eyes on him like a hawk. He knew there was no use keeping his secret any longer. "Well, I really shouldn't tell you this, but Mr. Oaks is a seventy-two year old millionaire virgin."

"What?" She jolted straight up. She had to snatch up her laptop because it almost slid off of the bed. "You're kidding me, right? Earl's a millionaire?"

"Yeah, I mean I don't know the extent of his wealth, but he has money. And lots of it. He told me about it tonight."

"How?" She stumped out her cigarette in the ashtray on the nightstand beside her bed and placed her laptop next to it. "What made him tell you? Is he going to give you any money? Is he about to die or something?"

"No! I would never ask him for any type of a handout." He quickly took offense to her asking if he asked the old man for a handout. "And he's not about to die!"

"Oh," she replied. She was slightly disappointed Jimmy's discussion with the elderly regular didn't include sharing the wealth. "Then what made him tell you about it?"

"We were just talking about our fathers, that's all. He told me about how his father and money kept him away from finding any real happiness from a woman. I mean, it was so sad. All he wanted was a woman he could call his own."

"Shoot, he must be don't know! Happiness is just around the corner. Why didn't you ask for no money, anyway?"

He gave her a disappointed look. "There's more to life than money, Kizzy."

She looked at him with a serious expression on her face but that quickly turned to an explosion of laughter. "Whatever, Jimmy! Money makes the world go around. Without it, you're just another loser trying to get it."

"So I guess that's what I am?"

"You said it," she said as she slid under the sheets and turned away from him.

His eyes stayed on her. "And what's all this talk about happiness is just around the corner?"

She sighed, "Jimmy, go to bed. I was only kidding." She fumbled to press the power off to her computer, then flicked off the lamp above it.

"Cut the alarm on for me, will you? I want to get to work early in the morning," Jimmy requested.

She hit the alarm. He stared at her motionless body as he wondered if she was really joking with her statement or if there was any seriousness to it. Her rendezvous with Trent Jackson placed plenty doubt in his heart about her.

****

The sharp rays of the morning sun pierced through the cracks of Jimmy's bedroom curtains and zapped him in his face, awakening him. As he batted his eyes, rolled over on his side and looked towards his alarm clock.

"What the hell?"

Jimmy bolted up as the clock revealed he had overslept by two hours, and Kizzy was nowhere to be found.

****

Jimmy pulled into the parking lot and to his surprise there wasn't a vacant spot left on the lot. The lot to his restaurant was overrun with vehicles and this was something he hadn't seen in over a year. As he spun around the lot, he couldn't help but notice the long line of customers waiting to enter his diner. On a normal day, with a crowd like the one standing outside of his door, he would've been overrun with excitement, but he knew this crowd was going to cost him something.

As Jimmy made his way into the restaurant he came to a freezing halt at the entrance. He scanned his diner and stood totally mystified by the loads of customers that were packed into his restaurant enjoying their breakfast. What was even more shocking, was the sight of seeing former members of his wait staff scattered across the restaurant floor serving the patrons. "What the hell is going on?" he asked himself. He looked towards the window and noticed his competitor's diner across the street was an absolute ghost town. The restaurant didn't even appear to be open.

Jimmy's befuddlement quickly transitioned to anger when he looked over to the bar and noticed Kizzy snuggled up closely beside Mr. Oaks with her arm around his neck. Mr. Oaks appeared to be rambling about something as Kizzy faithfully listened on.

"Kizzy," Jimmy yelled across the floor as he made his way towards the bar. Kizzy and Mr. Oaks quickly turned around, facing him.

"Jimmy," she responded nervously. "I thought you were..."

"Sleeping!" he swiftly cut her off. "For some odd reason my alarm didn't go off this morning. Care to explain?"

"Jimmy, your cook is back," Mr. Oaks interrupted as he pointed to the cook, standing at the grill, lining it up with bacon.

"Yeah, I see him," Jimmy replied, not removing his eyes off of Kizzy. "Well, Kizzy?"

She smiled and removed her arm from around Mr. Oak's neck. "Must we discuss this all in the open, Jimmy?"

"It doesn't matter where we discuss it, Kizzy, as long as it gets addressed. If you want to go in the back, let's go!"

She turned to Mr. Oaks. "Earl, I'll be right back. Don't go anywhere, hun."

"Hun?" Jimmy sneered while rolling his eyes.

"Oh, I won't," Mr. Oaks replied. "I understand."

"Thanks," she rewarded him with a peck on his cheek.

"My God," Jimmy mumbled in pure disgust.

Kizzy made her way to the back through the kitchen doors as Jimmy started to follow.

"Jimmy," Mr. Oaks called out.

"Yeah, Mr. Oaks," Jimmy responded.

"Go easy on the little lady, will ya?"

Jimmy nodded and proceeded to walk through the double doors to the back of the diner. Kizzy sat on the table, nonchalantly smoking a cigarette as Jimmy walked in. He stood in front of her with a face full of rage.

She gave him a slight look out of the corner of her eye and took a pull from her cigarette. "Well, say what you have to say. I'm listening."

"You know, on my way over here I wanted to believe there was a non cynical reason for you leaving me in the bed the way that you did, but when I walked through that door just now, all bets were off. You're trying to milk Mr. Oaks, aren't you?"

"What?" she snapped back with a huge frown plastered on her face. "I can't believe you just asked me that. Jimmy, you can be a real asshole when you want to be. I mean, I don't get any thank you's for getting your old staff back in here to serve all those people out there? And can a sister get any commendations for playing hostess and manger with that madhouse out there while you were away?"

"Woman, don't try to play me and change the subject. You know what the hell I'm talking about."

She smashed her cigarette in the ashtray beside her on the table. "Well, I hear you, but I don't believe that you're in front of me talking like that. Who do you think you are, my daddy or somebody?" She hopped off of the table and walked to the other side of the room.

"Look, stop all the run around and just answer my question. You're trying to milk Mr. Oaks, are you not?"

She grunted. "Bingo, Jimmy! I'm gonna milk that cow dry and there's not a damn thing you can do about it."

"Oh yes I can. I'm going to go tell him," he said as he walked towards the door.

"Tell him what, Jimmy?" she asked. "You think he wants to hear what you have to say, man? That what might be his last chance to get a piece of trim is out to scam him?" she laughed. "You think he wants to hear that? Hell no, Jimmy! He wants what I can give him, and I'm gonna give it to him," she smirked. "For a price."

"You're a goddamn gold digger!"

"And?" she smiled while folding her arms. "Ain't nothing free in this world, Jimmy. You know that by now?"

"He doesn't need this," Jimmy pointed.

"And who are you suppose to be, Jimmy? His guardian?" she rolled her eyes. "You're always walking around here like you're Mr. Perfect or somebody, but I got news for you Jimmy -the nice guy roles are played out. Just look at your father…"

"What'd you say? Don't you ever let anything about my old man cross your ratchet lips," he said while pointing at her.

"Or you'll do what? You know it's true, man. The nice guy role only got you in a world bit of debt, while doing something you really don't want to do." She knew bringing Jimmy's father into the fold was his weakness, but she felt if he could call her a gold digger, nothing was off limits.

"How in the hell do you know what I want?"

"I know it's not this."

"And who asked you?" Jimmy griped. "At least I'm not out here hopping from bed to bed, trying land the highest bidder."

She laughed, "Is that what I'm doing, Jimmy Tyler?"

"That's what the hell it looks like to me!"

"Well looks can be deceiving, Jimmy. I'm just trying to come up. Something you should try for a change."

"I work my ass off each and every day. That's all I know how to do."

Jimmy plopped down in a chair against the wall and folded his arms. There was an awkward silence between them. He was mad as hell, and Kizzy knew it. She didn't want to lose Jimmy before she could confirm what kind of money the old geezer was working with. Besides, she really did have feelings for Jimmy. She simply loved money more.

In an attempt to make amends, she grabbed him by his hand. "Jimmy, why don't you throw in the towel and help me get this money from this old buzzard before he croaks."

"What the hell?" he said as he snatched his hand away from her. "Are you insisting that I help you?"

"Yes, Jimmy! Don't you see, man? This is our ride. We can't let it pass us by this time. We can come up - together!"

"Are you fuckin' retarded?" Jimmy sat in awe as he couldn't believe what the woman he had just slept with the night before was suggesting. Jimmy was overcome with the feeling of being her sucker.

She took a step back. Jimmy's response clearly ticked her off.

"So you want me to turn my back on the only person that stuck by me and this place through thick and thin? I mean, have you really lost your mind?"

She approached Jimmy and stood only a few inches from his face. She couldn't believe he rejected her offer to finally come out on top for a change; a chance to leave the ailing diner behind. She thought Jimmy must really like to live struggling. It was clear to her that Mr. Oaks' riches was her route to financial freedom and she wasn't about to miss this opportunity. "When are you going to get tired of coming in last, Jimmy?"

"If coming in first means I have to stab people in the back that I care about, then I guess that means I'm always gonna come in last."

"Such a good guy." She nodded as she finally realized there was no getting through to him. She was on her own, but she really didn't care at this point. Jimmy had pointed her to the money train she had been searching so long for, and she wasn't about to let him nor anyone else get in her way. "Have fun dragging in the rear, Jimmy, because I'm not rolling with you back there anymore."

"Trust me, I don't even want you to roll back there with me anyway."

She chuckled. "You know, Jimmy, Trent was right. You really are a loser." After she served him with the biggest blow she could throw at him, she side stepped him and made her way towards the door. "Oh yeah, I quit."

"You can't quit," Jimmy responded as he jumped up out of his chair and faced her.

"And why can't I?"

"Because I already fired your ass," he yelled. "Get out!"

She smacked her gums. "Loser." She stomped through the door and left the room.

"Gold digging, bitch!" He angrily flipped the table over.

Kizzy hustled back into the dining area and grabbed her purse from behind the bar.

"Everything all right, Kizzy," Mr. Oaks asked.

"No hun, your boy, Jimmy just canned me!"

"What? Why?" Mr. Oaks quickly jumped off of his stool. "Let me go talk to him. I'll can try to straighten things out between you two."

"No, Earl, it's okay," she replied as she wrapped her arm around his and directed him towards the exit. "It's about time for a girl to find a new gig anyway. I've outlasted my welcome. Besides, I'd rather spend my day with you."

"You would?" he asked.

"Yes, Earl," She put her hand into his hand. "I've always wanted to know more about you, and now that I'm free to do whatever I want today, what better time to find out about you than now? Unless you have other arrangements today."

"Uh, no," Mr. Oaks replied, fumbling his words. "I don't have anything planned today."

She smiled, "Well, let's do it."

He stood amazed. It had been a couple of decades since a woman so much as winked an eye at him. Now he had one interested in spending the day with him. "O..Okay."

She wrapped her arm around his again, and they walked towards the front doors, making their way out of the diner.

Jimmy sat alone at the table as he had just got finished ransacking the entire back area. Tables, lockers, and sheets of paper were scattered all across the floor. He sat at the table sadly staring at a picture of him and his father that was taken when he was a kid.

The front line cook who had been patiently waiting on the other side of the door for all the ruckus to stop walked in. He nervously scanned the back room's wreckage in the aftermath of Jimmy's anger. "Whoa," the cook said timidly. "Mr. Tyler, you okay?"

Jimmy didn't answer.

"Mr. Tyler," the cook repeated.

"Yes, Samuel."

"Um," he replied nervously. "Do you have any more sausage patties stored somewhere? I'm down to the last box, and we still got people storming through the door wanting breakfast."

"We don't need any more patties," Jimmy answered in a low tone. "After lunch, we're closing."

"For the day, Mr. Tyler?"

"No," Jimmy looked up at the man and nodded. "For good."

****

Kizzy and Mr. Oaks walked down the apartment hallway arm and arm. They stopped at the last door down the hall as Kizzy dug into her purse and whipped out her keys.

"So this is where you live, Kizzy," said Mr. Oaks.

"Yup," she answered as she fiddled with the door lock and pushed the door open. "Come on in, Earl."

"Oh, Kizzy, I really shouldn't," he said nervously. "It's getting kind of late and –"

"You got a curfew, Earl?"

"Well, no," he answered.

"Then get your bottom in here," she demanded as she grabbed his hand and pulled him into the apartment. He eased into the living room as she flicked on the lights and locked the door behind him.

Mr. Oaks scanned the petite but well kept living area. "I'm not sure why, but I've always figured you to live in a bigger place. It's nice though."

She walked over to her stereo and turned it on. The subtle love making sounds of Keith Sweat lightly echoed across the room. He turned to her as soon as the music started.

"Kizzy?" he called out. She was staring at him like he was a piece of meat. He never had any woman look at him the way she was looking at him, so it made him feel flattered and uncomfortable at the same time. "You okay?"

"Oh, I'm okay, Earl," she said as she slowly walked towards him. "It's just a little hot in here, that's all."

She began unbuttoning her blouse. His eyes nervously followed her fingers down to the last button. He unconsciously paced a few steps backwards as she continued her path onward to him. Her blouse slid to the floor. She reached behind her back and unbuckled her bra. She slipped it off and threw at him. His old age didn't betray him with his reflexes as he caught it with cat like quickness.

"I know you've been wondering how these looked uncovered," she whispered as she caressed her breast. "Wonder no more, Earl."

"Good gracious," he muttered softly, as he salivated while staring at her perky golden brown breasts. He had seen quite a few bosoms in his old age via the internet and the secret porn stash he had tucked away in his closet, but he never saw any as perfect as Kizzy's and as close.

"You haven't seen good yet," she said as she gave him a firm push, and he fell backwards on the couch behind him.

She crawled on top of him and began to passionately kiss him. The old man was trying furiously to keep up with the young feline, but he knew he could only do his best. In the back of his mind, being this way with Kizzy was all he wanted since meeting her, and it was finally happening. He couldn't believe it. He wanted to pinch himself just to verify he hadn't passed away and went to heaven.

She pulled away from him and said, "Baby, I'm 'bout to rock your world."

"Uh, Kizzy, uhm," he fumbled on his words but she stopped him by resting her finger on his lips, signaling him to be quiet. She wanted to assure him, she had things under

215

control. She began pulling his shirt up out of his pants and loosening his belt buckle. "Oh gosh," he uttered as he felt the blood rushing to his head. His manhood had never been as rock solid as it was at this moment. He was so stiff it almost pained him.

"Ooh, Earl, you're so hard," she said while groping his private parts.

"Uhhhh," he let out a fierce groan as he suddenly began to tremble and shake. Worried, she backed away from him as he continued to shiver uncontrollably.

"Earl?" she said worried. She looked down towards his crouch and noticed there was a huge wet spot coming through his slacks. "Did you just?"

He nodded embarrassed while breathing heavily. "I'm sorry."

She smiled. "It's okay, boo. Don't worry about it, the first erection is always the quickest. The second one will take much longer." She crawled back on top of him, kissing his neck while unbuttoning his shirt. He simply laid back, allowing her to take control as he did his best to take his mind off of his initial misfire.

****

They both sat spread out on Kizzy's bedroom floor. Earl had his back against the base board of the bed, their bodies partially draped with a comforter that had somehow managed to find its way to the floor from Kizzy's king-sized bed. Kizzy had her head comfortably positioned on his chest as she ran her fingers through his shaggy, gray hairs.

"My goodness, what was that?" he uttered softly.

"That was the bomb, Earl," she replied.

He let out a long, relaxing breath as he leaned his head up against the base board. "I've never felt anything like the bomb before."

"You bragging or complaining?" she chuckled.

"I.. I.. I don't have any idea what I'm doing. I know I feel good, though."

She eased up off of him and sat up on her own. "Well, you surely can't be seventy-two years old, Earl. You are a stallion. I mean you wore me out."

"I did?" he asked, surprised.

"Yes," she said as she gave him a peck on his cheek. She knew every man enjoyed his ego stroked, no matter his age. She wanted him to know that he handled his business because a well stroked ego for a man uncertain of himself was worth its weight in gold. And although she thought Earl would just be a quick episode of bumping uglies, the old guy came to play. "A wild stallion."

"Wow," he giggled. He thought his performance was less than stellar, but he didn't have any other occasion to go off of, so he had to take her word for it. Her praise made him feel good inside.

She jumped up, grabbed her panties and slid them back on. "Boy, Earl, you really pack a wallop. You're just too much for a young lady like me."

"I am?" he said as he slid up from the floor and sat his naked rump on the edge of her bed.

"Yes, Lawd. I've never made love that felt so soothing and relaxing. I know you were a lady killer back in the day, weren't you?" she asked as she took a spot next to him.

"No," he shook his head. "Not at all." He bowed his head, uncertain if he should reveal to her the secret he had been keeping all his life. "You see, I'm kinda embarrassed to tell you this. Ah, what the hell?" He decided to come clean. "Kizzy, that was my first time."

"First time what? Having sex on the floor?" she asked, playing stupid.

"No, Kizzy," he answered, staring in her eyes. "Having sex at all. Kizzy, you just took my virginity."

"Earl, stop lying!"

"No, Kizzy, I'm not lying. I'm telling you the truth. That was my very first time."

"You're kidding me, Earl."

"I can't be any more serious," he said. He felt like a huge weight had been lifted off of his shoulders as he revealed to her his deepest, darkest secret. A secret, at this point in his life, he thought he would never reveal to any woman. "It felt so good, Kizzy. I..I..I liked the way it felt."

She smiled, "I did too, Earl."

"I mean, I really liked the way it felt. I want to feel that way every day."

"Earl, what are you saying?" she asked. She knew she had him hooked. The only thing left for her to see was how much her work was going to pay off.

"An old man like me, my time is limited..." He explained sadly as he bowed his head. He was upset about how long it took for him to get to this moment. He knew he lived a lifetime of regret. At last he experienced that wonderful feeling he had waited so long for, and it was all he dreamt it to be and more. He wasn't sure how Kizzy was going to respond to what he was about to say next, but he felt he was on a roll, so he let it out. "Kizzy, I would like for you to marry me."

Her lips begin to quiver. It was like someone had given her the winning lottery ticket, as she was overrun with excitement. Excitement she didn't reveal to him. "Earl, I don't know what to say."

"Say you'll marry me, Kizzy," he said as he inched closer to her.

"Earl, this is so overwhelming," she said in dramatic fashion as she jumped off of the bed and gave him her back.

She grinned, still ecstatic about his question, yet focused on not appearing too willing to say yes. It was imperative to her plans that he remained unaware that she knew he was a virgin at the start of the night. At least until they exchanged their "I do's". "I wasn't expecting this at all tonight."

"I know it's really sudden, Kizzy, but an old man like me don't have very long. Each day I get up in the morning is a blessing. I would love to spend whatever time I have left with you."

"But, Earl," she spun around. "A marriage costs money and requires preparation. We don't have any money."

"No…no. Money! I have lots of money," he explained. "I have several millions I've inherited. Money is no problem."

"You're kidding me aren't you, Earl?"

"No, Kizzy, it's true. Money won't be an issue. I just want us to be together. I can buy you whatever your heart desires."

"Earl, I don't know…"

He grabbed her hand. "Just say yes."

She smiled while nodding her head. "Yes, Earl. Yes, I'll marry you." Tears of joy slid down her face as she hugged him tightly.

****

Jimmy sat at the final table in the back of the restaurant. Papers scattered across every inch of the table as he thumbed through a large black notebook. It was the middle of the day, and Jimmy had the blinders closed at every window. The diner was deserted, as it had been closed for the past several months.

The chimes at the door rang, and Jimmy noticed the distinct tapping of heels approaching. He looked up, pissed that he had forgotten to lock the doors when he came in earlier, and even more pissed when he recognized the owner of those heels. It was Kizzy, and she was decked out in a skin tight skirt, fancy pearls around her neck and a gold ring that had a diamond in it that was the size of an almond.

"Having fun, are we?" Jimmy shook his head and returned to his reading. Even though he still thought she was sexy as hell, the mere sight of her made him want to gag.

She sat her fancy Dooney & Bourke handbag on the table and took a seat opposite of him. "I must say that I am, Mr. Tyler."

"Well, don't let me stop you. The door works the other way around, also."

She chuckled. "Jimmy, you've always been the jokester."

He slammed the book closed and looked up at her. "Look, what do you want? Why are you even in here? I sent your last paycheck to your old address months ago. Not that you even need it anymore."

"I just came to see an old friend," she answered. Her eyes swiftly zoomed across the empty diner. "Besides, I heard that you finally sold the place."

"What's it to you, Kizzy? I thought you were busy in the Bahamas having the time of your life or wherever you were. It makes me no difference."

"Oh yeah, we just flew back two days ago. I figured the old man does need a break every now and then, so I decided to come see how you were. After doing a little bit of shopping, of course."

"The joys of marrying for money. Well, I'm fine. Never been better. So now that you've done your status check, or whatever you want to call it, you can find your way out the same way you came in."

"Oh, Jimmy, you don't have to act all salty with me. I came in peace. I missed you."

"Why?" Jimmy asked perturbed. "I didn't and still don't have enough money for your ambitious needs. You got what you wanted, and no matter how difficult it was for me to keep my mouth shut, I didn't utter a word to Mr. Oaks about the real you."

"Well, Jimmy, I thank you kindly, but you have me wondering. Who's the real me?"

Jimmy laughed. "You're kidding me right?"

"No, I'm serious, Jimmy. Who's the real me?"

Jimmy's smile quickly wiped away. "You're an evil, sneaky, conniving, gold digging bitch, and one day you're going to get what's coming to you."

"Wow," she sneered. "Why don't you tell me how you really feel." She eased up out of her seat and grabbed her bag.

"Not enough hours in the day."

"Well, Jimmy, I was just a little concerned about you. I knew how much this place meant to you. I guess I wanted to make amends with you."

"Just get out," Jimmy shook his head tirelessly. "We don't owe each other anything. Just leave me the hell alone."

"If you want to be that way about it, I will. But let me correct you on one thing, Jimmy. I already have what's been coming to me. It may have taken awhile, but I got it, and I deserve it."

"You don't want me to tell you what you really deserve." Jimmy stood up and pointed at the door. "Now please, get the hell out."

"Once again, you ruined your chance to roll with the big dogs, Jimmy," she grinned.

"Out! Get the hell out now!"

"Later, loser," she mocked him as she made her way towards the exit.

Jimmy never laid a finger on a woman in his life, but Kizzy made him consider it. She said she came in peace, but

Jimmy knew better. She just wanted to flaunt what she gained in his face. He wasn't impressed, just disappointed in himself that he didn't give Mr. Oaks a heads up. But he knew if he told Mr. Oaks anything negative about Kizzy, he wouldn't believe it. So he just left well enough alone.

He walked to the window and peaked out of the blinds to make certain she was leaving. He watched as she jumped into her new Cadillac, the dealer tags still hanging on the car. He came to terms with the idea that she was exactly what his elderly friend wanted and who was he to intervene? She drove away.

****

Mr. Oaks was on the side of his bed in and old tee-shirt and some saggy boxers doing pushups. Each time he went up he let out a hard count as if he was being punched in his gut. Kizzy sat on the bed with her IPod speakers hanging from her ears as she flicked through channels on the huge television hanging from the wall on the opposite side of the room.

"Earl," she said as she ripped the headphones from her ears. "Don't you think you've done enough?"

Although she was married to him and she went on lavish spending sprees on just about every day since their simple exchanging of vows at the courthouse, she had agreed to sign a prenup with Earl. His health was important to her, at least for now. At least until she had enough time to confirm she was his only living relative, then after that, he could keel over for all she cared.

"I need to do all I can," he said, breathing profusely. "I gotta keep my heart pumpin'!"

She rolled her eyes without him noticing. "Well baby, I can keep your heart pumping." She enjoyed the idea of screwing him the death. She hoped she'd be as lucky to put it on him one night so good, it would send him straight to see his maker. She thought for him to go out that way would be more than fair.

He refrained from doing his pushups and quickly jumped to his feet. He began to stretch his arms. "I wonder how young Jimmy is doing. I haven't seen him since we got hitched."

"Well, you have no reason to," she said as she flicked her IPod to the side. Hearing Jimmy's name come out of his mouth sent chill bumps through her entire body. "I cook your meals now, just like you want them."

"That's true, honey, but Jimmy has always been like a son to me. A son I never had."

"Hell, Earl, I can arrange that for you too, boo," she laughed. It wasn't likely, she got her tubes tied long ago. She never wanted to risk getting knocked up by a random broke brother that she was simply attracted to and wanted to have a little fling with, so she made sure she eliminated the possibilities of a stray pregnancy.

"I know," he said as he refrained from his exercising and took a seat on the side of the bed next to her legs. "I guess I just feel guilty about how things came about with you and I. I was aware that you two had a thing together in the past, and I don't want him to feel like I betrayed him."

"Oh, Earl, you have nothing to feel guilty about. Jimmy and I, we just had a fling for a little while, but it was never anything serious."

"Really?"

"Uh-hum," she reassured him. "It was nothing serious at all."

"But how can that be?" he asked as he turned towards her. "You two were together for a long time."

She reached for the cigarette beside her on the nightstand and took a final pull from it. "Just because you're with someone for a period of time, Earl, doesn't mean you're in love with them. They may just be able to fulfill your needs when they need to be fulfilled."

"What about us, Kizzy?" Her statement had his father's voice rumbling through his mind, warning about women just wanting him for only his riches.

"Earl," she said as she smashed her cigarette into the ashtray. "You know you fulfill all my needs, every last one of them."

"I do?"

"Yes, you do." She explained as she wrapped her arms around him and placed her head on his shoulder. "I couldn't imagine living my life without you, Earl."

"Me neither, Kizzy," he was astonished by her proclamation to him. "I feel the same way, too! I couldn't imagine my life without you neither."

"Then why don't you get out of these sweaty clothes, jump in the shower and come back out here and show me how much you want me." she said while pecking on the side of his neck.

"Okay," he nodded. He gave her a short peck on the lips and made his way to the shower.

****

It was midday. Jimmy was standing on the side of his restaurant as he watched the movers take out the furniture to his restaurant piece by piece. Jimmy turned his attention to a sparkling red 68 Chevy Impala that had rolled into his lot. The vintage convertible didn't have a spot on it, and he was certain it looked the same way it did the day it rolled off the assembly line. The classic automobile was owned by no other than Mr. Earl Oaks. Jimmy was certainly surprised to see him.

Mr. Oaks slowly stumbled out of his car as Jimmy began walking towards him to shorten the trip for the old geezer.

"Jimmy," Mr. Oaks yelled as the two approached each other. "How are you?"

"Fine, Mr. Oaks," Jimmy replied. "I didn't expect to see you around these parts. How have you been?"

"I'm fine, son," Mr. Oaks said as he patted Jimmy on the shoulders. He took note of the movers taking out the restaurant furniture and packing it onto the moving truck. "I see you finally did it."

Jimmy nodded. "Yeah, Mr. Oaks, I finally threw in the old towel. Sold it to a family out of Richmond. They seem to be really good people. I know they'll keep up the place. Give it what I couldn't."

"This was never for you, Jimmy."

"Yeah, I suppose you're right," he said as they both turned towards the diner, standing side by side. "I guess the old place was a way for me to keep my old man alive."

"We all have our reasons for the things that we do. Sometimes we don't think thoroughly before we do those things. And some things we think through well, and we still end up not doing the right thing."

"So what brings you by today, Mr. Oaks," Jimmy asked while facing him. "I thought you'd be out enjoying married life. Congratulations, too."

"Thanks, Jimmy. I came by because I have something I need to give you." He dug into his back pocket and pulled out a envelope he had folded. "I think this is going to come in handy for you one day."

"What is it?" Jimmy asked as Mr. Oaks handed him the envelope. "You never stiffed me on any meals." He laughed as he examined the brown envelope that carried only his name on it.

"Let's just say that it's everything I owe you." Mr. Oaks didn't wait for Jimmy's response as he began to trek back to his car. He stopped and turned around. "You know, Jimmy…"

"Yeah, Mr. Oaks," Jimmy responded, puzzled.

"You have every bit of talent as your father had, only more. He and I both knew the restaurant business was never your cup of tea. We spent a lot of time guessing on what you would end up becoming. But one thing's for sure, you became one hell of a man. Don't stop being who you are." He smiled and carried on to his car.

"Thanks, Mr. Oaks," Jimmy muttered. He watched Mr. Oaks back up and drive out of the parking lot. Once the Impala was no longer visible from the highway, Jimmy focused in on the envelope again. He opened it, pulled out its contents and scanned through it. His mouth nearly fell to the ground.

****

Kizzy rustled through the front door with three huge shopping bags in each hand. It had been another day of binge shopping for her. Exhausted from carrying all the bags by herself, a task Earl would normally assist her with at the door, she dropped the bags in the middle of the floor.

"Earl?" she called out as she made her way into the living room. There was no sign of Mr. Oaks, so she made her way to the dining room. When she opened the door she came to a screeching halt.

"Hi dear," said Mr. Oaks as he had a chocolate cake on the table with one lone candle burning in it. "Happy six month anniversary!"

"Earl," she said with a phony smile plastered across her face. She dreaded the thought of him celebrating each six month period with an anniversary celebration and hoped this would be the first and the last one. She played along, thinking how many more six months his old body could reach. "You're so sweet."

He strolled towards her with two glasses of red wine in his hands. He handed her one of the glasses. "Let's have a toast, sweetheart."

"Okay?" she said, rolling her eyes.

"To eternity."

"To eternity," she repeated.

They both gulped the wine down.

"Wow, Earl, this is some good stuff." she said glancing at the empty glass. She thought it would be a great idea to get another swig of the stuff to get right before another night of him hunching on top of her. A nightly ritual. She didn't mind originally, but she quickly realized the old man had the stamina of a jackrabbit.

"The bottle is over fifty years old."

"Really? Well, I hope you got some more of that stuff because it really hit the spot."

He took her glass and placed it on the table with his.

"I've been saving it for this night."

"Better late than never, right?"

"Once upon a time, I thought I'd never share that bottle with anyone. But you changed all that, Kizzy." He placed his hand on her face and began rubbing her cheek with his thumb. She kissed the palm of his hand.

"Oh, Earl, it's only been six months. We have years ahead of us."

"You're right. We have an eternity."

She frowned, as she didn't recognize the old man's demeanor. "Are you feeling okay, Earl?"

"Never better," he said.

"Well good," she said as she started walking towards the hallway. "Because I just bought these shoes that–"

"I turned my entire fortune over to Jimmy today."

She froze in her tracks. A flash of anger ran rapidly through her entire body. "Okay. You're not feeling well tonight." She turned around to face him. "Why are you playing with me, Earl?"

"I'm not. I gave everything I own to Jimmy. It was something I had been planning to do for years."

Her eyes shot open as she thought he originally misspoke, but he said it again. He gave his fortune to Jimmy. "And why in the hell would you do that?" she asked as she clutched her stomach. She didn't know if she had to go use the bathroom, or if the news Earl was giving her just made her so sick she wanted to throw up.

"I thought it would be a true test of love."

"Negro, what the hell are you talking about!" she yelled. "Are you stupid or something?"

"No," he said smiling. He was slightly surprised by her angry tone. "We don't need it anymore."

"What?" she fumed. "What the fuck are you? Some kind of a moron? What do you mean we don't need money anymore? We have to fucking eat and pay bills, don't we?"

"I know you're upset, but we have to–" He grabbed his throat as if he was strangling.

"Earl?" she called out, worried, and still clutching her own stomach.

He fell to the floor.

"Earl," she ran to him and rolled his lifeless body over. "Don't your dumb ass be dying on me now." She got on her knees and felt for his pulse. She didn't feel one, and it scared the devil out of her. "Damn it, Earl," she cried. "Don't you fuck with me like this."

She began patting his face to revive him, but he wasn't responding. "Oh God! Oh God," she said as she began slapping him more violently, but she still didn't get a response. He was dead.

She quickly ran to the phone on the wall and began dialing, but she stopped as she felt a strong pain pierce through her abdomen. "What… what's wrong with me?" she yelled. She looked towards the champagne glasses on the table. Her hands began to tremble as the room began to spin. She began to gasp for air as she tried to stumble toward the hallway to find help but she fell. She fell dead.

THE END

The Trusted

He walked down the barren, country highway, covered in mud from head to toe. His walk was a determined one. His eyes focused on the rising sun that had just began to reveal itself on the other end of the highway. He was a white male in his mid thirties with short spikey, bronze hair.

Suddenly, he stopped in his tracks as he heard a sound, not of nature. It was the buzzing growl of a black and rusted 1978 Pinto that was streaking down the stretch of road behind him. He turned around and stared at the oncoming car. With no emotion on his hard, unshaven face, no movement from his slender body, he just looked on.

The car crossed into the wrong lane and headed straight towards him. He placed both hands on his filthy waist, as if he was ready to take on the impact. The Pinto quickly skidded as the driver slammed on brakes. The man kept his post, not budging an inch. The car stopped.

The driver was a black woman in her mid-twenties, wearing a baseball cap and shades. She gripped onto the steering wheel tightly, and revved up the engine with both feet on the gas and brakes. The man stood patiently with an angry scowl on his face.

She shifted the car into park and quickly rolled the window down. "Are you just gonna stand there forever, or are you gonna get in?"

The man turned his head and gathered all the saliva he could compose. He turned his head forward and spit on the center of the windshield.

"You bastard," she barked at him while shaking her head.

He slowly strolled to the passenger side of the automobile, opened the door and jumped in. A frown developed on his face. "Six hours."

She kicked the car in drive and continued to stumble down the highway.

"Six hours, I've been walking. Mud covering every inch of my body with soaked underwear riding up my ass. Six hours I've been walking."

"Rick, I thought you white boys loved to walk," she cracked as she snatched the shades from her face and stuffed them into her purse that rested between them. She had a short hair cut, caramel brown complexion and was very attractive.

"Damn you, Keisha, and your jokes. You always have jokes. I'm sick of your jokes."

"You weren't sick of my jokes when you were begging me to help you break out of prison, jerk.," she said as she gently smushed the side of his head with one hand, the other still gripped to the wheel.

"A man will allow for crazy things when he gets that magic." He placed his hand on her thigh and smiled. He started stroking her tightly fitted jeans. "In your case, that black magic."

"Red means stop." She glanced down at his hand and flung it back at him.

He chuckled, "Is it that time already? What great timing."

"It doesn't matter. I wouldn't give you any until you bathe a couple of days. You're filthy as hell," she said as she rolled her big, light brown eyes at him.

"More jokes. You should've been a comedian instead of a correctional officer. Talk about missing your calling."

"What happened anyway? Didn't you follow the map?" With her eyes glued to the road, she grabbed a towel resting on the back seat and handed it to him.

"The map," he grumbled. "Yeah, I followed the map, right into a hunting ground." He grabbed a bottled water from the floorboard of the vehicle and soaked the towel with it. After soaking the towel, he began to scrub the mud off of his face and out of his hair.

"No one saw you, did they?"

"No, but what does it matter? In about a hour or so, my mug will be on every television set in the southeast."

"It doesn't matter. We're hours ahead of 'em, and they don't know where we are or where we're headed."

"Did you get my guns for me?"

She grinned, "What? Of course not. You don't need them where we're going."

"Damn, Keisha! I feel naked without my babies."

"Maybe that's a good thing," she winked her eye at him.

He licked his lips and smiled, barely able to control his hormones as he began to salivate while staring at Keisha's perfectly rounded breasts. Her shoulders were exposed in the top she was wearing. The mere glimpse of a woman's skin aroused him. Keisha was physically fit and breath-taking. He placed his hand on her thigh again. "You black women are gonna be the death of me."

She looked at his hand and smiled, "Gone, now. I told you what was up."

"You know, I've had some women that..."

"Stop! Not this one," she snapped back. "I may be a freak, but I'm not nasty."

He shook his head and laid back in his chair, tossing the towel back to the backseat. "My blackberry pie."

She winked her eye and blew a kiss at him.

"You know, blackberry, my life has changed since I met you."

"Oh really? I thought it changed when they said they were going to shoot for the death penalty this time."

"Nah, that was just talk. They always gotta threaten you with something. But those threats were intended to be used against minorities and only them. Hell, all I had to do was tell them where I hid another body, or who put the hit out on the stiff and they'd spare me. I could've done that until I was old and gray. That's the system. That's the way the system works."

"You know a lot about the system, huh?"

"I know enough. My old man was a hit man, too, and his brother was a cop. A dirty cop. The dirtiest cop you would ever lay eyes on. Uncle Lou, he shared the knowledge. He taught me how to play the game." He studied the car's interior. "Why a Pinto?"

"Five hundred dollars, that's why." She rolled her eyes. "We do need money when we get to Mexico."

"Mexico, every convict's destination. Kind of like Canada to the slaves. Freedom, such a misunderstood word."

"What do you mean by that, Rick?"

"I was in that cell for two years, misunderstanding the meaning of the word freedom, wanting it badder than a punk wants cock in his ass. But I didn't see freedom until the day you passed by my cell."

"Is that so?" she blushed.

"Boy, Keisha, you were a sight for sore eyes. I wanted to stick it to you from day one; all the inmates did. But they weren't good enough, were they?"

"They weren't who I wanted, Rick. I had my mind set on you, babe."

"And you got me, suga'. You got me." He began to rub his own leg as he observed her perky breasts again. "When you came along, you gave a new meaning to being in the hole."

She grinned. "Couldn't keep you out, could I?"

"You had me kicking ass every time they returned me to general population. Just to get back in there."

"The things predators do to get their prey," she smiled.

He continued to stare. "Keisha?"

"Yeah."

"Why aren't you scared of me? Don't I scare you?"

"Not in the faintest way, Rick."

"What?" He fondled with his thin bronze mustache, baffled by her response. "Twenty-six murders don't scare you? Hell, I'm considered a mass murderer."

"You're a predator, just like my brother was. He killed many people, too. Unlike you, he didn't take pride, let alone any responsibility in his twisted trade. He blamed my family for making him the man that he was, so he disowned us."

"What happened to him?"

"He found out just like you will one day. There's always a bigger, nastier predator out there lurking, waiting for you to make that wrong step."

"So the cops got'em?"

"No, one of his friends did; shot him right in the head."

"Wow, that sucks. I killed a best friend of mine once. He was the coolest S.O.B. in the world, too." He flinched while recalling his memory of the man. "Well almost."

"Almost?" she gave him a quick glance and then returned her focus to the deserted road.

"We didn't eat together. Never. Not once!"

"You were best buddies, why not?"

"That's the reason I killed him."

She frowned. "For not eating with you?"

"No... Well, let me explain."

"Please do. You're confusing the hell out of me, Rick."

"We never ate together until this one day. I went over to his place. He fixed us up some soup, said it was his mother's favorite recipe. The most unusual taste I ever tasted, that soup."

"I thought you said you never ate dinner with him."

"Well, yeah, let me finish." He cut his eyes at her. "So while we're eating, his phone rings. Now the phone is in the other room. So, he goes and answers it. While I, being the cook that I am on the side..."

"You cook? Somehow I'm not seeing that," she chuckled.

"Yeah, let me finish. So me, being the cook that I am, I just had to find out what kind of ingredients he used in that soup. It was fucking delicious, you know? And I really had no idea that T-Rex was that good of a cook."

"T-Rex?"

"Yeah, stop interrupting," he said clearly frustrated by her frequent interruptions. "So I sneak into the kitchen, and I start snooping around in the cabinets, looking for any clues to his recipe."

"Why didn't you just ask?"

"I just didn't, okay? I'm a freaking tough guy, and I didn't want to ask him about it. All right?"

"Okay, Rick. Anger management," she sneered.

He couldn't contain the frustration shown all over his face. He stared at her and shook his head as he contemplated even finishing the rest of his story. "Anyway, I decided to peak into his fridge and that's when it happened."

"What?"

"I saw the most shocking thing I had ever seen in my entire life."

"What did you see?"

"I saw a freezer bag full of eyeballs in his fridge."

"No!"

"Eyeballs in the fridge. That's what I saw. He had the whole refrigerator loaded with body parts. The fucker was a cannibal and he was feeding me his shit."

"My goodness."

"Oh, there was nothing good about it because after I got over the fact that I was sipping down some poor souls gall bladder, I calmly walked into his room and I blew his fucking brains out. Pardon my French."

"How'd you know the soup wasn't legit?"

"I dumped out my bowl and part of a fucking ear was in it."

"Ooh, really?"

He shook his head. "Yeah. And I loved that bastard too."

"Uhhh, Rick, you're a cannibal," she laughed.

"Shit's not funny, Keisha," Rick said with his mouth balled up. "Shit's not funny at all."

"Well, it was your fault, Rick. Jesh!"

"How was it my fault?"

"T-Rex," she giggled. "Now come on, that didn't tell you anything? The T-Rex was a meat eating dinosaur. He ate other dinosaurs and everything else."

"What's that got to do with anything?"

"Rick, there's certain clues to life. It's up to you to pay attention to them. I mean, this guy was your best friend, and I bet you never once asked him why his name was T-Rex. I know that name wasn't given to him by his parents," she laughed. "Unless he was raised by a pack of dinosaurs."

"Well, I thought it was...." He thought hard for a moment. "I don't know. It never crossed my mind."

"That's why you got locked up. You can't see a trap a mile away."

"Hey, you win some, you lose some. How was I suppose to know that stupid sports bar was showing America's Most Wanted before the fight. I got the mind to blow that stupid bar up," he said as he made a fist and punched into his hand.

"Poor kitty..." She rubbed his scruffy chin. "...don't cry over spilled milk. You're out now."

"Yeah, but for how long?"

"Until you come face to face with destiny."

"Destiny's always been a bitch when it came to me."

"It brought me to you." She smiled. "Face it honey, I'm your destiny."

He placed his hand on her thigh. Suddenly a loud pop sounded off from the back of the car. The automobile swerved out of control.

"What the hell?" He grabbed the wheel in an attempt to help Keisha control the vehicle.

She slammed on brakes as the car swayed onto the side of the road. "What was that?" she asked, almost out of breath.

"I think destiny just gave us a blown out tire. You alright?"

"Yeah, I'm fine. Just shaken up a little bit." Her hands were trembling.

He jumped out and stumbled to the back of the car. She tossed her baseball cap onto the backseat and jumped out also.

"Yup!" He stared down at the tire. "With a deal so awesome I guess it didn't dawn on you that you may have needed to check the tires on this rusty piece of shit."

She walked around and stood beside him. "Damn!"

"And I bet you didn't get a spare with that awesome deal, either. Did ya?"

She slowly shook her head. "That was mentioned at the purchase," she sighed, "But nothing ever came of it."

He took a deep breath. "Fuck! Fuck! Fuck!" He began to furiously beat on the car.

"Rick!" She pulled him away from the Pinto. "Chill!"

"We're stranded in the middle of nowhere with the police hunting my ass down, and you're telling me to chill. I don't think so!" He swiped his arm away from her and continued to beat on the car.

"Rick, chill, I know where we are."

He paused and turned to her. With both hands on his waist he bowed his head and kicked at the ground.

"You think I'd be driving you from the pen not knowing where we're headed? The map! I planned it out, you prick," she smiled.

Realizing how stupid he acted, he shook his head. "I don't know, I'm sorry. I forgot. I'm sorry. Shit's just a little stressful right now."

"I know, baby," she placed her arm around his shoulder and began caressing it. "It's alright."

"It's the pen, Keisha. It changes the way people think. It makes people hard to trust. I trust no one."

"But me, Rick."

"Yes, you. I trust you. I've always trusted you."

She walked to the middle of the road and pointed down the highway. "Now we're not that far from this little town called Stony Creek. If we start moving now we can make it there before it gets dark."

He approached her. "So what happens when we get to Stony Creek?"

"Well, about three miles outside of that town is the interstate, so we can either lay low in Stony Creek for a day or two or go for the gold. But that's up to you. We have a long journey ahead of us just by making it there. On top of that we have to find another ride when we do get there."

"And how are we suppose to do that?"

"Jesh, Rick! You're a convict aren't you? Must I spell out everything?"

"More jokes, huh, Keisha?"

"As long as you continue to set them up. Now come on. Even though this road is rarely traveled, I'd hate for a state trooper to get lucky."

He balled up his fist. "Trust me, there wouldn't be anything lucky about it."

"Anyway," she walked to the trunk and unlocked it. "You better put on some clean clothes."

"You're right. I don't want to inspire any of the locals in that hick town to ask any questions as we pass through." He kicked off his pants and shoes as she threw him a change of clothing.

****

The sun had began to lay amongst the trees as Rick and Keisha walked pass a dusty, worn out sign that read, "Welcome to the Town of Stony Creek". They paused and looked around the small deserted town, which showed no sign of life. All the small buildings were boarded up and the landscaping was overrun with wild weeds.

"You said you know this place. What happen to everyone? Not a hillbilly in sight." Rick said as he spun around in a circle in the middle of the road. "It's just dead."

Her mouth opened widely as she stood amazed. "I don't know. I don't remember it like this. It's been a long time since I been here, though."

"It looks like it's been a long time since *anybody* has been here." They slowly walked down the barren road. "No people, no lights, no nothing. Maybe that's a good thing, though."

"It's just ghost town, now," Keisha said to herself.

"Hello!" Rick yelled. He smiled as he heard his echo. "Did you hear that?"

"Yeah, Rick. Welcome to the third grade." She looked down to the edge of the road, intrigued by what she saw. "I don't believe it."

"What?"

"A sign of life." She pointed to the last house on the road.

"Where?"

"Down there," she continued to point. "There's actually a truck in the yard down there that isn't laying up on cinder blocks."

Rick looked towards her, "You think we can trust them?"

"We have to see if someone's even living there first."

"Well, we walked several miles today and didn't see a soul while doing it, so we ain't gotta worry about any coppers coming fast if whoever lives there does become a problem."

"Well," she said as she gave the other empty buildings one last stare. "What are we waiting for? Let's go."

They began walking towards the house, and after a short trek, they wandered onto the front porch of the old southern styled two story home. They crept onto the old wooden porch, standing side by side. Then, they looked to each other, not knowing what to do next.

"You knock," said Keisha.

"Why do I have to knock?" Rick questioned.

They dropped their bags.

"Because you're the man, that's why."

"Well, what am I gonna say? Excuse me but my girlfriend and I are running from the law..."

"Halt! Who goes there," yelled a voice from behind them.

"Ah," Keisha mumbled as they turned around simultaneously.

A fifteen year old boy wearing dirty overalls stood before them with a shotgun pointed at Rick. "I don't know who you people are, but you better tell me something quick."

"Look kid, we just need a little help. Our car broke down on us a couple miles down the road," replied Rick.

"Me and Pa ain't see no broke down car down the road," said the young man.

"Ah shit, he said Pa. Are you serious?" Rick said from the side of his mouth. "Okay, I'm going back to turn myself in." Rick attempted to walk off of the porch.

The young man cocked the hammer back on the old shotgun. "I wouldn't do that if I were you, mister. I'm aiming to shoot you if you move any further."

"Rick, be still," Keisha said as she pulled onto the back of his shirt.

"Alright, boss. I'm not moving. Just be careful at how you're waving that thing around," Rick paused and held his hands up.

"Young man, what's your name?" asked Keisha.

He gave her a puzzled look. "Michael... Michael Haverty."

"Michael, where's your Pa?"

"Right over here, princess," said a middle aged black man wearing overalls, also. He approached the porch and walked pass Michael. "Michael, take that gun out of these people's faces." He grabbed the edge of the shotgun and motioned the boy to put the weapon away.

Michael lowered the shotgun as the older man walked onto the porch. "My name is Raymond Haverty. How can we help you good people this evening?"

Rick extended his hand to the man and they shook. "My name's Rick Reed. Our car burned a flat several miles down the road. We were just looking for some help or a hand perhaps."

"You got a spare?"

"Uh, no sir," said Keisha. "We don't even have the tools to put a spare on."

"Well, all the stores in this town are closed down. I'm sure you noticed that while passing through. Not much of anything here anymore." Raymond scratched his head. "The closest parts store is about thirty miles out. About time we get there, it'll be closed."

"Well, thanks," smiled Rick as he preceded to walk off of the porch. Keisha followed.

"You folks don't look dangerous or nothin'. You could spend the night with us, and I can take you out there in the morning, if you like."

"You don't have to go...," uttered Rick.

"That'll be great," interrupted Keisha as she nudged Rick.

Raymond smiled. "Michael, get the bags for these kind people and take 'em upstairs."

Michael grabbed the bags from the couple and walked into the house. Rick rolled his eyes at Keisha.

"Y'all come on in here and meet Mable," said Raymond as he walked into the house behind Michael. The hardwood floors cracked with every step.

"Keisha, I don't trust this," Rick whispered.

"It'll be fine. Come on." Keisha followed Raymond around the house.

"Mable," Raymond yelled towards the rear of the house.

"What in God's name are you fussin' 'bout, Pa," yelled a heavy set black woman, with flour scattered all over her face and apron.

"We got guests," smiled Raymond.

"Well, that's something we don't see every day," Mable smiled and observed the couple. "Hi there. How are you two?"

"Fine, mam." Keisha shook the woman's hand.

"We're okay." Rick walked to the woman and shook her hand also. "A little aggravated after getting that darn flat down the road, though."

She stared deeply into Rick's eyes as she held tightly onto his hand. "Everything happens for a reason, young man." She smiled and released his hand.

Rick appeared a little dumbfounded and uneased by the woman's remarks and her firm grip.

"I put their things in the guest room, Pa," said Michael as he sat down at the top of the stairs.

"Well done son," replied Raymond.

"Well, if you folks don't mind, I'm gonna go back into the kitchen and finish up dinner. Great goodness it's a good thing I've always been in the habit of overcooking." Mable began making her way back towards the kitchen. "Raymond show these good people around our happy burrow and make them feel at home. Dinner will be ready soon."

"Come on, princess, let me show you and your man around the place." Raymond motioned his hand for them to follow him.

"Alright." Keisha trailed Raymond into the den.

Rick looked up to the top of the stairs and noticed Michael staring at him. "You coming, Michael?"

He didn't answer. He just gave Rick a cold empty stare.

Rick became unnerved by the look and walked towards the den. "I guess that means no."

****

"He just stared at me. He didn't say a damn thing. He just gave me this weird scowl," Rick whispered as he sat on the edge of the bed. "Does this kid realize that I've killed people for less than that?"

Keisha combed her hair in front of the mirror, while playfully smiling at Rick's comments. "I don't think he meant anything by staring. Kids tend to stare at people they don't know all the time. As filthy as you looked I would've been staring, too."

"Not like that Keisha. He stared at me like he wanted to kill me. I know that stare. I've killed, over and over again. It was that look of death. I know what it is. I think he knows who I am."

"He does not know who you are," Keisha rebutted. "You're getting too paranoid, Rick. These people don't even own a television."

"Damn that! I say we take that raggedy truck of theirs and haul ass to that interstate tonight. Take that truck straight to Mexico, that's what we should do."

She placed her comb on the dresser and sat next to him. "Negative, Rick. This is what we want, time to lay low. These people don't know a thing about current events. For goodness sakes, I bet they still hunt their food, Rick."

"The food that we're suppose to go down there and eat. No thank you. I'll pass on the char-grilled possum tonight."

"Oh, Rick, you're just being silly and paranoid!"

"I just don't trust it Keisha." He shook his head. "Remember what you said about the clues to life? Well, I'm thinking this is one of 'em. It's burning inside me."

She placed her arm around his neck. "Come on Rick, are you gonna let some kid rattle your nerves like that? Do you want me to let you shot him? Would that make you feel better?"

"No. It was just that look. And why are these people so damn nice to us? I mean you're black. Have you ever met any black people that acted this strange in the damn country?"

"Now, I know you just didn't bring race into this," she responded somewhat annoyed.

"I'm just saying, do you realize how many people I've murdered because their mistake was their kindness?"

"It doesn't matter now, Rick. We're not far away from our destinies."

He shook his head. "I sure hope so."

She gave him a quick peck on his cheek. "We'll be there soon."

"Lovebirds!" Mable's call was faint from below but enough for the two to hear.

"That's Mable." Keisha jumped off of the bed. "We better get down there."

"Yeah, I'm starving, but I'm not eating no damn possum." Rick rubbed his belly. "That's just out of the question."

"Come on, dummy," smiled Keisha. "Let's see what the old lady has cooking."

"I sure hope it's good."

They left the room.

****

"So Mr. Reed, how long have you and princess here, been dating?" Raymond smiled at Rick who sat on the opposite end of the table.

Rick, almost finished with his bowl of stew, paused, with his spoon halfway to his face. Surprised by the question, he smirked and laid his spoon next to his bowl. "Oh, for a couple of months now. Greatest time of my life, too." He looked over to Keisha as she blushed.

"So you like black women," chuckled Raymond.

"Pa," Mable yelled, offended.

"What?" Raymond frowned. "He got himself a black woman! He must like 'em. I like mine."

"But that's a private question, Pa," Mable replied.

"No, really, it's okay. I don't have any problem with answering those types of questions." Rick looked towards Raymond. "Yes sir, I do love me some black women. To tell you the truth, I think a black woman is going to be the death of me one day because I love them so much."

"And a long time ago, they would've, son," countered Raymond. "At least for her, dealing around with you. That type of stuff didn't bid well around these parts back in my day."

"Well, thank God we ain't back in your day anymore," he chuckled.

"I agree," replied Raymond.

"I'm aware of the mistakes my people have made in the past." Rick sighed.

"Still making, son. Still making," Raymond interrupted. "Why if you two had to have passed through this town and onto the next, you would've ran right into Lynchburg. One of the most racist towns in the south. It's always been that way." He laughed, "I mean the name speaks for itself."

"I thought the interstate was next to this town." Rick glanced at Keisha.

"Yeah, about a hundred miles away." Raymond laughed. "I know you two weren't considering walking to the interstate. Why, it would've been a few days before you would've made it there."

Rick's traditional angry scowl surfaced onto his face, "Are you serious?"

"Lived here all my life. I know this here town and everything surrounding it like the back of my hand," replied Raymond. "In case you didn't realize this son, but you guys are in the middle of nowhere."

"Unbelievable," muttered Rick as he gawked at Keisha.

She sighed and shrugged her shoulders. Her expression spoke for itself. She had made a mistake.

"So, Raymond, what time do you think that parts store opens up," asked Rick, burning inside.

Raymond looked towards the ceiling as he took a moment to think. "Oh about nine or ten. I haven't been there in a spell, but I know that's around the time Old Man Stevens opens up. Ole Betsy hasn't been acting up on me since I replaced the transmission, so I haven't had much need for automobile parts lately."

"It's going to take forty-five minutes to get there, though," Mable added.

"Yeah, you're right about that, Mable," sighed Raymond. "We're gonna have to be up rise and shine in the morning if we want to get to the shop and have enough time to get back to your car to repair it."

"It's kind of strange that you guys don't have a parts store here in town," said Rick.

"Not strange," Raymond responded. "There's never been a real parts store here in town."

Rick grinned. "To be honest, Ray, this town isn't much of a town. What happened to everybody, and why did you all stick around?"

Raymond sneered. "We've never had a reason to leave, Mr. Reed. This is our stomping grounds. We belong here. To heck with what everyone else did."

"The town is inside of us." Michael replied.

Rick looked over to Michael with a slight frown.

"Where you folks headed anyway?" asked Raymond. "What is strange is to see visitors around these here parts. Now that's something you don't see every day. Ain't that right, Mable?"

"Yeah, Pa," Mable responded.

"Texas," Rick quickly spat out.

"Oh, I heard that's a nice place," said Mable.

"I never been to Texas, but I had a Cowboy's cap once. My old man gave it to me," smiled Raymond.

"That's really interesting, Raymond," Rick frowned. "Well folks, if you don't mind I think I'm going to go get an early start on sawing those logs. I want to be well rested for our little journey tomorrow." He rose from his chair. "Mable, the dinner was delicious. I loved the stew."

Everyone looked towards him.

"Well go ahead without me, honey. I'll be up later," said Keisha. "I'm going to sit here with the Havertys for a little while longer."

Rick had a puzzled look on his face. "Ah, okay."

He looked over to Michael who was smirking.

"Goodnight, folks." He headed towards the exit.

"Have a nice night, Rick!" yelled Mable.

"Goodnight, son. Don't let the bed bugs bite," laughed Raymond. Mable let out a chuckle, also.

****

Keisha quietly tip-toed into the dark bedroom. Suddenly a lamp flicked on. Rick had flipped on the lights as he sat on the bed, fully dressed. He angrily stared at her.

"And why didn't you come up here with me when I left?" he asked.

"Oh, Rick," she sighed.

"Oh, Rick, what?" He jumped off of the bed as she began undressing. "A hundred miles. I know that hillbilly didn't say it's a hundred miles to get to that damn interstate."

"He did Rick, and he's not a hillbilly!"

"Hell if that's so. I feel like I'm trapped inside of the black Mayberry."

"You can be such an asshole sometimes."

"You know what? I can be! I thought we were well on our way to our destination but no! We're stuck in this damn ghost town."

"Okay, Rick, I made a mistake. Shoot me for it." She put on a tee shirt.

"Not long ago I probably would've."

"What's different now?"

"I'm taking a break."

She giggled and pulled him by his hand. They sat beside each other on the bed.

"Look, Rick, I admit that I made a huge mistake. I don't know how I got the mileage mixed up, but in the morning we'll go get a new tire and go back and fix our ride. Then we'll ditch this place, alright?"

"I say we take their truck and forget about the damn Pinto."

"These people need that truck more than we do."

"Says who? I need to get my ass down to Mexico before these cops start coming. And how am I suppose to know if the cops aren't on our trails right now, anyway? These country bumpkins don't even have a television set."

"Rick, we can't screw these people over. It will only cause more problems. If we steal these people's truck, they're gonna call the cops. And they may not have a television, but they do have a phone. And how far do you think we'll get if they call the cops on us in that old heap of junk? Not far, Rick. Not far at all."

He shook his head. "Maybe you're right. But that kid's spooking me out. *The town is inside of us!* What type of crap is that? I didn't ask him that. I wasn't even talking to him. Damn Eddie Munster clone! I got the right mind to..."

"He's only a child, Rick."

"They kill the same."

"Have a little compassion, okay?"

267

He placed his hand on her thigh. "Every time I try you keep pushing me away."

She lightly shoved his hand away. "And for good reason, Rick. Now, we do need to get some sleep. Once we get the car fixed, we'll have a long ride ahead of us."

He sighed. "I guess you're right again"

She crawled to the top of the bed and slid underneath the covers. "I'm always right."

He grinned. "What about the map? You were wrong on that."

" Even when I'm wrong, I'm right. Don't you know anything about women."

Rick smiled, "I guess I don't know enough."

"You don't," she added. "Now cut the lights off."

He leaned over to the lamp and turned it off.

****

Hours later, Rick laid on his back on top of the covers, staring at the ceiling. He'd been staring at it for hours. Then, he looked over to Keisha, who was quietly sleeping beside him. He softly ran his fingers through her hair and smiled. Afterwards, he quietly rolled over and carefully eased off of the bed. He walked to the other side of

268

the room and stared at her for a moment, then silently exited the room.

The house was dark. He gently crept down the stairs and slid into the kitchen. He walked to the refrigerator and opened it. It was empty. "What the fuck? What do these people eat around here?" He scratched his head and looked around. He noticed a door behind him. He slowly eased towards the door and opened it. It led down to the basement.

He took one step inside and stroked the wall for a light-switch, he found it and flicked it on. His eyes shot wide open as he spotted a television in the room. "Son of a bitch!" He walked down the stairs and strolled to the television. He rubbed the screen. "A new model, too! Something doesn't smell right in black Mayberry." He looked around and observed everything.

The room was cluttered with two televisions, a washer and dryer, a leather sofa and a large freezer. He walked to the sofa and sat down. "Soft. I wonder why all this stuff is down here and not upstairs. Crazy ass people." He stared across the room at the large floor model freezer. "That must be where all the grub is." He jumped up and quietly crept over to the freezer.

He attempted to open it, but it was locked. "Damn!" He looked around the machine and felt the back of it. He smiled when he realized that he'd found something. He pulled off a key from behind the machine. "Just like Uncle Lou." He stuck the key in and opened the freezer. An abundance of cold air rolled out. "Food!"

He reached into the bottom of the freezer and pulled out a plastic grocery bag. "What's this?" He opened the bag and pulled out a frozen human head with the eyes plucked out. He dropped it immediately. "What the fuck? What the fuck?" He stumbled backwards a few steps while covering his mouth. He glanced back towards the basement stairs then charged towards the freezer again. He furiously dug into the freezer and pulled out more bags, all containing different body parts. "What the fuck is this?"

"Michael," he faintly heard Raymond's call from upstairs.

Rick paused and looked towards the ceiling. His breathing was fierce and harsh. "God, where the hell am I?"

"Michael, is that you down there," Raymond's call was closer this time.

"Keisha!" He said as he quickly became concerned about the safety of his accomplice. He eased the freezer closed. He ran up the stairs and exited the basement. He ran straight into Raymond and froze in his tracks.

"Rick, what are you doing up? It's three in the morning."

"You crazy son of a bitch!" He punched Raymond in his mouth and shoved him to the floor.

Raymond fell backwards and Rick kicked him several times on the side of his stomach. Raymond groaned in pain. "You sick son of a bitch. If you did anything to Keisha, it's gonna be worse when I get back."

He ceased his punishment on Raymond and ran out through the kitchen doors. He glided up the stairs and into his bedroom. "Keisha?"

She was gone.

"Oh no, Keisha," he yelled. He ran out of the room and started to run down the steps.

"Hold it right there, Mr. Rick," yelled Michael from below.

Rick stood frozen with his mouth wide open. "Keisha!"

Michael had his shotgun pointed towards Keisha's back as Mable stood beside him.

"Keisha's with us now," replied Michael.

"You let her go, you little bastard," Rick replied.

"Keisha, these bastards are crazy as hell. They got heads and all kind of body parts chopped up in the basement. We got to get the hell up out of here."

Raymond stumbled into the room, clutching his stomach. "What makes you think she wants to leave us, Mr. Reed?"

"What the fuck are you talking about, man," yelled Rick, "You sick bastard."

"Well, princess, do you want me to tell him or are you gonna tell him?" Raymond looked towards Keisha.

"Tell me what?" Rick questioned. "What is it, Keisha?"

Michael lowered the gun and stood beside Keisha.

"The clues Rick," Keisha explained, while shaking her head. "There are certain clues to life that you just don't pay any attention to."

Michael handed her the shotgun. She cocked the hammer back on the gun back and pointed it towards Rick.

Rick had a puzzled look on his face. "Keisha, what the hell are you doing? Why are you pointing that gun at me?"

"I'm doing what the law would've never done. You even said it yourself, Rick. Remember, in the car?"

"Keisha? What the hell are you talking about?"

"You're still too stupid to figure out what's going on," she sighed as she rolled her eyes. "T-Rex had a sister, you asshole!"

His eyes split wide open. "What?"

She quickly pulled the trigger and shot him in his chest before he could utter another word. His arms spread out as he looked down at his bloody chest and then back at Keisha. He slowly fell over and stumbled dead down the stairs. He stopped sliding down the stairs at her feet. Mable smiled.

She handed the shotgun to Raymond. "I'm going back to bed, daddy." She walked over his body and stomped up the stairs.

"Okay, princess. Sleep tight," Raymond replied.

The End

He Beats Me

When her eyes parted, she had no idea how long she had been lying there, dead to the world. A sharp jolt of pain ravaged throughout her body as she cautiously lifted her face from the cold, hard floor. She let out an agonizing moan as she rose to her feet and backed up onto the edge of the bed. With her head ringing and her entire body sore, it all suddenly came back to her–he beat her again.

After taking a few moments to gather herself while caressing the small lump on the side of her head, she carefully crept into the bathroom. She grabbed a towel, threw it in the sink and ran the water. She gazed at herself in the mirror as she contemplated her reason for allowing him to do this to her again. While examining her face for any noticeable bruises other than her small lump, she despised the reflection looking back at her that actually found relief in the fact that he didn't leave any visible marks on her face this time.

She picked up the towel, but before she could wipe her face with it, she burst into a fit of tears. She couldn't understand why he always found reasons to hurt her when all she ever wanted him to do was love her–nothing more, nothing less. All she wanted, all she ever asked from him, was his love.

Flashes of him with his hands around her neck as she helplessly struggled to breathe and claw herself out of his overwhelming grasp replayed through her mind. The demented smirk on his face as he forced her into unconsciousness was etched within her head. His words, "I should kill you right now, bitch," that slithered from his lips while they were pressed snugly against her cheek, still rang in her ears.

The thought of him gaining pleasure from tormenting her was enough to have her march from the bathroom and rush to her closet. She ripped her clothes from the racks and threw them onto the bed. She then turned to her dresser, grabbed as much of her items as she could from the drawers and tossed them onto the bed also. Dropping to the floor, she dragged out her only suitcase from underneath the bed and slapped it onto the mattress. She flung it open and threw everything she could into it as quickly as possible. As she filled the suitcase, reality swiftly struck, and it slowed her down. *Was there any way to completely disappear from him? Where in the hell would I go? Who would help me?* She managed to cut herself off from the rest of the world over the past few years, wagging around with this man that somehow found it so easy to put her through so much pain.

She froze. The anger that spread throughout her body was nearly impossible for her to contain as she propelled her suitcase onto the floor. She dropped onto the bed and buried her face into her pillows. It was the pillows that muted the screams that bellowed from deep in her gut as she laid there punching into the mattress while crying to herself. She felt so helpless, so weak, and so alone.

Her sadness and anger was quickly transformed into fear when she heard the door slam from the front of the apartment. She briskly hopped up from the bed, scurried into the bathroom and twisted the faucet off to stop the water she had left running. She then made her way to the bed in an attempt to clean up the mess she had made with her clothing, but the bedroom door sprang open. She halted as he eased into the room through the door carrying a single red rose.

"Hey, Ma," he greeted her.

"Keon," she answered nervously.

"Baby, I'm sorry," he said as he approached her. "I know I said I wasn't gonna get mad like that no more, and I winded up doing it again. Man, I know I fucked up."

"It's…" she stopped as her heart pounded ferociously while he approached. For once, he actually sounded sincere, but she knew if he assessed that she was trying to leave him, his mood would swing in the blink of an eye and all hell would break loose. He always made it his business to tell her that it wasn't going to be a good thing if she ever left him. He warned her that the people she loved the most would get hurt, and she would most definitely feel his unforgiving and complete wrath–if she was lucky. With his aggressive behavior, she didn't have any reason not to believe him. She couldn't keep her eyes from wandering towards the mess all over the floor behind him as another empty apology bounced from his lips.

"Nah, nah, it's not okay. Take this," he said as he handed her the rose and swallowed her with a hug. "I ain't shit to be taking my anger out on you like that–as good as you are to me."

"Keon, don't worry about it," she said.

"Nah, baby," he said as he backed away from her. "This shit I got going on got me so fucked up right now. I need to treat the people who really got my back with the most care. I can't be doing this shit to you."

"Keon, really," she said. "I understand."

"Nah, baby, I ain't shit," he said as he threw up his hands and turned away from her. When his eyes fell on all the clothing that was scattered across the bed, they quickly zoomed across the room to the suitcase and all of Ashley's remaining garments hanging out of it. "You 'bout to fucking leave me?"

It was almost like she got punched in the gut; the air left out of her body so quickly. She didn't know how to answer him as she just fumbled on a few sounds of gibberish. She knew the sight was enough to set him off again. "Keon, I..." Before she could get another word out, the back of his hand cracked the side of her face.

"Really bitch? You fucking trying to leave me?" he asked. His face was filled with rage. His high yellow complexion turned beet red as he scowled at her with his fists balled.

"Keon... don't," she cried with one hand against the side of her face and the other held up high in an attempt to block the barrage of punches she was expecting to follow.

He slowly raised his hand as if he was about the smack the daylights out of her, but he opted to just shove her away from him instead. He said, "I done told you before.

You ever leave me, not only am I gonna take your ass out, but I'm gonna take out some of your people, too. You think I'm playing with you about that shit? You think I'm a liar?"

"No, Keon," she said. "I believe you."

"Then why the fu…" he said, directing his finger towards the side of her head, then smashing it into her temple as hard as he could. "Just give me back my shit." He snatched the rose from her, balled it up and threw it right back at her.

"I'm sorry, Keon."

"You right about that. Your ass is sorry as hell," he said. "Just go'on and take your lousy ass in there and cook me that steak I just brought in there. Make sure you cook that shit well, too. I'm a black man. I ain't no goddamn peckerwood. I don't like no damn bloody ass meat. Last time you cooked me a damn steak, the shit could've donated blood. You hear me?"

She nodded nervously, careful to not make eye contact with him again as she hustled towards the door. "Yes, I hear you, Keon."

"And cook both of 'em, too. I brought one for your disloyal ass, too, feeling all sorry for your ass. So since your ass up in here thinking about leaving a nigga, I'mma eat yours, too–right in front of your trifling ass. Them damn corn flakes is gonna be your meal tonight, and you better not touch another crumb of any other food but them damn corn flakes, too."

"That's fine, Keon," she said with her head still hanging downwards, somewhat grateful he didn't make things physical again.

"I know it's fine. Now make the shit snappy," he yelled. She quickly left the bedroom door as he just shook his head, disgusted by her existence.

****

As he chomped and smacked on the well done T-bone steaks she prepared for him, she quietly stared at the knife that resided beside his hand. She didn't want him to see her staring at it for too long or too often, but she couldn't keep her eyes off of it. She hadn't even touched the bowl of cereal that sat in front of her that he demanded she prepare for herself for supper. The desires to reach across that table, grab the knife and stab him right in his throat were just

281

running too rampantly through her mind for her to have any kind of appetite.

Just one poke in the right place, that's all it would take for her to be free from the evil shadow he reigned so heavily over her life. But she was too scared. She thought with her luck, he'd beat her to the flippin' knife and stab her with it as fast as she could jump for it. Or even worse, she'd grab it and somehow fall on top of the sharp object, puncture herself and just bleed to death, knowing Keon would no doubt graciously watch the blood ooze straight from her body until her final breath.

No, if there was one thing she understood about herself, it was that she was no killer. No matter how bad Keon would beat or abuse her, she just didn't have it in her to end his life, even though the opportunities seemed plentiful. More importantly, she understood she just couldn't allow things to go on like they were with his violent treatment towards her because eventually he was going to wind up killing her. She knew it. There wasn't a day that went by that she didn't have fears about it. Every morning she woke up, she thought this was going to be the day she'd die by his ratchet hands. When her eyes trailed upwards, Keon's eyes were locked on hers.

"You getting some ideas?" he asked with a slow chew matched with a pair of suspicious eyes.

"No," she uttered nervously, somewhat afraid that he could somehow see her thoughts with his evil stare.

With a nod and a chuckle, he said, "If you feeling froggish, go'on head and jump. Now when your ass jump, you better jump like a motherfucker though, because when I catch you, and believe me when I tell you this shit–I will catch you, I'm gonna put your ass in so much pain and agony, you gonna wish you ain't never crossed my yellow ass. You're gonna beg me just to kill your dizzy, black ass. I promise you that."

She just shook her head while he gazed at her, smirking. She couldn't believe the words that managed to escape from the lips of the man with whom she once wanted to spend the rest of her life. As his wicked eyes rested on her, she prayed that God would just do her a divine favor of having a piece of that savory steak she had just prepared for him to slip and get stuck down the wrong pipe and choke him right dead, finally freeing her of the misery of being with him.

His last disrespectful statement made it just too difficult for her to resist asking him, "What happened to you?"

"Bitch, ain't shit happened to me. You need to be asking your damn self that question. Me–I just finally started realizing that you're a goddamn disappointment. When we first met, I really thought you were a ride or die chick, but eventually, I realized all the fuck you do is die. You're like a pack of fucking Dollar Store batteries. Put 'em in, and their ass will work great for about fifteen minutes, but then all the sudden they just die on a nigga–completely fucking useless– just like you in every way imaginable. Anymore fucking questions?"

His words forced her to fight back her tears. She couldn't look at him any longer. Although she fell out of love with him long ago, his words still cut deep. He hated her with all his soul and somehow she still had something in her heart for him.

There was a knock at the front door. He looked back at the door and then back at her. She knew that was her signal to go answer it. She hopped up out of her chair, but before she could make her way towards the door, he grabbed her arm. "Look here, you look through that fucking peephole before you open that goddamn door. Don't act like your nosey ass don't know what's going on."

"I will," she replied. She scurried to the door, and as he instructed, she looked through the peephole. When she opened the door, Porkchop was standing on the other side of it.

The tall, lanky man with a low box haircut proceeded to speak, "Hey, Ashley. Keon here?"

She stepped back from the door and threw her hand out in Keon's direction towards the dining area on the other side of the apartment. Before closing the door behind him, she stuck her head out of the door to see if anyone else was downstairs.

"Goddamn dude, where you been at?" Porkchop asked as he hurried towards the kitchen table.

"Minding my own fucking business, nigga," he said while slicing his meat into smaller chunks.

Porkchop took a seat at the table and said, "Damn, that smells good."

"It is good, nigga," he laughed. "The old lady can cook her ass off when she's motivated."

"You got some more of that?"

"The hell this look like, a restaurant or something?"

"Nah, man, I was just asking."

"Well nah, we ain't got no more," Keon spat. "Anyway, nigga, you heard anything from, Angelo?"

"Hell, you heard anything from him?"

"Hell no, that's why I'm asking you. I thought that's what I sent you to do anyway–to find his thieving ass."

"Man, I can't track that nigga nowhere. Nigga got three baby mommas and eight kids, and ain't none of 'em even seen or heard from him. It's like the nigga just vanished into thin air."

"Really?" Keon asked as he dropped his fork and just gazed at Porkchop.

Ashley grabbed the remote control off of the coffee table in the living room area behind them and flipped on the television, but before her bottom could hit the couch, Keon called, "Ashley, this trash shole looking full over here."

She took a deep breath and dropped the remote on the coffee table. "I'll get it."

She walked over to the trash can as Keon still had his eyes locked on Porkchop, not flinching an inch. The stare made Porkchop feel uneasy, so uneasy that he took his eyes off of Keon and glanced over to Ashley and the trash bin.

"And don't forget you got some shit to clean up back there in that bedroom when you get back," Keon added.

She didn't respond as she tied the ends of the big, black trash bag and struggled carrying it to the front door.

"Damn, blood, you got your old lady taking out the trash in the middle of the night? You raw as hell."

"What's it to you, nigga?"

"Nothing… I mean... nothing."

"Alright then," said Keon. "At least she can do what the hell I send her out to do, unlike some other motherfuckers."

"Man, the last thing we need to be doing is jumping down each other's throat."

"Nigga, I ain't jumping down nobody's throat, and you damn shole ain't jumping down mine."

"I'm just saying."

"Don't just say shit. Just explain to me how in the hell you come back with nothing on this nigga? Speak on that shit."

"Man, look, we've been looking for this dude for over two weeks now. We ain't gonna find him. We just need to haul ass like he did before Max sends his goons out lurking like we both know he's gonna do."

"Haul ass? Haul ass to where?"

"Why is you playing with dude?"

"Playing with dude? I ain't playing with nobody, bruh. This nigga breathe and bleed just like I do. My heart don't pump no Kool-aid. Yours might do, but not mine."

"Nigga, if mine did, I don't wanna be laid up nowhere leaking blood and guts to find out."

"What? So you think you can hide from niggas like Max? How long do you think it would be after you go calling yourself *hauling ass* before one of his dudes show up wherever you think you're hiding at, ready to split your damn wig?"

"Well it's better than being a sitting duck!"

"Nah, hell with that. I got a plan."

"A plan, huh?"

"That's what the hell I said," Keon replied with a slow nod and smirk on his face.

When Ashley stepped onto the sidewalk leading out from her building, she couldn't help but notice a black sedan backed into a parking space with no other cars around it. There appeared to be two figures inside the vehicle, and the occupants seemed to be looking right at her. She bowed her head, walked off the sidewalk and into the street slowly. Her gut was telling her they were staring at her building, possibly even looking for Keon about whatever crap he found himself into this time. Her nerves had her praying that they wouldn't try to shoot her to get back at him because that would most definitely be a fail. She figured if they did that, they'd only be doing him a favor, yet in a twisted way, doing her one, also.

With the big, black bag of garbage in her hand, she tried her best to keep the car in her periphery and not look directly at it. When she walked in front of the car, the car started and sprang its bright lights right on her. She froze. The car pulled slowly out of the parking space. Her heart raced as she accidently looked right into the face of the brawn white man with his big, scruffy red mustache in the driver seat. She couldn't take her eyes off of his cold, pale face as the black car simply passed her by.

"Please tell me that shit you just told me ain't really your plan."

"No, that's exactly what the plan is."

"Nigga!" Porkchop jumped up out of his chair and threw his hands in the air. "What in the world makes you think Ashley's momma is gonna give you eighty grand when she don't even like your ass? None of her family does."

"She's not gonna give it to me. She's gonna give it to Ash."

"The woman you just made drag a big ass bag of trash out to the dumpsters all by herself in the middle of the night?"

"Negro, calm down with all that yelling in my house like that. Where the hell you think you're at?"

Porkchop took a deep breath and sat back down at the table with his partner in crime, staring wildly at him.

"Alright now, nigga, I told you I got a plan. I got it all worked out with Ashley. Hell, I know her people don't like me. I can't stand none of their snooty asses neither," he continued while digging into his food again, "But they love Ashley. We're gonna tell her momma we need the money to put a nice down payment on a house."

"A house with you?"

"You got any better ideas?"

"Yeah, getting the hell out of dodge."

"Porkchop, we ain't running nowhere. Now, didn't you say that nigga Angelo got three baby mommas and eight little ones?"

"Yeah."

"And don't that chick Keisha we know from way back got five rug rats with that nigga?"

"Yup."

Keon took a moment to think. "She locked the nigga up a few times for not paying child support, too."

"Yup, that's her."

"Alright then, I need you to go back and put some major pressure on her ass. Scare her ass up, do whatever the hell you have to do to make her give you a lead on this chump. Maybe even try and bribe one of them rug rats of hers with some gummy bears or some shit," he said. "A nigga with that many seeds in one spot is gonna keep his ass close to the nest with the highest potential child support payment. Besides, if we can find that nigga maybe we can beat his ass until he tell us what he really did with that money, and we can get that shit back."

"And when we don't find him and you don't get the money from Ashley's family, then what are we gonna do? Max is giving us till Friday to have his money, and nine out of ten that cat ain't really gonna give us that long. We're probably already on the chopping block as we speak."

"Nigga, stop being so damn pessimistic," said Keon. He turned towards the door when he heard Ashley returning through it and whispered to his partner. "If shit falls through, then I got a contingency plan. I got my cuz down in Rock Hill. He got some connects where he can get us a clean ride, some credit cards and a couple of fake IDs, but if shit goes like it should, we won't have to worry about none of that. You feel me?"

Porkchop, still weary of the plan, nodded in agreement. "Alright, I'll follow your lead."

"Good," he said. "Porkchop, I need your head in the game, bruh. I can't get through this shit if we're not on the same page. We're in this shit together, my nigga."

He nodded again and said, "Alright... I'm game."

****

Ashley sat on the bed drifting off at the television as Keon took his shower. Dinner at her mother's house the following day was stuck in her mind. She figured there was no possibility on God's green earth her mother was going to give them the amount of money Keon was putting her up to ask for. Besides, her mother and the rest of the family had always known Ashley to be the loner type and never the one to ask anyone for anything. It was one of the reasons her relationship with the family was so strained in the first place, in addition to leaving and shacking up with a man they all collectively considered to be no good.

Keon eased out of the bathroom with a towel around his waist and his frame still dripping wet. He immediately walked to the edge of the bed, picked up the remote and cut off the television.

"You know if you work this thing out for me, it will make me forget about the stunt you tried to pull on me earlier today. Matter of fact, I won't ever bring the shit up again. It'll be like the shit never happened."

"About the money, Keon, I don't think…"

He cut her off. "At-at-at, don't you call yourself up in here talking about you're thinking. That's what I do. I do all the thinking around here. Now, when your daddy passed away, out of all his kids, you ain't get shit, and you and I both know, it's well beyond time for you to collect what's due to you."

"But Keon, my momma's not gonna buy this story you want me to tell her."

"Well, you better sell the shit as best you can, because I'm tellin' ya', it ain't gonna be a good thing if we don't get this money, Ash. I'm just gonna be straight with you."

All Ashley could do was shake her head as he marched out of the bedroom and into the living room. Keon was bent on making something happen that just wasn't going to happen. It would be a cold day in hell before her mother would give her anything while she was still with the man she believed was abusing her own flesh in blood. It was the only reason she didn't receive any of her inheritance from her father when he passed years ago, and it would remain the reason she wouldn't receive any of it now.

****

Ashley checked herself out in the mirror one last time to make sure the bump on her head from the day before was no longer visible. It wasn't. Relieved, she charged through her bedroom, grabbed her purse from the bed and headed for the front door. When she placed her hand on the doorknob, she paused. She quickly remembered where she was headed and what she was about to be put up to do. Armed with an idea failed at its creation, Ashley hustled over to the phone and dialed her mother's house. The phone rang three times, and after a soft hello, Ashley slammed the phone down without saying a word. She knew the voice on the other end to be her unsuspecting mother, and she wasn't quite sure why she even called. She was just thankful Keon always had the caller id blocked on the house phone.

Keon kept one eye on the entrance going up to his apartment and the other on his phone he had resting on his knee below the steering wheel as he searched for any new text messages. Disappointed, he quickly dialed a sequence of numbers and placed his phone up to his ear, but the other party wasn't picking up as the call went straight to voicemail. He quickly called again only to receive the same results. Before he could dial the number once more, he saw Ashley coming around the corner of their building, and he slid the phone into his pocket. She hopped in the car.

"What took you so long?" he asked.

"Stomach's a little upset."

"What the hell–you got butterflies?"

"No, but I'm good now."

He stared at her suspiciously. "Man, we ain't got all day and night to be spending at your moms. I know she's gonna want us to do that yuppie dinner thing she like does with company, but we're just gonna throw it all out there as fast as possible and wait for a response. Hopefully, it's quick so we can just get the hell on," he said.

"I understand, Keon."

"And oh yeah, I gotta make a quick stop before we get down that road."

"Where to?"

"Don't worry about all that. It's just a little business I gotta handle."

As he started the car, tears nearly formed in the wells of her eyes as she veered her gaze through the passenger's side window. She knew that the trip was destined to be one big waste of time. There would be a better chance of icicles forming in the most obscure reaches of Hell before the day she would witness her mother handing her one red cent for anything while she remained in a relationship with Keon. She hated the man and wasn't shy about making her feelings felt, but she was always respectful about it. She never went out and told Keon directly that she couldn't stand his guts, but he knew. Just like her mother knew Keon's feelings towards her were mutual.

It was a damned if you do and damned if you don't situation for Ashley. If she didn't agree to go down to her mother's house and ask her for the money, Keon was going to be mad and probably do his best to beat her brains out, and then when they arrived to her mother's house and she most certainly denied them any funds whatsoever, he was going to be even more irate and most likely beat her brains out when they returned home.

****

Keon eased into a parking space of an upscale apartment complex not too far from they're own. He shut the vehicle off, turned to Ashley and said, "I gotta check on this lead. I'll be right back."

She looked at him with a slight grin and didn't say a word. She knew exactly what he was there for and who he was there to see. Raven was her name, and she knew he was seeing her on the side for a little over a year now. She didn't care, though. As long as he was sneaking around with his side piece, he wasn't in her face trying to smash it in. As far as she was concerned, if his mistress really wanted him she could have him and all that went along with being his. She had just about her fill of the man.

As he jumped out of the car, she repositioned herself to get comfortable, and reclined in her spot, ready to get the entire day over with. Shortly after Keon disappeared into the walls of the apartment complex, her eyes fell on the passenger side mirror, noticing the same black car from the night before had slowly rolled up and briefly paused behind their vehicle. She quickly turned around in her chair, trying to stay snug behind the seat to see the passing car with her own eyes. Without a doubt, they were being followed.

Raven opened the door wearing a tight t-shirt that barely came down over her belly button and some pink jogging pants that fit snuggly around her perfectly round bottom. When she opened the door to Keon's smiling mug, she groaned and left him standing in the doorway.

"Damn, baby," Keon said as he walked in. "Nigga don't get a hug?"

"You think you deserve one?" she grunted as she walked to the sofa and plopped down on it.

"I'm just saying, a nigga ain't been through in a couple of days. It seems like you would miss a nigga or something."

She sucked her teeth and began flipping channels on the television set which was located on the other side of the room.

Keon was so uncomfortable by her cold reception when he walked up to the sofa, he chose not to sit. He said, "So, why your phone been off all day? Nigga been trying to call you and check in, but all I kept getting was your voicemail."

"Maybe that's all you deserve."

"What's all this talk about what a nigga deserve and shit?"

"You figure it out…playa."

"Oh, I guess you're all up in your feelings today." He dropped down on the other end of the plush leather chair and asked, "Man, you know I got some major shit on my plate right now. So what the hell a nigga do this time, Raven?"

She turned to him with the most disgusted stare and said, "Nigga, it ain't what you did. It's what you ain't doing?"

"And what's that?"

"You're a smart guy, you figure the shit out," she said as she threw the remote in his lap and stormed off towards the kitchen.

He shook his head and said under his breath, "This shit right here—never satisfied." He hopped up and made his way into the kitchen to join her. When he stepped in, she was at the counter slicing tomatoes. The sight of her with a knife made him feel slightly uneasy with the way she was acting.

"So where that chick at?" she asked not giving him any eye contact.

He let out a hard grunt and blurted out, "Shit, she out there in the car."

She dropped the knife and let out brief chuckle. "She's outside?"

"Yeah," he replied with a nod and goofy look on his face.

"So you brought her to my house?"

"No... no. Let's get the shit straight. I didn't bring her to your house. She's outside in the car. I gotta take her over to her momma house for something."

"They shole make some bold niggas these days, I tell ya." She laughed and returned to cutting her tomatoes. After a few seconds of intense tomato slicing, she dropped the knife again as her anger towards him became too unbearable for her to contain. She took a few moments to think about what he just revealed to her and said, "Let me ask you a question."

"Yeah."

"How in the hell does it even remotely seem like a good idea to bring another bitch to my house? I mean, what is it in your simple ass head that made you think bringing her over here was a good idea? Please tell me now, Negro, because I'm beginning to think you're fuckin' retarded. I just wanna know."

"Damn, why you tryin' to handle me like that," he asked. "I mean, shit, you're the one not answering your phone and shit."

"It's because you're constantly doing stupid ass shit like this."

"Look, you weren't picking up your phone, and a nigga just got concerned—and right now a nigga is just trying to do his due diligence and check on your ass."

"Well, I'm fine, nigga. So now that you know that I'm fine, you can leave now and take your extra baggage on down the road with you," she said while pointing towards the exit.

"Awe girl, why you trying to be all hard and shit?" He eased up behind her and palmed her hips with both hands.

"Nah, don't touch me." She backed away from his lips as he attempted to kiss her on the side of her neck.

"You gonna let a nigga get a quickie while she out there waiting in the car? I'll straighten out that little attitude you tryin' to have."

She whipped around and tapped him on his lips and said, "Sorry, boo boo, but my little friend came early this month."

He chuckled, slowly slid his arms around her waist, and then pulled her into him. He said, "So, is it light or is it heavy?"

"Nigga," she said as she pushed him away by pounding both her knuckles into his chest. "You ain't getting up in me like that. I don't know what you're thinking."

"Awe, come on. It ain't like you ain't never did it like that before."

"Hell, even if I did, it ain't going down like that today," she said. "Go'on back down there and ask that bitch you brought over here that you got waiting on your stupid ass in the car to let you hunch on her while she's leaking blood."

"Awe, baby, why you gotta be like that," he asked while trying to grab the arm she was quickly pulling away from him.

"Cuz, Negro, I'm tired of being your side bitch!"

"Side bitch? Girl, come on, now. I done told you over and over again, you're my main lady. I ain't touched Ashley in over eight months."

"Yeah, nigga, you'll tell me anything," she folded her arms and issued him a disgusted frown.

"It's the truth!"

"Whatever!" she replied. "It shole look like I'm over here holding down the side bitch status while your ass is out there parading around Charlotte with her and going to family functions and shit. Boy, if you only knew how many niggas that just begged for the chance–just a sniff of it."

"What?" Keon barked.

"Nigga, I don't know what you getting all swole up for. You got the wrong bitch. Ain't none of that Mista-Miss Celie shit gonna fly over here with this bitch right ch'ere," she laughed. "You touch anything over here with force, and you gonna need a GPS tracker to find your fucking balls, nigga. Don't try and play me like that."

"Girl, whatever. Ain't nobody coming at you like that," he said as he pulled her close to him. "I'll never put my hands on you–not in a bad way—you my baby."

"And you never will, nigga. You best get that thought out your head if it ever find a way in it."

"Awe, girl, get up off that now," he replied. "Now look, so just to let you know, I'm taking her to her momma house so we can get this money."

"Money for what?"

"To pay back, Max."

"Pay back Max? I thought you said you handled that mess already."

"Nah, I said I was working on it. I ain't handle shit just yet."

"Boy!" she punched him on his shoulder. "And your ass rolling up over here knowing you still owe that nigga money!" She rushed to the small window over her sink to get a glance at the cars in the parking lot below.

"What the hell you getting all scared up for?"

"You owe a drug lord money, that's why, fool! You better stop playing with that dude."

"Man, fuck, Max! Everybody acting like that nigga don't breathe the same air and bleed blood the same way everybody else does. I told him we'll get him his money when we get it."

"Yeah, well if you don't get him that money, you gonna be one dead nigga. Don't try to play that role with me, I know ya'. You and your flunkies 'bout to be dead real quick if you don't get that man his money," she added, "And on that note, I'm sorry, Keon, but you gotta get the hell outta here with that mess." She positioned herself behind him and began pushing him down the hall towards the living room exit.

"So you just gonna turn your back on a nigga that quick?" he asked while mildly resisting her guidance towards the front room. "As much as I do for you—pay your rent, get your hair and nails done, buy you all kinds of shit that the next chick would love to have, and this is how you turn around and do a nigga? For real?"

She swung the front door open and said, "Get out your feelings, Keon. You can't do nothing for me dead," she rebutted. "That's exactly what you're gonna be if you don't straighten your mess out. I'm down for you and all, but I'm not trying to die for nobody. For real, you *gots* to go."

****

When Keon returned to the car, he did his best to conceal his frustration of being thrown out of the apartment by the women he considered to be his main chick. In front of Raven, he took her rejection in stride, but it pissed him off on the inside as he resented her for acting as if Max was more than the mere mortal that he saw him to be.

His gaze was straight forward as he slid his key in the ignition but froze before turning the switch. Ashley could tell something apparently didn't go his way. She didn't ask him how he was feeling because she really didn't care. She figured the love birds must've had a quarrel or something. She long suspected he didn't treat Raven like he treated her. Knowing him, she figured he probably worshipped the ground she walked on as she treated him like unadulterated crap in return. She assumed that's how it usually worked with a cheater and a beater like him.

"So I guess we gotta get on down the road."

"What?" he said as he finally snapped out of his spell.

"My mother's house. We probably should get moving."

He frowned, "Hell, I know that. I don't need you to be reminding me of nothin'. You just make sure you figure out a way to get that money we need. That's all the hell you need to be concerning yourself with." He started the car and began backing out of the parking space.

****

Ashley took deep, slow breaths as she could sense that a panic attack was coming on. They were parked outside of her mother's house, and Keon had already made his way out of the car as if they were at his own homecoming with his own family. She couldn't move. As her hands trembled, she found herself gawking at the two story brick house and its well kept shrubbery that wrapped around the residence as it had since she was a child. It was home, but she'd been away for so long she knew it wouldn't feel that way. She was reluctant to entertain all the questions that resided behind the brick walls that stretched before her.

Keon turned around towards the car once he realized she wasn't following him. To his displeasure, she hadn't even exited the car. A look of disdain sprawled across his face. "You gonna get the fuck out?" he asked as he swung his arms out.

The sight of his furious demeanor was an instantaneous fix to her nervousness. She quickly became less concerned about the mysteries that awaited her behind the walls of her mother's home and more cautious of the potential wrath of her chauffeur. Ashley took one final, deep breath, hopped out of the car and speedily joined him up the walkway to the front door.

"Don't fuck this up," he whispered to her.

Her mother, Rose, opened the door to them and a smile the size of Texas erupted across her face once she set eyes on her youngest daughter. "Ashley," she said as she slowly stepped out onto the porch and grabbed her daughter, embracing her tightly. "Oh, my child, my child, my child."

Her mother's excitement took her by surprise as Keon looked on with a smile followed by a brief nod. Rose's ecstatic response to seeing her daughter was exactly what he wanted to see. He could almost feel the money he needed to get from her gracing the palm of his hands.

"It's been so long, child. Too long," Rose exclaimed with watery eyes as she pulled away from Ashley. She scanned her over from head to toe, questioning herself about the reality of the moment. "I still can't believe you're standing here."

"I'm here, Momma," Ashley added, humbled by her mother's warm embrace.

The magic of the moment swiftly began to fizzle for Rose once she looked over to her daughter's companion. With a straight face, her only greeting to him was meek and uninspired, "Keon."

"Rose," he replied just as coldly as she spoke. It tickled him whenever he got the chance to see the displeasure of Ashley's family's faces when they saw him. He knew they couldn't stand him and that they yearned for the day that Ashley would leave him. He knew he would never let that happen because he felt that he owned her mind, body and soul, and he had no plans in ever letting her go. There wasn't a damn thing they could do about it.

Rose led the way into the home down the lavish hickory hardwood floors towards the dining room. "Your sisters are in the dining room already. Shall we join them?"

As Keon's eyes fell upon the luxurious oil paintings and exquisite décor that laced the walls of the foyer, he was not only reminded about how loaded Ashley's mother was, but he also recalled the original reason he wanted to make Ashley his in the first place. She was the little rich girl that was supposed to be his ticket out of the hood. His aspirations was for her to be the direct link to him and her parent's money. He just didn't factor in how critical her parents would be of their relationship when they discovered their precious darling had somehow managed to hook up with somebody from what they felt was the wrong side of town with a moderate criminal record they somehow used their money to dig up. It also didn't help that he was six years her senior.

Her father was so demanding that she leave him alone, he threw her out of the house and cut her out of his will right before he passed away. With him cutting her out of all that money, Ashley quickly went from being his prized blue chip stock to an inexperienced burden that essentially became his personal slave that was made to do whatever he requested, from cooking, cleaning and sex whenever he saw fit. If she disagreed with anything he positioned to her, he always had the remedy waiting for her in the form of his bare knuckles across her face and body, or his old school favorite, a strap across her backside. He wasted no time in letting her know that he was in charge when she found herself with nowhere else to go.

Draya and Shanice, Ashley's older, fraternal twin sisters sat at the end of the long dinner table and barely batted an eye to her as she greeted them. They were just too busy and transfixed in their own conversation to truly acknowledge her, but it was no surprise to Ashley. They were never close to her nor did they ever pay her any attention for the short time they all lived under the same roof. She wasn't certain if it was because of their differences in age, that being nine years, or if it was just that eerie twin bond she figured all twins had with each other.

It had been years since Ashley was graced by the aroma of her mother's succulent country cooking, and despite being on edge from the instance she arrived, she took a moment to take in the smells from the dishes that stretched across the table from end to end. She and Keon took the chairs opposite of Rose as they all sat in unison.

"Your brother should be arriving at any moment, so we'll give him a few minutes before we begin eating," said Rose as she sipped on a glass of wine she already had prepared prior to answering the door.

When Keon realized Ashley's younger brother, Dexter, would be joining them also, he immediately felt irritated. While Rose provided slight hints of her dislike for him in a subtle manner, Dexter made it no mystery that he couldn't stand him one bit, and he was always extremely vocal about it. Things were like that since the day he came over to inform Ashley about their Dad's passing, and she opened the door to him with a pair of black eyes. He didn't buy the story Keon instructed her to tell anyone asking about how she looked—that she'd been robbed and beaten at an ATM machine from some random street punk. Dexter had absolutely no doubt in his mind that her bruises were from Keon's hands as he aggressively made claims that he'd noticed marks and bruises on her before. Ever since that day, he had been begging for the chance to square off with Keon in a fair one. He just didn't know Keon was evenly eager to go one on one with him, also, just to teach the young, hot-head a lesson.

"So how have you been, Ashley?" Rose asked after a few moments of staring at her daughter. Her daughter's coyness wasn't sitting well with her as she remembered her child as always being a bit of a loner, but one that was confident and full of life.

Ashley didn't make any eye contact with her mother. Her vision was strictly focused on the wedding ring that was wrapped around her mother's finger. Her father told her so many stories about how hard he had to work to buy the symbol of love and commitment during her childhood. When she was young, she imagined she'd grow up and marry a dignified, hard working man like her father, but unfortunately she ended up with Keon–the exact opposite of him.

"Ashley?" her mother repeated. "Do you hear me speaking to you?"

Ripped out her of her daze by her mother's voice, she raised her head to her mother, then looked over to Keon, and then back to Rose. She was at a loss for words and didn't want to say the wrong thing. The mere anxiety of trying to figure out the right time and place she would ask her mother for the money she needed had her insides rumbling and her mind everywhere but at the dinner table.

"She's been doing alright, Rose," Keon answered.

After Keon's words, there was complete and utter silence. Ashley bowed her head. Her two sisters at the other end of the table ceased their conversation altogether and looked on to their mother, anxiously anticipating her response.

The old, bronze skinned lady raised her eyebrow at her daughter's companion and said, "I don't mean any harm, Keon, but I was talking to my daughter." She then turned her focus to Ashley. "I raised her to speak for herself as I did all my children, so I am confident she knows how to answer me when I'm speaking to her. Ashley—"

"I'm doing good, mom," she interjected before Keon could fix his mouth to say another word.

"I hear your mouth saying that you're good, but your posture tells me otherwise. To be frank, with all of this looking down, around and away, you almost look as if you're fearful of something," Rose looked Keon dead in his eyes. "Fearful in the one place you don't ever have to be fearful of anything or anyone—your home."

Keon let out a short grunt as his eyes crawled up the wall and onto the oil painting of Ashley's father that hovered

315

over them and the dinner table. The portrait of the stern faced man made Keon feel even more uneasy as it almost appeared to him that the man was looking directly at him, straight from the grave. Keon contemplated if the trip was even worth it at all. His blood was beginning to boil from the elevated tension in the room. He thought if they could get through the visit and obtain the money he needed, they would never have to see his black ass again. Unless, of course, Rose kicked the bucket and left his old lady with the money–that would definitely be the next and final time they'd see his black ass again.

"What the hell is he doing here?" Dexter yelled out as he dashed towards Keon. All the young man could see was red the moment he entered the dining room and laid eyes on the man he'd been yearning to square up with for past few years. Keon quickly jumped up and backed away from the table, sending his chair flying to the floor while clinching his fists, anxiously waiting to defend himself.

"Dexter!" Rose yelled as she and her twin daughters rushed towards him to prevent him from connecting with his first swing at Keon.

"You better back up, son." Keon warned him as he continued to back away from the muscular young man. "Ain't nobody come here to be fighting nobody."

"Well that makes one of us," said Dexter while attempting to escape the tugs and restraints of his family.

"Dexter! Dexter!" yelled Rose as she worked herself in front of him while pushing him backwards towards his sisters who managed to finally get a secure hold of his arms. "Settle down, son! You settle down right this minute."

"Nah, Ma," Dexter replied. "Ain't nobody stupid. We know what he does to her. I've seen his handy work with my own damn eyes. He beats her. He beats the hell out of her."

"Dexter, you watch your mouth in my house and cut out all of this foolishness right this minute," Rose demanded while wagging her finger in her son's face. "I didn't raise any hoodlums in this house, now cut it out, I say."

"You know what, let's be real for the first time since I got here" said Keon. "I ain't family. We all know that. There's no reason for me to even be up in here trying to impose. This is yall's time together. I'm 'bout to go outside

317

and let y'all do y'all family thang. I didn't come here to stir no trouble."

"You damn right you ain't family," Dexter said.

"Dexter!" Rose called to him with a firm look.

"I'm sorry, Ma," he replied, still angry but no longer requiring his older sisters to restrain him.

"Keon," said Rose, "You don't have to leave. Despite our differences, you are a guest in this house, and I made enough food for everyone."

"Nah, Rose, I insist," Keon replied.

"Nobody begging him to stay," said Dexter.

"Dexter, that's enough," said Rose.

Ashley never moved a muscle as she kept her seat and looked straight ahead as if there wasn't any commotion at all in the home. Keon leaned into Ashley's ear and whispered, "You make sure you talk her into giving you that money or his ass whoppin' belongs to you." He kissed her on her cheek. "I'll see you in a few, babe." He added loudly, just for put-on purposes for the rest of the family.

She nodded as he looked to the rest of the family and said with a short wave, "Folks. I'll see myself out."

They watched silently as he retreated from the dining room.

"Momma, we got to go, too," said Draya.

"Already?" Rose asked with a surprised look on her face. "We're finally all in one place, together as a family. We haven't been like this since before your father passed away."

"I know, Momma, but Draya's right, we gotta go," Shanice added. "We're running inventory tomorrow night and nobody's trying to be in that store past midnight like the last time."

"I know that's right," Draya added. "We can't leave those types of responsibilities to the help. Their slack behinds will have us all over budget."

"Well, I know you girls stay busy with your boutiques and all, but you can't leave until I make you both a plate."

"Girl, we didn't say we were leaving without taking a plate of your food, Momma," Shanice laughed while giving her twin a high five.

"Amen," Draya added with a brief chuckle.

"Well, you come on here and follow me to this here kitchen," said Rose. "Dexter, Ashley, I'll be right back." She led them into the kitchen as Dexter took a seat at the table across from Ashley.

"That's cool, Ma," Dexter replied.

"Nice seeing you again, Ash," said Draya as she bent over to give her sister a short, cutesy hug that barely included any actual touching.

Dexter grabbed a roll from the bread basket, took a huge bite from it and watched his sister look away and around at everything in the dining room but him. He said, "So why'd you bring that filth up in here? You for one, should know he's not welcome here–ever!"

"Look, Dexter, I know what you're going to say, and you're wrong. Keon doesn't hit me," Ashley said, almost in disbelief she could put those lying words together and allow them to escape from her own lips. "I've told you this over and over again. You should stop spreading this mess around the family."

"My ass," Dexter replied. "How you gonna bring that clown up in Momma's house, knowing good and well she can't stand him? We all know how he treats you? You're nothing but his punching bag. He doesn't love you, and you know it. I didn't dream up them black eyes I saw on you nor the bruises on your arms. I know what the hell I saw."

"Dexter, whatever goes on in my house, I can handle."

"Yeah, right," he shook his head while frowning at the sight of her. He couldn't believe she was so loyal to such a lowlife. It sickened him down to his stomach. "Dude is beneath you. He never deserved you, and somehow you can't even see that. To hell with what everybody keeps trying to tell you."

Her brother's words cut deep but not because he was saying them so bluntly and without any regard, but because all of his words were true. She couldn't even keep a straight face and try to pretend she wasn't going through hell every day she lived under the same roof with Keon.

There wasn't anything she wanted more than to send Keon on his way without her, but in her heart she knew it wasn't an option. She feared for her brother's life and the rest of the family with what Keon might do to them and her if she left him. Dexter was a hot head and even trained to fight by way of Taekwondo, but he wasn't a street dude like Keon. Keon was tough enough to take a well-deserved beating, but he'd be sure to come back and sneak you and take you out another day. She understood that all of the special training and fighting in the world could never prepare him for someone like Keon–not his kind of evil. If he couldn't get you face to face, he'd still get you–one way or another.

"I mean, what happened to you," Dexter asked, with an disgusted expression. "You were the one that taught me how to stand up for myself when we were growing up. Now look at you."

She remained silent as her mother reentered the dining room. "Okay, well the girls are squared away and on their way home," said Rose as she took a seat next to her son. "I guess that just leaves us three with some good eating and some overdue catching up."

"I've done my share of catching up for one night, Ma." Dexter proclaimed as he rose from the table, his concentration on his sister unbroken.

Rose turned to her son with her mouth open and her hands out. She said, "Wait a minute, you haven't even eaten anything."

"You know what, Ma, I'm not even hungry."

"But, Dexter," she said.

"I need to shower," he said as he stormed out of the room.

Rose didn't even try to stop him as she finally threw in the towel on the disaster of a dinner. She shook her head and took another sip of her wine, while wishing she had poured herself something a little stronger if she'd known the night was going to turn out the way it had.

"Well, Ashley, I guess we need to start eating as much of this food as we can so it won't go to waste," Rose said while scooping up a spoon of green beans and dropping them onto her plate.

"I'm not really hungry, either, Momma."

Rose let out a tiring sigh, "Well, I'm not really surprised child. Seems like no one came to dinner to actually eat dinner tonight."

"Momma, Keon and I came over to ask for a loan," she blurted out. It seemed like the longer she waited to bring it up, the worst the night got. She just couldn't keep thinking about the different ways to position it any longer and decided just to let it out raw and ugly.

"Really," she said while dropping her utensils beside her plate as she took a few moments to digest her daughter's revelation.

"Yes, mam," she answered while looking down at her own reflection in her empty dinner plate. "We wanted to put a decent down payment on a home we just fell in love with once we saw it. One that we could perhaps even start a family in," she lied. The words that came out of her mouth made her feel like the lowest scum on the earth. She just hated lying to her mother, especially in the form of the bull she was sifting out by portraying a happy and promising future with Keon.

Rose's eyes hadn't left her daughter since the moment she asked for the money. She wondered what was going on in her daughter's head. The woman before her looked like her Ashley, but she was far from the young lady that she'd remember raising. "Well, I guess we need to mosey on down to your father's office and find my check book."

Ashley eyes shot opened as she thought her ears had deceived her. "Huh?"

"Well, come on." Her mother eased up from the table and said, "Let's get to it."

Ashley rose from her chair and began to cautiously follow her mother out of the dining room and down the hall. She felt relieved she had finally coached herself into asking her mother for the cash, but she was also suspicious of mother's willingness to oblige. She didn't even ask how much she needed. Although her mother had plenty money, it just didn't feel right for her not to ask how much money she was actually requesting from her. Nevertheless, she was mere moments away from getting the finances she needed to get Keon off her back, and she just couldn't believe it. She felt like pinching herself to make sure she was awake.

Keon sat on the back of his car blowing smoke circles in the air as he waited for a text response from Porkchop. After a few moments without a reply he flicked his cigarette to the ground and dialed Porkchop's number. To his surprise, his ally's phone went straight to voicemail. Infuriated, he spoke into the phone once prompted by the voicemail box, "Aye man, what the fuck? You suppose to hit me back with the word on that bitch nigga, and I ain't hear

325

shit from you all day. I hope your punk ass didn't leave town. If you did, you know you're on some fuckboy shit, for real. But I know you know better than that, so hit me back when you get this message. Don't disappoint a nigga." He ended the call and mumbled, "Shit!" He looked towards the house and said, "Girl, you better come through for a nigga."

When Ashley followed her mother into her father's office, a frightening streak of nervousness came over her. The last time she was in her father's office her, old man was alive, kicking and determined to sculpt his children's lives the way he saw best fit. It was in this very room that he gave her his final ultimatum to leave Keon or be banished from his house forever. He explained to her that he didn't want to see her again if she wasn't going to abide by his wishes of leaving the overgrown career criminal, whom at the time was everything she thought she wanted in a man. Leave him or he wanted no part of her in his life, he told her. It was all a pile of regrets now, and although she was mad as hell at her father for trying to force her into choosing between him and Keon, she finally realized he was only looking at the man she loved without the infatuated eyes she couldn't take off of him. It was now that she wished she'd listened to her father as she lived most days regretting not being able to tell the stubborn old man that she was sorry and he was actually right.

"Have a seat," her mother stated as she walked around her deceased husband's cherry oak desk and pointed to the chair across from it, signaling Ashley to sit.

"No, I'd rather stand, Momma."

Rose grinned, "You're gonna ask me for money and not adhere to at least one of my requests?"

Ashley begrudgingly sat in the chair. The chills just wouldn't stop flaring up across her arms and down her spine. She sat in the spot where her father leaned against the desk before her and pleaded for her to not walk out on the family— to use her head and not her foolish heart. It was his last request to her, the final day she saw him alive. The guilt was agonizing. Her heart raced as mounds of grief weighed down on her soul as she thought that if she only had listened to him, things would've turned out much differently. She couldn't help but think that somehow he could've lived a little longer if she only obeyed him and broke away from the man he warned would bring her so much pain and heartache. He was so right about Keon.

"Did you hear me child?" Rose asked.

"What's that?" asked Ashley.

"You didn't hear a word I just said, did you?" Rose said while shaking her head. "I asked how much money do you need."

Apprehensive, she asked, "You're not going to ask me about where the house is located, or how it looks?"

"Why should I? You said that you and Keon loved the place."

"And you're just going to write us out this check and not even ask when we'll be able to pay it back?"

"Sure," she said as she pulled out her checkbook from the drawer on the side of the desk and sat it on the table. She uncapped her ballpoint pen and asked, "Now how much do you need?"

"Well, we need eighty thousand dollars, Ma. We should be able–"

"That's fine. Don't even worry about paying it back." Rose began filling out the check.

"Are you serious, Momma?"

"Absolutely."

Ashley couldn't believe it. It was almost too good to be true. She watched her mother carefully as she wrote the check out. After her mother graced the paper with her signature, she slid it across the cherry oak desk.

Before Ashley could pick it up and grab it, Rose said, "This check is yours under one condition."

Ashley took a step back and sat back down on the edge of her chair. She replied, "And what's that mother?"

"I will give you this money and you won't ever have to worry about paying me back if you take this here check, walk it out to that man outside and tell him this is his to keep as long as he leaves this home without you and call this so-called relationship you have with him over–for good!"

Ashley quickly realized her mother was determined to finish what her father wasn't able to complete. She knew her mother's urgency to write her out a check was just too good to be true. The craziest thing about it was there wasn't anything in the world she wanted more than to be rid of the man she despised so much. There just wasn't a way he'd let her go that easy–not without a fight and not without someone dying. It just wasn't going to happen without some type of tragedy, and it didn't matter what dollar amount was thrown at him

"Momma, I know this may be difficult for you, but you gotta respect..."

"Respect what? Your relationship, Ashley?" She rose from her deceased husband's executive leather chair and leaned over his desk with both her hands planted on top of it. "You don't think I know that man out there abuses you? That he puts his filthy, stinking hands on a child of mine–a child that I raised? Every time I see that man, it takes the unrelenting strength of the Lord to keep me from killing his black ass."

"Mom..."

"Don't Mom me," she wagged her finger towards her daughter. "Don't you do it. Don't you dare do it," she yelled. "That man got you in here acting like a shell of yourself. I don't even recognize my own child anymore with all of this looking down and around and everywhere except for in the eyes of the person that's speaking to you. I didn't raise you like that. I didn't raise any of my children like that. You're better than this, Ashley. You're better."

"Momma, we need this money."

"And you can have it—ever last cent. You can have it all. But in order to get it, you have to agree to my terms."

Ashley was stunned. She rose from her chair, fighting back tears. Once she looked into her mother's eyes, she couldn't hold them back anymore and nor could Rose. They both stood still with tears streaming down their faces, stubborn in their own separate ways.

"I'm giving you an out, Ashley. That's all I'm trying to do. I know his type. I've known it all my life. There is no good in that man out there. He will drag you down into the depths of hell with him if he can—further down than he's already taken you."

"You don't understand, Momma," she cried, while shaking her head. "You guys don't ever seem to understand." She yearned to take her up on her offer, but no figure she wrote down on that check would be enough to recapture her freedom from Keon.

"Oh I understand, child. More that you could ever imagine." Rose picked the check up and held it before her daughter. "Take this money to him and get your life back. End it while you can."

****

When Keon noticed Ashley approaching the car, he put away his phone and sat from his reclined position in the driver's seat. The expression on her face didn't appear to be a pleasant one, but he hadn't seen her smile in quite some time so that was nothing new to him. He really didn't care how she was feeling as his only concern was if she had come through for him or not, and he was certain she did. She surely understood the agony that awaited her if she failed him.

Ashley hopped in the car with her nerves shot and chest feeling as if it could explode. She could feel Keon eyes on her as she bowed her head, let out a deep sigh and said, "She didn't give us the money."

"Wha…Really."

She looked at him and gave him a bit of a nod and said, "Yes." She knew she was in deep trouble. She was just hoping he'd have enough decency to drive out of her mother's yard before he started his rampage.

He looked at her with a hopeless expression as he couldn't believe his ears. She came back empty handed. Plan A through Z for him had fallen apart. He wanted to call her every foul name in the book, but the shock of her coming back empty handed made him choke back his words. She had to be kidding him. As he gazed at her with her hanging head, he was hoping she'd raise her head and tell him she was only kidding, but she didn't. He could tell by her tense demeanor she was waiting for him to go ape crazy, but he didn't. He simply said, to her surprise and his, "Well, I guess you tried."

There was a deadening silence in the car for a few moments as he just sat there gazing at her mother's house, still in disbelief, contemplating requesting the money himself. She looked towards him but not in his face, only towards his knee where his tightened fist sat idly. He started the car and backed out of the driveway. As they moved down the road, she remained terrified to look at him. She thought he would've gone ballistic once he got about a mile from her mother's residence, but he was still calm–too calm.

The further away they travelled from her mother's home, the more relaxed she started to feel. She thought maybe he was just trying to scare her up to force her to be more inclined to ask her mother for the money he needed. She figured he had to have known the odds of her mother just giving them the money in the first place weren't good due to the fact that she was practically exiled from the family for years, and the only reason for it was for being with him.

After driving about five miles down the barren stretch of road, Keon slammed on the car brakes and quickly jabbed an unsuspecting Ashley square on her chin, forcefully propelling the side of her head against the passenger side window. He put the car in park in the middle of the road and yelled, "What the hell you got me way down this road wasting my fucking time for?"

"Keon, I.." she attempted to explain, but Keon struck her across the bridge of her nose with the back of his hand.

"Bitch, don't try to explain shit to me," he said. "You understand me?" When she didn't immediately respond, he held his hand near her face at striking distance. "I asked you if you understood my ass, heffa?" He lowered his hand once she tearfully acknowledged him by nodding her head.

Tears raced down her cheeks as she regained her composure from the brief dizziness she sustained from his strikes. She rubbed her chin as he continued on with his rant. She didn't look at him, fearing he'd hit her again out of his own paranoia, believing that she was looking at him in a disrespectful way.

"I told your ass you was gonna pay if you didn't come through for me with this money," he angrily professed. "Got your brother in my goddamn face talking all this cold cash trash, like he can beat my ass. Boy is your ass gonna pay when we get back to the crib. Your sorry ass had just one goddamn thing to do. Just one goddamn thing to do, and you couldn't even do that shit right. You're a goddamn disappointment. I don't know what the fuck I'd ever seen in your lousy ass."

"Keon, I tried."

He chopped her across her forehead with the side of his hand and said, "Don't you talk back to me woman!"

As the tears flowed she simply nodded, trying her earnest not to break down completely.

"You know I'll fuck you up out here on this road. Don't you tempt me," he warned her while pointing at her forehead. "I told you what was gonna happen before we even got down here so you may as well get ready for what's coming to your ass. And I know your ass didn't really wanna get me that money because you would've gotten it. I ain't crazy. You just ain't good for a goddamn thing!" He slung the car in drive and began barrelling down the road again, his expression embodied with rage. "Can't do shit I tell you. You're worthless. You're fucking worthless. Good for shit."

He went on and on until she didn't even hear his hurtful words anymore. She was numb to it. She only wished she was numb to his physical attacks. She also wondered if she should've just taken her mother up on the offer and bring him the check in exchange for her freedom from him.

****

Keon didn't yield his onslaught of derogatory words towards Ashley since he attacked her a few miles down from her mother's house. His only shift in focus was when his stomach started grumbling because he hadn't eaten anything all day. He got mad at her for that, too. He ripped into her for not thinking enough of him to bring him a plate out, knowing good and well she failed at getting him his money.

He backed his car into a parking space facing the side entrance of his favorite hood restaurant, Biggie Burgers. "You go in there and get me a Biggie Max Burger with cheese. Tell them I don't want no mayonnaise on my shit. If they put mayonnaise on my shit, I'm already warning you– I'm not gonna be a happy camper so you best stress that shit to them inside." He slapped a twenty in the palm of her hand and warned, "If a nigga try to holla at you in there, you better act like the mother fucker don't exist. You got me?"

She nodded and slowly eased out of the car. Her ribs were sore and it pained her if her arm merely rubbed up against them. Slowly walking towards the entrance, she instantly became nauseous from the burnt grease smell that always exuded from the former McDonalds building rebranded with graffiti that embellished the Biggie Burger moniker on every wall that kept the deteriorating structure standing. She wondered how he could even eat out of such a place as the outside of the building was in need of a severe litter pickup, and the inside was normally no better.

He watched her slowly walk into the building. Once she entered the restaurant, he slid his phone out of his pocket. He was disappointed when he realized he didn't receive a single text message or missed call from neither Porkchop nor Raven. Right before he could dial his side chick to get on her case for not checking on him, there was a hard knock against his window.

He immediately hurled over towards the passenger side of the car, fearful that he was about be under attack from one of Max's men. "What the…" He looked towards his window to a sparingly dressed woman standing just outside of his car. He felt a sigh of relief, but he quickly rolled the window down halfway to angrily ask her, "Fuck you want?"

"Hey, handsome," she replied with a smile that didn't include any front or bottom teeth, just brownish fangs hanging from the corners of her mouth. "I can make your dreams come true for fifteen dollars."

He looked the filthy woman from head to toe, thinking at best she was probably a six or a seven during her good years, but she was far from it today. "Bitch, I'll pass," he replied.

"Well, fuck you then, faggot!" she yelled. She then pressed on away from his car. He just shook his head, without any aspirations to bother with wasting a response on the woman as he rolled his window back up.

Before she could make it into the restaurant, a car stopped right in front of Keon's. The driver tapped on his horn a couple of times in an attempt to get the woman's attention. She halted, smiled and jogged over to the driver's window. She bent over into his window after looking around the immediate area to see if anyone was paying them any attention. After exchanging a few words with the driver, she glided over to the passenger side door and jumped in. The car sped off.

Keon thought the driver of the vehicle must've been mighty hard up for a trick. "Niggas." As he chuckled to himself, he noticed a young man wearing headphones, and bobbing his head, while sitting on a couple of crates alongside the wall on the backside of the restaurant. He then noticed Ashley approaching the car with his food. He looked over to the man and then back at Ashley. He had an idea, but he wasn't sure how much it would benefit him.

Ashley jumped into the car and handed him his food. "I made sure they didn't add any mayonnaise, and they made the burger fresh just how you like it."

He snatched the bag from her with the wheels still turning in his head. Looking into the bag, he grabbed the burger, checked it to see if it had any mayonnaise on it and then took a big chomp out of it. His eyes then returned to the guy sitting on the crates.

Ashley bowed her head as she waited for him to finish his meal so he could drive them home and begin her punishment. The sooner he was able to do whatever he was going to do, the sooner he could leave for the night and be with his other woman.

He took a swallow from his drink and pointed towards the guy on the crates. "I want you to walk up to that nigga right there and tell him you'll give him head for forty dollars?"

"What?" Her head quickly popped up, alarmed and shocked by his request. "Huh?"

"Bitch, what'cha looking at that nigga for?" He backhanded her across the bridge of her nose with the same hand he was holding his drink, spilling the beverage all over her chest and lap. "Fuck you pop your head up so fast for? You wanna do it or something, bitch?"

"No, Keon, I didn't even know what you were talking about," she cried.

"Bitch, you been out here playing me? You been having some nigga in my crib with you while I'm out here hustlin' in these here streets?" His eyes were almost bulging out of his head as Ashley attempted to explain herself.

"No, Keon, no... I was just trying to understand what you were asking of me."

"Bitch, you lying," he said as he smacked her across her lips.

Blood immediately began to trickle down from the corner of her mouth as she held her hands up in an attempt to block his barrage of jabs. She screamed and pleaded for him to stop as she tried to deter his punches. When she successfully blocked her face from getting hit, he would then direct his punches towards her midsection.

"You wanna give that nigga some head, don't ya? I knew I couldn't trust your scandalous ass."

"No, Keon. Stop! Stop hitting me," she begged him.

"Stupid, bitch," he yelled as he poured on his vicious bombardment of strikes. He struck her as hard as he could from his side angle, furious with himself because his punches weren't more on target.

"Keon, stop it, please!"

One of his jabs slipped through her guard and plowed her face against her window. There was silence as her hands fell to her lap, and her body went limp. When he realized she wasn't moving, he held off on his punishment and began examining her. "Ashley?"

Silence.

He looked her idle body over and a slight stroke of fear overcame him. With her head lying against the passenger window, he thought he might've killed her. He repositioned himself in his chair, not believing he actually struck her hard enough to really kill her. He then picked his burger up from his lap and bit another chunk from it—his angry eyes still piercing through her. "Girl, stop all that damn playing and get your ass up."

She didn't utter a word nor did she move an inch. Her silence infuriated him.

"Alright, then, just lay your stupid ass there. Play dead. I like it quiet in this bitch while I'm driving anyway," he said as he stuck his key into the ignition. There still wasn't any movement from her as he faced her again, now even more irritated that she wasn't responding to him. "Ash," he called as he nudged her shoulder. "Stop fuckin' playing and get the hell up… Ashley! Now that black out shit is getting played," he pushed her again, this time more forceful. Her limp body fell forward and the collision of her head against the dashboard sounded off an unnerving thud. When he noticed the stream of blood coming from the side of her head, it alarmed him, "Girl, what the fuck?"

He pushed her upright and began to softly pat her on her cheek. "Ashley… Ashley… Wake your dumb ass up. Ashley…"

****

Darkness.

"I knew he was gonna do it to you, child. I knew it."

"Momma," Ashley called out to her mother's voice. She couldn't see a thing as she was surrounded by darkness. She couldn't even see her own body. All she could feel was the coldness against her body from wherever she blindly stood. She could hear light whispers surrounding her as the voices intertwined themselves with the darkness. "Girl, why'd you let him do this to you?" she heard the hurt in her mother's strained voice. "I told you he was gonna do this to you!"

"Momma, what he do? Where are you," she asked frantically. "I can't see anything. Where am I? What happened, Momma? What happened to me?"

"That mother fucker," was the sound of her brother, Dexter's voice.

"Dexter?"

"You let that bastard put you here, Ashley. Nobody could tell you nothing," said Dexter. "That mother fucker!"

"Dexter, tell me what's going on, please," she cried. "It's so dark, so cold. Please tell me I'm not..."

"You stupid, bitch!" It was Keon's voice.

Fear overcame her at the sound of his voice. She couldn't utter a word. She didn't know where she was, but she figured he put her there.

"You had to fuck things up again. I didn't even hit your stupid ass that damn hard. You don't have to play dead, bitch. I can turn your fantasies into a reality. Come here!" She could feel again, the feeling of his hands clasping around her neck. "This time you die."

"Noooo!" She bolted up from the bed. Her eyes shot open as she was awakened to see a nurse standing at the foot of her bed holding a tablet with a stunned expression. She was lying in bed at the hospital.

"You're awake," said the nurse. "That's great. I'll get Dr. Ramirez."

"Wait! What happened?" she asked as she stroked the top of her head to fell a bandage plastered just above her eyebrow.

"You were in an accident," said the nurse.

"I was?"

"Yes mam," the nurse answered in a deep southern voice as she nodded. "You bumped your head pretty hard. You had your husband quite terrified when he brought you in."

"My hu..." she stopped herself. She was trying to put the events leading up to her lost of consciousness together as best as she could, but her splitting headache wasn't giving her any relief whatsoever. She slowly eased backwards onto her pillow and began caressing the spot of her forehead that was bandaged. "How long was I out?"

"Just a few hours, hun."

"Oh," she answered as a sharp stroke of pain moved through her head. "Mam, please tell me you have some type of pain reliever."

"I'll get something for that headache of yours in a few shakes. Why I know the pain has to be excruciating. By the way, what's a smart young lady like you doing riding around without wearing a seatbelt anyhow?"

She figured that must've been the cause of her injuries according to Keon, his explanation to the hospital—some type of a car accident. She just shrugged her shoulders to the old nurse, not disputing anything she'd been told. Ashley began to recall the flurry of punches Keon threw at her before smashing her skull into the window, and she couldn't remember anything else after that. She expected him to try to harm her some kind of way because she couldn't provide him with what he wanted, but that didn't make what he did right.

"Here you go, sweetheart." The nursed handed her two aspirins and a small cup of water. "I'm heading off to notify Dr. Ramirez that you've finally awakened from your slumber."

Keon laid back in a chair located in the small lobby with his clothes wrinkled from several hours of trying to position himself comfortable. He was nodding in and out of consciousness until he caught a glimpse of Dr. Ramirez pacing down the aisle, almost passing him by. He quickly hopped out of his seat and began tucking his shirt into his pants as he yelled, "Doc! Doc, did she wake up yet?"

Dr. Ramirez quickly ceased her stride and spun around. "You are?" the middle aged Puerto Rican woman with shoulder length graying brown hair asked as she looked through her tablet.

"Keon... Keon Robinson."

"Oh, yes, Mr. Robinson. You and ahhh—your wife were in that car accident last night."

"Yeah," he answered with a nervous grin.

"I haven't received any further updates about Ms. Parker's status, but when I do you will be notified. Oh, and there's no restriction on visitation. You could sit in the room with her. The chairs are far more comfortable."

"Nah, nah, I don't like to see her like that," he nodded.

"Her injuries weren't too severe," Doctor Ramirez added. "Some bumps and bruises and a mild concussion."

"Yeah, I always tell her about wearing that damn seatbelt. She don't ever listen, though. And then some asshole came right out of nowhere–almost sideswiped the shit out of us, doc."

"Hmmm," she looked over her tablet. "With the injuries she sustained, it's amazing she didn't fly through the windshield—with her not wearing her seatbelt and all."

"Yeah, you're right, doc," Keon agreed with a bit of a frown. He was suspicious the doctor was letting on to something else. There was a brief, uncomfortable pause between the two.

"Well, I've reached out to Ms. Parker's family to notify them that she's here."

"What the hell did you do that for, Doc? I'm her family."

"Well, we couldn't locate you on any of Ms. Parker's files as a point of contact even though you claimed to be married."

"Common law, Doc, you know that's still a thing around these parts."

"Not so much in this state, Mr. Robinson. Besides, legally we have to follow hospital protocol." She took a deep breath and added, "And with all due respect Mr. Robinson, I do have my reservations about the entire incident."

"Reservations?" Keon said, "About the incident? What? You calling me a liar, Doc?"

"No, Mr. Robinson, I'm not making any accusations whatsoever. I just have my reservations. Now, if you'd prefer that I notify the authorities to discuss the details of the incident instead of the family members Ms. Parker has listed on file, I could oblige."

"Nah, Doc, you've done enough." Keon said.

"Alrighty." The doctor shrugged her shoulders then walked off.

Before Dr. Ramirez could get two steps away from Keon, she was approached by Ashley's nurse. Keon overheard the nurse advising the doctor that Ashley had awaken, and Dr. Ramirez swiftly followed the nurse to Ashley's room. This worried him because he was unsure if Ashley was going to go along with his story or not. He had enough problems to concern himself with than to be worrying about some cops questioning him about some type of domestic assault. He knew Ashley wasn't crazy enough to rat him out, but he wasn't one hundred percent sure of her loyalty after the way he mangled her around in the car.

As he stood in the hall, his eyes didn't leave Ashley's room door. When Dr. Ramirez finally exited the room with the nurse, he hustled back into the lobby until they left the area. He, then, walked down to her room door, stormed in and rushed to her bed, "Alright, what did you tell that fucking wetback, doctor?"

"I didn't tell her anything," Ashley nervously answered, startled by his chaotic entrance.

"Um hmm, um hmm," he pointed towards her and in a lowered but commanding tone he said, "When your damn momma come up here, you better tell her you weren't wearing your damn seatbelt. It ain't gonna be a good thing if they come running up in my face today. I won't hold shit back on their asses."

"Who called momma?" she asked.

"Your damn doctor did, that's who!"

"Why?"

"I don't fuckin' know. She just did," he said, "With her nosey ass. You sure you didn't elaborate on anything with that woman?"

"No, I didn't. I just went along with what the nurse said you told them."

Keon nodded as he raked his fingers through his hair, still uptight, but slowly calming down. He walked over to the window and gazed down at the parking lot. The sky was dark orange from the rising sun.

"I ain't got no time for no extra shit. You passing out in that car set me back some serious time. Time I needed to fix this shit."

She took a deep sigh and lowered her head, not saying a word. She simply listened as he blamed all his misfortunes on her.

"It fucking looks like Porkchop done skipped town on a nigga," he said as he whipped around to face her. He threw his hands up in the air and added, "After all the shit I've done for that nigga—all the shit I've done for his ass. He was the last nigga I ever thought would do me like this."

"He hasn't called you?"

"Are you listening to any fucking thing I'm saying," he replied. "No. Hell no, he ain't called me—that motherfucker! I told him I had a fucking plan, but no, this nigga done went dark—his black ass."

There was a knock at the door. It captured their attention as the door sprang opened and Rose eased in. However, complete chaos broke out as Dexter zipped right in from behind his mother and yelled, "You!" His gaze was set on Keon as he dashed across the room and nailed Keon with a right jab that forced them both onto the floor. The two began to tussle as Dexter fought like a man possessed. Rose and Ashley both screamed for the two to stop battling as a couple of male nurses rushed into the room to separate the men.

"You son of a bitch," yelled Dexter as he was forced towards the entrance by one of the nurses.

"Rose, you better get that boy of yours," Keon said as he wiped a splattering of blood from the corner of his lips. He was totally out of breath as the young man was a little too much to handle than he originally imagined.

"Knock it off, Dexter" Rose demanded.

All Ashley could do was watch from her bed. She was happy to see her brother get the best of Keon, but she didn't want him to get hurt or sent to jail.

One of the nurses yelled, "Okay, you both are gonna have to leave the premises. This is a hospital not a wrestling arena."

"Oh he can stay," Keon said as he walked towards the door. He casted an angry glance at Ashley and added, "I'm going downstairs to get into my car. I'm leaving in thirty minutes."

Ashley didn't say a word but bowed her head when her mother faced her with a stern look as she waited for her to respond to Keon, however there wasn't a response.

"Tough guy," Keon looked towards Dexter. "We'll get up. We'll get up."

"Anytime, Negro, anytime," Dexter answered repeatedly nodding, anxious to get his hands on him again.

"Chill out, dude," said the nurse as he pushed Dexter backwards a bit to allow Keon to walk by to prevent the two from tangling again.

"I got plenty more helpings for you—believe that," Dexter emphasized.

Keon responded with a chuckle as he slowly exited the room. The staff that had entered the room to control the ruckus exited behind him. Dexter was so upset he punched into wall.

"If you want to go run behind him, you won't be getting an escort from me," said Rose.

"What are you talking about, Ma?"

"A car accident, Ashley, really?" she said. "We passed right by his car on the way in, and there was no damage on that car that wasn't there already. What kind of a fool do you take us for? And to make matters worse, that man didn't have a mark on him until Dexter put hands on him."

"Ma, I got hurt by him trying to avoid the accident," she lied while shaking her head closing her eyes, already fed up with discussing the situation. "I wasn't wearing my seatbelt, Ma."

"Oh my flippin' God," Dexter barked. "This crap is useless with her, Ma. She's protecting this clown once again. She's doing it again."

"Dexter, please," begged Ashley.

"Look, I'm out of here." He pointed at her and warned, "You can let that clown beat your goddamn brains out if you want to—I'm done with it."

"Dexter!" Rose interjected.

"What, Ma? Why should we care? She doesn't." He slammed the door shut behind himself, angrily leaving the room.

Their focus rested on the door that Dexter had just stormed through. Neither knew what to say to each other, but they both had a lot churning on the inside. They just didn't know how to say it. Ashley wanted to reassure her younger brother and her mother that she had everything under control, despite the fact that she really didn't. Rose, simply wanted peace and happiness for all her children, and she wanted to demand Ashley stay away from Keon as long as eternity.

Rose sat on the edge of her daughter's bed. "He put you on the clock. What are you going to do child?"

There wasn't an immediate response from Ashley as the room stood awkwardly silent for a couple minutes. Rose's attention never left her daughter, despite Ashley never looking back at her. Instead, her focus just bounced from the edge of the bed and from wall to wall during the silence.

"I gotta do what I have to do, Ma," Ashley finally responded as she began to ease out of the bed.

"Child, where are you going?"

"I'm about to catch Keon before he leaves," she said as she walked towards the chair, grabbed her jeans, and slid them on.

"What?" Rose hopped off of the bed and moved towards her. "After all of this, you're really considering leaving with this man?"

"After all of what, Ma?" Ashley asked. She looked directly at her mother and explained, "He didn't touch me. I know it seems hard for you to believe, but the story is true."

"And you expect me to believe that?"

"You have no choice."

Her mother had no answers as she helplessly watched Ashley slip on her shirt and gingerly creep towards the door. Suddenly, she stopped. "I told you back at the house before I left, I got this, Ma."

"Ashley, don't..." Before she could complete her sentence, Ashley left the room. Tears began to roll down her cheeks because once again, she wasn't sure if she'd ever see her daughter living and breathing again. It infuriated her to be so helpless, but she knew her daughter to be bullheaded just like her father was. She was destined to do things her way and her way only.

Keon examined the corner of his mouth in the rearview mirror. There was only a light bruise there as a result of one of Dexter's jabs slipping through. The bleeding had stopped, but his desire for revenge was still burning fiercely. He was determined for a rematch once he got his issues with Max resolved. He knew the young buck would be a challenge straight up due to his fighting skills, but there was nothing straight up about his plans for vengeance. Next time he saw him, he would sneak him and make sure he'd regret the day he ever laid a finger on him.

As he repositioned his mirror, he caught a glimpse of Ashley walking out of the hospital, scanning the parking lot for the car. He tapped the horn a couple of times to get her attention. As she slowly began her trek to the vehicle, he said to himself, "Humph, your ass know what's good for you, don't you?"

She eased into the car. He turned to her with a smug look on his face. "I knew you weren't dumber than you look." She bowed her head as he went on to say, "That brother of yours." He began wagging his finger towards her face, "I promise you I'm gonna fuck him up real good when I get the chance—I promise you that. Ain't no nigga gonna get off with handling me that kind a way and not pay for it."

She wanted to smile, but she wasn't crazy enough to do so. She knew it was killing him that he couldn't get back at Dexter, and with him feeling that way, it gave her a sense of redemption. Dexter was able to do some things in that hospital room she had been longing to do for a very long time. However, he didn't he didn't do as much as she'd desired.

****

They didn't go home immediately as they drove around town for hours until dark. Keon cruised around and waited outside Porkchop's mother's house for a while, hoping to catch his homeboy to question him about why he wasn't answering his calls or texts. To his displeasure, there wasn't any activity there, and the residence appeared to be completely abandoned. He then drove around all the places he'd known Angelo to frequent, including all of his baby mother's cribs, and came up with absolutely nothing. It was like his former crew had dissolved into thin air, leaving him as the sole person to handle their debt with Max.

The ride home was a quiet one as neither said a word to the other. Ashley had absolutely nothing to say to him. Sitting in his presence after what was by far the most brutal attack he had ever made against her, she couldn't help but feel foolish. It sickened her that she left her mom behind at the hospital after she pleaded for her to come back home with her. Her family wasn't stupid. She knew they could tell what really happened, and it embarrassed her. She was so ashamed of herself for running back behind him, but she knew if she didn't, it would only be a matter of time before Keon would show up at her mother's doorstep, at first begging for her to come back to him. If she resisted, he would find some way to threaten her or her family. It was getting to the point that she couldn't underestimate his evil, and she couldn't put the burden of her tumultuous relationship on her family.

He circled around their apartment complex several times before backing the car into a space across from their building. She could tell the paranoia of possibly being watched was getting to him. He was right to worry just from the couple of times she saw Max's men on her own. His eyes bounced from one end of the community to the next in search for anything suspicious in the parking lot. Ashley carried on with her own inspections, also. If someone was waiting or following them, it wasn't the men she'd seen previously.

"Look," he said as he turned off the car. "If I don't get Max his money back to him by tomorrow, we're probably gonna have to leave town for a little while. I'm letting you know ahead of time."

His revelation unnerved her. It just made her more hopeful that he would straighten out whatever he had going on with the gangster known as Max because the last thing she wanted was to be in some foreign place with him.

As they headed upstairs to their apartment, halfway up the steps, Keon stopped in his tracks. "You see that shit," he asked pointing towards their apartment door.

"What?" she asked as she tried to look around him.

"There's a box in front of our door." He nervously looked around the dimly lit corridor to see if anyone was watching them or hiding out in the shadows.

As he continued up the stairs, Ashley followed closely behind. There was a small cardboard box that was sealed with electrical tape sitting in front of their door. They cautiously crept towards the door and stood over the box.

Keon scratched his head as he took a couple of minutes to contemplate what the contents of the box could be. He looked around again, suspicious they were being watched. "Pick it up," he said.

"What?" Ashley answered. She was just as nervous as him. She had no idea why he wanted her to pick up the box.

"It may be my money. Angelo's scary ass may have left it here." Keon now smirking, "His bitch ass is too scared to face me and hand me my shit like a real man, knowing he'd get a fine tuned taste of these hands."

"Or it could be something else... like a bomb."

"Shut the hell up," Keon's smirk quickly disappeared and transformed into an angry scowl. "That nigga ain't gonna leave no damn bomb at the front door. You see how stupid you sound?"

"How do you know it's from him?"

Keon sucked his teeth as he wondered why he was even consulting with her about anything, let alone discussing with her about what was in the box. He considered her clueless about how things were done in the world he was conducting business in. He slowly stretched his leg out and gently kicked the box. Ashley was ready to run on contact, but she was promptly relieved when nothing happened after Keon's contact with the package.

"Pick it up," Keon said. "If it was a bomb, the shit would've blown my fuckin' foot off."

Ashley didn't budge. She just gazed at the box, totally ignoring his request as he scowled her way. Her nerves were wrecked as she knew he wasn't going to rest until she grabbed the package.

"Did you hear me? Pick the motherfucker up."

Stunned, she couldn't believe he was trying to make her pick up a box that only God and whomever left it there knew what was in it. He wasn't man enough to grab the package himself. Instead, he was asking her to put her life at risk by picking it up, knowing good and well whatever it was, it wasn't left for her.

"You want some more of what I gave you yesterday or something?" He cracked his knuckles. "I ain't got no problems hooking you up with some more of it."

She shook her head and placed her focus back on the box. It was going to be hell to pay if she didn't pick it up as he asked. She took a deep breath as she carefully placed her hands on the side of the small package. Trembling, she held it as far away from herself as she possibly could while lifting it.

Keon nervously backed away. "Don't put that motherfucker that close to me."

Before attempting to open the door, he looked around to see if anyone was watching them. He then unlocked the door, pushed it open and told her to go in. Ashley slowly walked in with the box. In her mind it was a bomb, and if she made the wrong move it would blow her up into smithereens. Keon closed the door behind them as Ashley walked to kitchen table and gently sat the box on top of it. She'd already begun perspiring under her arms and forehead in the matter of seconds.

Keon rushed to the kitchen drawer and grabbed a box cutter. They stood at the table with their eyes glued on the package. He was flicking the blade in and out as he considered making her do the honors of slicing it open.

"What do you think it is?" she asked.

"Hell if I know," he answered. "It needs to be my fucking money. That's actually what I think it is. It's probably not all of it, though. Angelo ass must've dropped it off. It ain't gonna save him from this ass whoopin' I got planned for him, though. He can duck and dodge all he wants. It don't matter because he's getting his ass beat— that's a fuckin' fact!"

They continued to ponder over the box quietly for a good five minutes before Keon stepped forward and placed the razor at the top seam of the box. He gave Ashley a quick stare as she took two steps backwards. He then swiped the razor across the center of the box along the middle of the tape and then sliced it along the sides. He gave Ashley one more glance before opening the flaps of the box. There was something inside the black garbage bags that were stuffed inside of it, appearing somewhat the size of a butterball turkey. He ripped the bag from around the object and immediately fell backwards to the floor once his eyes laid witness to Porkchop's bloody, severed head with his eyes carved out. Ashley immediately fell to the floor and threw up.

"Porkchop... Porkchop," Keon cried. He jumped back to his feet, his entire body trembling as he hovered over the box in utter disbelief. "Porkchop, they did this to you, nigga! Oh God, they fucked you up, man. These niggas fucked you up!" He looked towards Ashley with a stray tear sliding down his face and yelled, "They fucked my nigga up... Oh God!"

As she wiped her mouth and stared up at him from the floor, she was unfamiliar with the expression of fear on him. The message Max sent him knocked him down to size, and it put him on notice that he wasn't playing. She then looked towards the box, mystified that someone could butcher another human being the way they did Porkchop. She could only imagine the terrible things they had planned for Keon, and or anyone they thought was close to him. She wanted no parts of it, but she was stuck smack dab in the middle of it.

Several hours had passed, and Keon sat at the table, lost in a trance with the box that he'd now closed the flaps on so he could no longer see the mangled face of his best soldier. After cleaning up the mess she made on the floor,

Ashley sat idle on the edge of the couch waiting for him to do or say something besides repeating himself about how he couldn't believe what they did do his friend.

Suddenly, he popped up from his chair with a deranged expression and stomped into the bedroom. She could hear him ransacking the room for a few minutes until things got completely quiet again. When he returned to the living room, he was carrying a big, black gun in his hand. His nose flared from his intensely exhaling. She didn't even know he kept a firearm in the home.

He held the gun up, wagged it around and said, "These motherfuckers think I'm a joke. I ain't going out like no sucka." he looked towards her and added, "You understand that?"

She gave him a soft nod, thinking that he'd finally lost it. He had gone from fearful to delirious. The sight of him with a gun and the crazy expression he wore on his face while toting it scared the daylights out of her.

"This nigga Angelo need to turn up. He need to turn up now." He stuffed the weapon in the small of his back and demanded, "Let's roll. We got shit to do."

Her mouth dropped. Why he thought it would be a good idea to bring her into this situation with people getting their heads chopped off was beyond her rationale. He walked to the table, grabbed the box with Porkchop's head stuffed in it and marched to the door. She hadn't moved an inch.

He looked at her like she was crazy. "What the hell? You gonna sit there all night, or are you gonna move your ass? I told you we got shit to do."

She begrudgingly followed him out of the apartment and down to the car. Prior to leaving the apartment complex, he stopped at the garbage compactor at the front entrance. Before he stuffed Porkchop's boxed up remains in the machine, he looked down at it and promised, "You won't die in vain, my nigga. You won't die in vain."

****

Keon spent most of the day bouncing across town scoping out the residences of Angelo's assortment of baby mothers, and there were no signs of Angelo at any spot. As he advised Porkchop days ago, he figured Angelo would rest his head with the woman he had the most children with and that was Tasha. Angelo had been locked up by her several times in the past for not paying his child support, and it was common knowledge that he wanted to stay in good terms with her to prevent getting locked up again. Besides, he'd always referred to Tasha as his main chick, and the amount of kids he had with her supported that claim.

He cruised around the parking lot of Tasha's apartment complex several times throughout the day but had yet to actually knock on her door to ask her if she knew where Angelo was. After receiving Max's deadly message, he knew it was time to turn things up a notch.

He backed his car into a parking space on the side of the building's entrance that had very little lighting due to the street light being knocked out. The complex consisted of mostly section eight housing, but it was a development where mostly older people resided so it was literally a ghost town at night. When he took a moment to really think about it, the spot was the perfect place for someone in Angelo's situation to be hiding.

"When I'm up in that motherfucker, I need you to be down here with your fucking eyes peeled," he said to Ashley as he turned off the engine. "I don't need you to be falling asleep or your mind wandering, thinking about whatever fucked up fantasy your mind be channeling when you're by your goddamn self. I need you to be watching for shit. If you see that nigga Angelo anywhere in damn sight while I'm up there, I don't give a hot damn if you wake up this whole fuckin' complex, you blow the shit out of the horn so I can get his ass."

He waited for a response, but she didn't give him one. She was too worried about the possibility of getting tied up in some type of homicidal mess now that he was toting a gun around and looking for blood. She didn't want to be an accessory to anyone's murder. Keon was dangling on the deep end, and he was spiraling out of control.

"You fuckin' heard what I said, didn't ya?"

She gave him a nod.

"Then acknowledge what the fuck I'm saying—shit! I don't need your ass to be acting retarded on me now. This shit is real, goddamn it."

He hopped out of the car and headed towards the building's entrance. He didn't leave her sight until he disappeared into the building's stairwell. He climbed up the metal steps with much haste and rage. His search for Angelo, and Max's owed money was bearing down on him immensely. He knew if he came up empty here he would have no choice but to skip town before Max tracked him down.

He crept up to Angelo's baby mother's door and quietly stood in front of it. Putting his ear against the door, he could faintly hear some music. Finally, he knocked.

"Who is it?" a female voice yelled.

"Is Angelo home?"

"Who?"

"Angelo. Is Angelo home?"

After a few moments the music ceased, and he could hear footsteps moving towards the door. The woman on the other side of the door said, "Angelo? Angelo don't live here? You got the wrong building."

"Tasha, this here is Keon. I don't have time for the bullshit. I need to talk to Angelo."

There was more silence and after a few seconds she said, "Keon?"

"Yeah, Keon, he answered. "You know who this is."

She cracked the door open and peaked through the opening. His head was just above the chain lock that she kept attached to the door. "Keon, you know Angelo don't live here. Besides, I ain't hear shit from him in weeks."

Keon attempted to look over her head to get a glimpse of the inside of the apartment as she rambled on with what he suspected to be all lies. "Damn, Tasha, I thought we went way back. You scared to open the door for a nigga?"

"Keon, you know it's late—nothing personal."

"Nothing personal for you and me, Tasha, but your man, that's another thing. I really need to holla at his ass, Tasha. He got us all tied up in some real serious shit."

"What kind of shit."

"Some serious shit! That's all you need to know," he chuckled then added, "So me and him need to vibe together and figure out how we're gonna work this shit out."

"Well, if I see him, I'll let him know that you're looking for him," she obliged as she attempted to close the door.

Keon slipped his arm through the door. "Nah, Tasha, I need to see that nigga right now."

"Keon, what the fu…" she complained as Keon shoved the door open, snapping the chain latch.

"You just broke my shit. You're paying for that, damn it."

Keon walked into the apartment and whipped out his gun. Her eyes bolted wide open as she took a few steps backwards when she saw the firearm. "Keon, what the hell are you barging up in here with a gun for? Nigga, is you crazy?"

"The kids sleep?" he asked, completely ignoring her question as his eyes scanned every inch of the walls around the living room.

"They at my mommas," she shouted angrily. "Keon, what the hell are you trying to prove, man?"

"That sounds about right," he mumbled to himself as he focused on the hall where the bedrooms were located. "Where the nigga at, Tasha? You know we go back further than you and him. I expect more out of you than for you to be hiding and protecting this lame ass nigga."

"I told you I ain't see him in weeks."

"Don't lie to me, bitch." He pointed the gun at her. "I know you know where the fuck he is."

"Keon, you better get that gun out of my fuckin' face. I know that much, nigga." Tasha was about five feet tall, wearing a pink robe and pink rollers to match.

He took a hard sniff of air and asked, "When you started smoking?"

"I always smoked. How else is a bitch gonna stay relaxed with a sorry nigga and a shitload of kids?"

"Yeah, right," he signaled her with his gun to go to the bedroom area. "Lead the fuckin' way."

"Keon, you can't be doing this," she said as she began leading him down the hallway to the bedrooms.

"I can do whatever the fuck I want as long as that nigga got my fucking money. Now walk slowly to the back. I'm gonna need for you to open them doors nice and slow so I can see for myself if that nigga's here or not. I can't believe shit that you say right about now.

Ashley feared the worst of what Keon could be doing in the building totting around that gun with fear in his heart and a whole bunch of hatred to go with it. She wanted to be brave enough to just jump in the driver side seat and take off without him, but the thought of him catching up to her was the one thing that always plagued her mind, not the fact there could be a possibility that he wouldn't be able to catch up to her. She knew she should've listened to her mother and returned home to her.

From the woods, she noticed a slender man wearing a dark jogging outfit and a hoodie covering his head run up to the same entrance that Keon entered. She couldn't make out if the man was Angelo or not, but he was certainly tall and lanky like him. She considered blowing the horn to alert Keon as he requested, but she wasn't certain if the man was him or not.

Tasha pushed opened the door to the master bedroom, threw her hands in the air and said, "See, I told you he wasn't here. His ass ain't been around in weeks, nigga."

Keon stepped into the room and carefully looked around. He walked to the closet and swung open the door. There was nothing but clothes and mounds of junk stuffed inside from the floor to the ceiling. He took a deep breath and stuffed his gun in the small of his back before punching the wall in fury. Tasha's place was his last hope at finding Angelo and him not being there took everything out of him.

"You got a lot of nerve, Keon, coming into my fucking house with a gun and pointing it all in my face and shit. As much child support that nigga owe me, you think I would be protecting his ass?" she asked as she walked down the hallway towards the living room.

"Damn, Tasha, that's my bad," he said with his head hanging as he followed her down the hall.

"You damn right, it's your bad. A bitch in here trying to get her beauty sleep and you're barging in here worrying me about some sorry ass Angelo!"

The front door swung open. "Tasha, I'm back. Damn store fresh out of rolling papers," Angelo said as he swiped his hoddie from his head and walked into the home with his back turned to Keon and Tasha.

Their mouths were wide opened by the sight of him. Keon couldn't believe his eyes.

"Lying bitch," Keon said.

Angelo turned around to see a red hot Keon standing across the room. It was as if he seen a ghost as he stumbled backwards towards the front door. "Keon... the fuck, man?"

"What's up, nigga?" Keon's high yellow face was redder than a bottle of hot sauce. "Glad you remembered my fuckin' name. Too bad you couldn't remember my fucking phone number."

"Man, I... I...," Angelo couldn't stop stumbling over his words as he slowly began to inch towards the door. Before Keon could make his move on him, Angelo snatched the bookshelf from the wall beside the front door and shoved it to the floor in front of him. He then grabbed the door handle and charged out of the apartment. Upset that she lied to him about everything, Keon shoved Tasha to the floor but he ended up falling over the bookshelf trying to get at Angelo. He quickly made his way to his feet and through the apartment door, hot on Angelo's trail.

Angelo skipped down the stairs to the ground floor as Keon hopped down the steps right behind him. As Ashley waited patiently in the car, she noticed the men running from the apartment building and into the woods. It was then that she realized the man in the dark clothing was indeed Angelo. The first thing she thought about was what Keon would do to her for not warning him when she first saw him entering the building if he didn't catch up to him.

When Keon got close enough to Angelo, he pulled out his gun and threw the pistol directly at the back of his head. Angelo gasped and fell face forward onto the ground. Keon quickly stomped on him in the small of his back causing Angelo to bellow in pain.

"Motherfucker!" Keon yelled, seriously out of breath as he scooped up his pistol. Angelo began pleading with Keon, begging him not to hurt him as he began crawling on all fours away from him. Keon dove down on his back with his knee and smashed him in the back of his head with the butt of the pistol. He hopped up and said, "You turn your fucking ass over! If your ass try to run I'm putting two in you without a second thought, you bitch ass nigga."

"Keon, brotha… I can explain."

"I don't wanna hear that brother shit. I told you to turn your bitch ass over!"

Angelo rolled over frantically and unable to breathe steadily. "Keon, wait, man. A nigga fucked up," he pleaded. "I know you're pissed off at me, man. I'm pissed off at me, cuz."

"Me being pissed off at you is a fuckin' understatement right now, nigga." Keon dropped onto

Angelo's chest, cradling him. He stuffed his gun in the small of his back and began pounding Angelo in his face with his bare knuckles. Angelo hollered in pain as his face began to get scarred up and bloodied. "Where's my fuckin' money, nigga? Where is it?"

"Keon... stop, man... stop," he pleaded between punches. "It's not... it's not... what you think... I didn't try to screw you over, man."

Keon pulled back from his onslaught on his weakened prey and looked down at his battered face. The moonlight gave him just enough light to see his handy work, yet he wasn't actually satisfied with the beating so far. "Really, nigga? You ain't try to screw me over? Then what the fuck you call it? You got another name for it?"

"My cousin....Bam...," he said while coughing up blood. "He said he could make some major moves with the cash—major moves! Four times what we had already made off the work we got from Max. He had this partner with really good connections."

"Bam, huh?" he shook his head. He was familiar with Bam and knew him as a bullshitter—always a lot of talk and promises but never any legitimate actions. "So what the fuck happened, nigga?"

There was a pause. Angelo sighed as tears began to flow down his beaten face. "Man…"

"You got fucked, nigga. Your punk ass cousin scammed you out of the goddamn money. My money! You ain't gotta say shit!" Keon backhanded him. "Your stupid ass got us all fucked!"

"Keon, man, wait..man." he cried. "I've been all around town looking for them niggas—trying to get the money back. I was just thinking in the best interests of us, man—the crew. You gotta believe me, man. Brotha!"

"Best interests, huh?" Keon smashed him in his face with a three punch combo and then spit in his face. Angelo didn't make any efforts to fight back. He just helplessly took his pounding.

"Chill man, please," he pleaded while crying like a baby. "I…I know… I fucked… I fucked up."

Keon backed off with his onslaught. "You were thinking in the best interests of Porkchop? You got my nigga head chopped off. So was that in his best interests, nigga? The best interests of your brothers, bitch?"

"Porkchop? Wait, what? What they do? They killed Porkchop?"

"Yeah, nigga they cut my nigga head off and sent the shit to me in a box like it was some priority mail or some shit." Keon hopped up off of him and jumped to his feet. "He dead over your dumb shit, nigga—your dumb shit."

Once Keon climbed to his feet, Angelo sat up on his behind. His face was covered in bruises and blood, but he was relieved that Keon had stopped the attack. He said, "We gotta get the fuck outta here, man. Max ain't gonna let this shit ride if we can't get him his money. We're good as dead if we stick around."

"That I do agree with you on, partna. But there ain't no we in the shit, nigga," Keon said as he removed his gun from the small of his back. Angelo eyes shot open.

Ashley scoured the wooded area where Keon chased the man she believed to be Angelo. She jumped when she heard what sounded like several loud gun shots. Her entire body shook fearfully as she wondered what had happed in those dark woods. Did Keon shoot Angelo or did Angelo shoot Keon? She didn't know what to think. She quickly realized that Keon was no one's victim when she spotted him calmly walking away from the woods and towards the car moments after the gunfire.

Keon jumped into the car. He was heavily breathing, and his hands trembled as he placed them on the steering wheel. After a few moments of silence he said. "I thought I told you to blow the fucking horn when you saw that motherfucker."

"I didn't know it was him," she said softly. She feared he had just killed Angelo in those woods, and she didn't want to be his second kill for the night.

He turned his head towards her, still breathing ferociously. "What the fuck do you know?" She didn't answer him as he just sat and stared at her for a couple of minutes anticipating a reply. Then, he started the car and began making his way out of the apartment complex. After driving a few miles he pulled over to the side of the road. He slipped out his phone and dialed. When he heard the man on the other end of the phone answer, he said to him, "I'm gonna need that thing we talked about."

The low, raspy voice answered back, "Say no more. You know where to be."

Keon ended the call, took a deep breath and looked over to Ashley. "We're gonna have to relocate for a little while."

A stroke of fear drilled down her spine when he mentioned relocating. She didn't want to be with him where they currently resided, let alone being on the run with him to God knows where. She wanted to just tell him no—just no, better yet hell no, but she was just too scared. Her mind couldn't stay in one place because she didn't have a clue as to what was about to happened next. Keon had most likely killed someone, and now he was talking about leaving town, and she wasn't even sure if she was next on his kill list or not.

Keon drove them to a Wal-Mart that was about twenty miles away from their home. He didn't say a word the entire drive. When he initially arrived at the supermarket, he drove around the entire parking lot at least six times before he finally decided on a spot that wasn't too far from the primary entrance. It was late but this particular Wal-Mart was near a couple of college campuses so it was still packed with people.

Keon shut off the car and ordered, "You follow close and don't wander off any fucking where, you understand?"

She gave him a nod, and they exited the vehicle. Keon was so nervous, he couldn't mask his trembling hands and the twitching of his head. When they entered the store, he frequently looked right to left, suspicious of everyone they approached and walked by.

Ashley followed him to the back of the store as Keon carefully and slowly looked down each aisle, obviously looking for something or someone. Once he moved to the sporting goods aisle, they noticed a man in the middle of the aisle observing the bicycles that were hanging from the racks. Keon stopped his stride and stood still for a couple of seconds. The man wore a dark brown Ivy cap and a black leather jacket. He motioned Ashley to remain where she stood as he cautiously approached the middle aged gentleman.

Keon stood side by side with the guy and looked up at the bikes along with him before speaking. "A desperate man can get but so far on only two set of wheels."

The man turned to him and said, "Let's go—quickly!" The man took off towards the back of the store.

Keon waved to Ashley to follow them as they headed off into the back. They walked to a fire exit that didn't sound off when the man opened the door. There was a box truck that had its engine running and was parked right next to the door. The man slid the back door upwards and motioned Keon and Ashley to hop into the back of the truck. The man closed them in and looked around to make sure no one was watching them. He then hopped into the passenger side of the truck and the truck took off.

The ride was a bumpy one for the couple as they tried to stay in one place with the crates they sat on. The only light they had was a dim red bulb that hung from the front wall of the truck. Ashley had no idea where they were headed. She was exhausted from the lack of sleep, and she was frightened by not knowing where they were headed. She looked toward Keon who wore an angry scowl on his face as he looked straight ahead at the truck's back door.

"Don't worry. When we get to where we're going you're gonna love it. New place, new surroundings—a brand new start. We could probably even get started on making a little family."

The thought of starting a family with Keon at this stage of their relationship made her want to gag. She looked up at him for a moment wondering if he made the comments as a joke, but his face was straight and serious. She looked towards the floor and thought that there was no way she'd have his baby after all that he'd put her through, even if she had to perform an abortion on herself somehow.

"We wouldn't have to be doing this if you had gotten that fucking money from your momma," he added.

There it was—the real Keon. She knew he'd find some way to blame all of his misfortunes on her. She knew it would come out at some point.

The speed of the truck slowed down. They heard what appeared to be a mechanical door, similar to a home garage door opening but louder. They felt as though they were driving into some type of building as they could hear men just outside of the truck giving the driver instructions as to where to park.

The truck stopped and after a couple seconds of being parked idle, the engine shut down. The doors on both sides of the truck opened and closed from the front of the vehicle. After a few moments of silence, there was banging on the back door of the truck that sounded like it was coming from a metal pipe. They both rose from their respective spots on their crates and crept towards the front of the vehicle. The door slid upwards, and a tall, stocky build man with a short afro and an open sports jacket stood behind two heavy set balled men dressed in two piece suits.

The man removed the short, stub cigar from his mouth and spoke, "You must like it in that motherfucker—you ain't trying to get out."

"Big Percy!" Keon yelled out with a huge smile on his face.

He chuckled and pointed at Keon. "You know better than to call me that shit, ya jackass. You family, but I'll still kick your scrawny little ass. Maybe even do you worst than what Max is aiming to do to you."

"Damn, BP," Keon laughed. "You'll do me like that?" He waved to Ashley to follow him. "Just because your little cuz called you by your goddamn government?"

Keon hopped off the tailgate of the truck, leaving Ashley to struggle to get down on her own.

"I'll do that and a whole lot more, motherfucker," he laughed and embraced Keon with a huge hug. "You dumbass! You got your ass in some brand new dumb shit, I see."

They were in an old body shop. An assortment of cars were scattered throughout the garage—some with their hoods and doors opened, others freshly painted and tricked out, and a few completely hidden under car covers. BP wrapped his arm around the back of his cousin's neck and guided him to his office at the rear of the garage. BP's goons stayed behind as Ashley followed behind the men.

Just before opening the door to his office, BP looked back at Ashley with a bit of a frown. "'Sup, Ashley."

"Hi, how are you BP?"

"Just fine, sweetheart—never better actually. Look here, I gotta talk business with your man for a few. He'll be back in a minute. Have a seat," he said, pointing to the brown sofa just outside his office door.

She took one glance at the old, rugged chair and opted to remain standing with her arms folded. Keon followed BP into the office and shut the door behind himself.

The office was small with an old, shabby desk and a flashy sixty inch high definition plastered on the wall that seemed somewhat out of place with all the other old furniture. There was a huge, tinted window that provided the office a view to the garage area allowing BP to see everything going on in workplace but leaving the work area blinded to him.

While staring at Ashley through the window, BP suggested, "You know it's a lot easier to make this thing work travelling solo."

Keon looked back at Ashley and chuckled, "Yeah, but what the fuck would she do without me?"

"She'd probably live, motherfucker," he laughed.

"Well, ain't nobody dying tonight—especially not my black ass."

"You sure about that nigga?"

"Fuck yeah!"

BP shook his head. "Boy, I told you about doing business with them fuck-boys. You could've been doing business with me, doing organized, thorough business—the type of shit people ain't thinking about and not in the news every goddamn day. But you wanna be a dope boy—a fuckin' dope boy—like it's nineteen ninety-five or some shit." BP took a seat in his executive chair behind the desk. "Fuck you wanna be, Nino Brown?"

"Look, man, I ain't got time for all these lectures and shit. I ain't down with that fucking night club shit, and my mind ain't savvy enough for that credit card shit you got going on."

BP hopped up and leaned over his desk. "But you coming over, *needing my shit*, though." BP sat back down. "You know, Key, a nigga out there wasting his time dope selling on the block, ain't got but a limited amount of time before his dopey ass ends up in some white man's prison doing hard time on his cell block," he chuckled and asked, "Did you even find the nigga that ran off with the money?"

He nodded, instantly furious at the thought of Angelo and the whole ordeal. "Yeah, I found his ass."

"And?"

"I had to put two in him. He got ganked for the dough."

"You're a stupid, nigga, you know that?"

"Yeah, I know."

BP opened the drawer under his desk, pulled out a small, dark satchel and slid it across the desk. Keon grabbed the bag, but he hesitated to do anything else.

"Open the motherfucker," said BP.

Keon unzipped the satchel and pulled out a stack of identification cards and credit cards. A smile arose on his face.

"You know you can't come back here. Not while Max is alive and running these streets. The motherfucker can't stand losing, and he took a loss with your ass. And trust me, it ain't about the money because the bastard got a lot of that. It's the principle. He ain't never gonna let that shit go. Not until your ass is dead."

"Yeah, I know," Keon grinned. "You can always send your dudes to tighten him up for me."

"I'm too old for wars, cousin. I got a family and a good thing going. Besides, if your stupid ass had to have taken me up on my offers and rolled with me, you wouldn't even be in this shit in the first place."

Keon bowed his head and sighed. "Shit, you're right—can't argue that."

"You're family, and this here is the best I can do."
BP rose from his chair and walked around his desk to face his younger cousin. He gave him a pat on his shoulder and said, "Wherever you end up, please stop doing dumb shit."

Keon grinned then raised the satchel in front of him and said, "It's appreciated, cuz. It really is. I fucked up, I know that."

"Yes you did," BP nodded and added, "Now get the fuck out of my place before that son of bitch track you here."

"I gotcha'," Keon headed for the door.

Just before Keon could walk out the door to leave, BP stopped him. "The brown Three Hundred parked right at the garage door has the keys in the ignition and a full tank of gas."

"Thanks, cuz," Keon walked out of the office and approached Ashley. "Come on. Let's get the fuck out of here."

****

The interstate was empty under the night sky, and Keon was coasting down it like a bat out of hell. Although they were on the road for a little over an hour, Keon didn't have a specific destination in mind. All he knew is that he was headed west, as far west as he could go to feel comfortable that he was far enough from Max.

Ashley sat quietly on the passenger side. She didn't want to be with him at the place they called home the past few years, and she definitely didn't want to be with him on the run for what could potentially be forever. On the run for something she had nothing to do with. Ultimately, she felt trapped with no way out.

She was at the point that she was no longer angry at Keon but angrier at herself. She couldn't stand the way she always allowed it, and now, she was allowing him to relocate her against her own inner will. She didn't say a damn thing about it—she simply cowered again. She was so fed up with herself, she just couldn't take anymore. It was at that moment her lips released a formation of words that stunned her own ears.

"Keon, you gotta let me out."

He nearly gasped, turning to face her with his mouth gaping open, believing he was hearing things. "What?"

A tear slid down her face. She realized what she said, and she knew there was no way she could step away from it.

This was her moment to put her foot down. It was going to be now or never. She continued, "This isn't my fight. I don't know what's going on with you and these gangsters, but it doesn't have anything to do with me." She looked towards him and added, "I don't want to be on the run, Keon."

"Oh my fuckin' goodness," he said, switching his focus back and forth from the road and her. "You must be done lost your fucking mind."

She bowed her head. Something in hopeful her heart thought that he may have responded differently, that for once he'd consider how she felt about things again. She looked straight ahead and kept speaking, "I'm tired, Keon. I'm tired of living in fear. I'm tired... I'm tired of being..." She paused as more tears continued their path down her face. She then looked at him and confessed, "I don't want to be with you anymore. Please, let me out."

He began to laugh hysterically. "Oh my God. Out of all the times in the world you could've pulled this shit." He looked over to her and said, "I guess I need to give you what you're asking for, huh?"

She didn't know what he meant by his words—if he was really going to let her out or if he had something sinister in mind. There was complete silence in the car for at least ten minutes. After a few miles down the highway, he yielded his speed as they approached a dimly lit rest area. He drove the car into a parking space at the entrance in front of the restrooms. The spot was abandoned and a bit eerie with the tall trees surrounding it. If he was really about to let her out, she preferred he let her out at some place like a gas station. The previous exit was about fifteen miles back at it was well lit with plenty stations.

"Whelp, your black ass wanted to go. Here's your stop."

A gush of relief overcame all her fears as she couldn't believe he was actually agreeing to free her of him. It was almost too good to be true. He unlocked the door, but when she grabbed at the handle, he locked it again.

"Keo…"

Before she could finish saying his name, he drilled his fist right to the center of her nose. Her head smashed into the window. He then leaned over her and wrapped both his hands around her neck. "Bitch, how many times I gotta tell you that you'll never leave my ass and live. Huh? Huh, bitch?"

"Keon... Keon, stop," she pleaded. She was frantic as he continued to apply pressure around her neck. She became dazed, and the pain around her neck and head increased immensely while she thought that this moment was the one she expected to come about one day—the day he would try to end her life.

She grabbed him by his wrist, scratching and trying to push him off her. He was so strong and overrun with hatred. He called her all kind of names and demanded she die as he applied more pressure around her neck, telling her that he should've killed her long ago. Ashley began to phase in and out of consciousness as her vision began to blur. She wasn't ready to die, and she surely didn't want to go out by his evil hands. She couldn't die by his hands.

Her fear swiftly turned into anger, and in a last ditch effort to get him off of her, she kneed him in his crotch. The strike propelled him backward into his seat as he grabbed his manhood while squealing in pain. She began stomping at it even harder, smashing his hand, legs and penis repeatedly. She reached over him, unlocked her door and climbed out of the car.

He grabbed her by her foot. The momentum sent her face first onto the pavement. "Bitch, I'mma kill you." He then crawled out of the car behind her and drove his fist to the back of her head. She gulped in agony, but the pain didn't stop her from attempting to crawl away from him.

She continued to claw her way towards the restroom area as he rolled over on his back with his hand massaging his crouch. She finally was able to make it to her feet, and she began to run. Keon also made it to his feet and whipped out his pistol. As she approached the restroom door, he yelled "Stop bitch!" and let off a shot towards her.

"Keon...what!" She froze in her tracks, just in front of the door. She was too scared to turn around to face him fearful he would let off another shot, but this time in her face.

"You stupid, ungrateful bitch," he yelled before shoving her through the bathroom door. She went tumbling to the dingy floor. The bathroom was filthy, barely lit and smelled like a pigpen. "All that I've done for your ass and you want to leave me, bitch! Are you fucking shitting me?" He kicked her in her behind and yelled, "Turn your stupid ass over."

She slowly turned over only to see him pointing his gun right at her face. She cried, "Keon... you don't have to do this."

"Don't tell me what the fuck I don't have to do!"

"All I asked..."

"Bitch—shut up!" He took several deep breaths and continued, "You've been dead weight for far too fucking long."

Just before he could squeeze his trigger, a shot rang out and he dropped his gun. He looked towards his left shoulder and saw that he was bleeding out. He slowly turned around and was greeted with a big white knuckle that propelled him backwards, sending him crashing to the floor next to Ashley.

"Take her outside," said the stocky man. It was the big bald man with the scruffy red mustache from the apartment complex.

The man with him, whom was just as big and stocky as he was, ordered her up. "Come on." He pulled her up from the ground.

"Hey, man what the fuck," Keon yelled toward the man that shot him.

"You know that fuck this is, Robinson. Pay up time."

"Man... look, tell Max I just need a little more time," Keon cried while fearing the worse was about to happen.

"Ain't no more fucking time," said the man as he dove on top of Keon and began pulverizing his face.

Ashley could only get a glimpse of his beating as the other henchmen guided her towards the exit and out of the bathroom. "Sit here," he demanded as he forced her onto the grass. She could hear Keon begging and pleading the man to stop beating him. As she sat there, she feared for her own life but it brought her much pleasure to hear Keon screaming for his. The enjoyment she received from his pain immediately stopped when she heard the three gunshots in rapid succession echo from the bathroom.

After a few moments of silence, the man walked out of the bathroom with Keon's lifeless body over his shoulder. Ashley could only watch the man in fear as he walked towards the car BP had given them and threw Keon's body in the trunk. The black sedan they arrived in was parked right next to the car. She watched the man remove and throw his blood soiled shirt in the trunk with Keon. He then slammed the trunk shut and grabbed another shirt from his car.

Finally, he walked up to his partner and said, "Alright, that's fucking done. Let's get out of here."

"What about her?" The man asked pointing to Ashley.

"What about her?"

"We ain't gonna handle her like we did the rest?"

The man with the scruffy red mustache chuckled and asked Ashley, "Hey, did you see us come here and beat the shit of your boyfriend right before I blew his fucking brains out? Did ya?"

She looked towards the vehicle she rode to the rest stop in and then back at him, prompting her to shake her head.

"I can't hear you."

"No," she said softly.

"I thought not," he said to his partner. He held out his palm as if he was signaling her to give him something. "Alright, I'm gonna need that back now."

His request stemmed from the night she first saw them passing her by at the apartment, but only they didn't make it all the way out of the apartment complex. Instead, that night the brake lights of the car lit up as the automobile backed up to her as she remained motionless.

***

The man with the scruffy red mustache rolled his window down and said, "Hi, Ashley."

She was befuddled by the man's knowledge of who she was.

"Would you like to do us a favor?" he asked with a devious grin on his face. "One that would actually benefit your life in a whole new way, possibly even extending it. Step a little closer darling."

She remained frozen, terrified to move one single inch. He waved her closer with a pistol after his initial request fell upon deaf ears. "Sweetheart, if I wanted to kill you, I could've gotten you right before you saw us while you were struggling with that big ass bag of trash. Could've popped you right in the head. You wouldn't have known what hit ya'."

She slowly walked a few steps closer, convinced that the bald man could've indeed ended her if he desired.

"Good girl," he smiled.

"What do you want?"

"We may need your help."

"Why would I help you? I don't even know you?"

"That is true. You don't know us, but your man does," he said. "And like I said a few moments ago, helping us can only help you. You see, I don't know if he let you in on this or not, but your little boyfriend back there is in debt with my boss for a substantial amount of money, so much, we're beginning to get the feeling that he's not going to be able to pay up before his deadline."

"And what does that have to do with me?"

"Everything, sweetheart," he said. "You see, guys like us, we get paid to observe and eventually execute. So while we've been observing Mr. Robinson the last couple of weeks, we started noticing that you don't appear to be a particularly happy woman. Now, if you've been observing things about your man like we've been observing things about him in this very short period of time, we're pretty certain that you're aware that his time ain't that exclusive to you."

She held her head in shame as the man insinuated Keon was cheating on her.

"We figure if he decides to run, maybe you can help us out, and in return, we can take some of that drama out of your life… and we can even assure you that you'd have a life to have the drama removed from." He removed the aim of his gun from her and held up a black device that resembled a thumb drive. "You see this right here? This fancy little do-hickey is what they call a GPS tracker. All we need for you to do is turn this little contraption on if he tries to sneak off with you somewhere without us knowing and then we'll handle the rest." He threw her the gadget.

She observed it carefully after she caught it. After giving the gadget a quick look over, she looked at him and questioned the whole idea, "If I don't?"

He shrugged his shoulders and momentarily bobbled his head with a silly look on his face. "Well, that's your decision, sweetheart. I just can't guarantee you we'd be this sociable with you the next time we meet, that's all." he said.

"Besides, why wouldn't you?" he laughed. "We'll be seeing you, Ashley." He drove off.

***

Ashley dug into her pocket and handed him the tracker.

"Thank you, sweetheart," said the man as he stuffed the contraption in his pocket. "A deal's a deal. It's been nice working with you, Ashley." He turned to his partner and said, "Let's get the fuck outta here."

She watched the men walk away as they took off with their car and the car BP gave Keon. She then climbed to her feet, took a deep breath and gazed back at the restroom. Keon was finally gone. She began walking towards the main highway.

She sat on the edge of the walkway, just in front of the door of a twenty-four hour gas station she discovered at the exit a few miles down from the rest stop. She sat silently—hair mangled lips sore and busted along with a throbbing pain along her rips. With her hands clasped together on top of her knees, she ignored every late night patron that found their way into the spot, whether they had genuine concerns about her battered and bruised face or if they merely thought she was a late night trick looking for a John to pick her up.

It wasn't until a late model Mercedes rolled into the parking space next to her that she made any movement. She hopped up and briefly gazed into the lightly tinted windows of the luxury car. She then approached the passenger side door and opened it, easing into the ride.

"Did they get him?" asked the driver.

She turned towards the driver and calmly replied, "They got him, Ma."

"Well, I guess I shouldn't have doubted you when you said you could take care of things back at the house."

Ashley let out a deep breath, totally exhausted by the events of the past few days. Then, she let back her seat and motioned forward. "Let's just go home, Ma."

"You got it sweetheart," Rose smiled, relieved to finally have her daughter back. As Ashley reclined in her chair with her eyes closed, her mother scanned her over, enraged and woeful over the bruises that sprawled across her daughters face and arms. She gave her daughter a gentle rub on her knee before backing out of the parking space, grateful she had her daughter back.

THE END